Organically Yours

Sanctuary, Book Five

USA Today Bestselling Author

Abbie Zanders

Organically Yours

First edition. May, 2021.

Written by Abbie Zanders.

Cover Design: Graphics by Stacy

Cover Image: Eric McKinney, 6:12 Photography

Cover Model: Taylor S

Editor: Jovana Shirley, Unforeseen Editing

ISBN: 9798504885124

Acknowledgements

Special thanks go to members of my readers group, the Zanders Clan for all of their love, help and constant support. In particular:

- To my friend and fellow author, Tonya Brooks, for always being there, no matter what.
- My reader group, the Zanders Clan for coming up with such great ideas for Lottie's big adventure with Gertie Handelmann.
- My amazing ARC Angels team, who help ensure that what you're reading is as close to error-free as it can get, and for providing such great snippets and quotes for teasers and promo.

And thank YOU. You didn't have to pick up this book, but you did.

CHAPTER ONE

~ *Tina* ~

Tina left Ziegler's farmers market, feeling tired and hungry. It was hard enough, standing on her feet all day, but pasting on a smile and dealing with people were exhausting. The townies weren't so bad. She knew most of them by name, knew their families, and a quick and friendly hello was always welcome.

But the tourists? The ones who had come from out of town and thought venturing to the farmers market on the weekends was a rustic adventure? Not so much.

On the plus side, they were willing to pay premium prices for organic produce.

The best and worst thing about working the market every Saturday was having to smell the slow-roasted rotisserie chicken from the Amish place a few stalls down. Mouthwatering and delicious, it was hands down the *best* chicken around.

Tina wasn't the only one who thought so.

Zook's sold out every week without fail. The locals knew to get their orders in early, before the place opened its doors to the public.

Those enticing aromas were now filling the cab of her truck, whispering suggestively that she didn't have to wait until she got home to have a taste. Her stomach growled loudly in hearty agreement. Why should she wait? The chicken was hot and fresh now, and when she got home, she'd feel compelled to unload the truck before settling in for the night. It could be an hour or more before she had a chance to sit down and enjoy it.

That was how Tina found herself in the back corner of Ziegler's parking lot, ripping into the foil-wrapped goodness of a Zook's chicken as if she hadn't eaten in days.

The first bite was practically orgasmic. The skin was crispy and dripping with hand-churned butter. The meat, melt-in-her-mouth tender and perfectly seasoned. She closed her eyes and savored the moment before she took another bite. And another.

She was tearing the last piece of meat from the bone when there was a knock at the window. She turned, ready to rip her brother a new one for ghosting her all day, and promptly froze.

Because it wasn't her brother standing there.

No, it was so much worse. Dirty-blond hair, brushed back from a sculpted face, just long enough to skim the collar of his plaid flannel. Amazing hazel eyes so focused that she felt his penetrating gaze on the inside.

Doc.

At least, that was what Kate Handelmann had called him. Tina didn't know his real name. All the Sanctuary guys had nicknames.

But none of *them* made her heart beat faster on sight like he did.

And none of *them* were currently standing outside her truck, looking on as she tore into a chicken like a savage.

She scanned the interior of the cab for a paper napkin, a tissue—anything she could use to mop up the butter currently dripping down her chin—and came up empty.

Summoning as much dignity as she could, Tina moved the bag to the passenger seat, wiped her greasy lips with the back of her sleeve as discreetly as possible, and put the window down.

"Yes?"

"Is everything okay?"

His voice was just as buttery as the chicken. Smooth. Calming. But it wasn't enough to erase her embarrassment, and her knee-jerk response was to go on the defensive. Growing up with three older brothers probably had something to do with that.

"Yes," she snapped. "Why wouldn't it be?"

"You've been sitting here for a while."

"So?"

He shifted his weight. "So, I just wanted to

make sure everything was all right."

"Well, it is."

He hesitated, almost as if he wanted to say something more, but simply nodded. "Okay. Sorry to bother you."

He started to turn when she said, "What are you doing, skulking around the parking lot anyway? Ziegler's closed an hour ago."

He smiled, and damn if it didn't make him even more gorgeous. "Helping a friend."

Tina immediately wondered who that friend was, followed shortly afterward by a wave of envy. She imagined those broad shoulders lifting crates into the back of *her* truck. Not only would she have enjoyed the view, but she also would have appreciated a second pair of strong hands since her brother hadn't bothered to show.

The Good Samaritan walked away. She groaned and banged her forehead on the steering wheel.

Nice going, Tina. Way to make a great first impression.

She lifted her head and followed his progress in the side-view mirror, curious to see where he was going, but another knock, this one on her passenger window, garnered her attention and made her jump.

"Damn it, Rick!" Tina yelled. "You startled me."

"What did he want?" her brother asked, tilting his head back toward where Doc had disappeared into the shadows.

"He just wanted to see if I needed help."

He snorted. "I bet he did."

"What's that supposed to mean?"

"It means, you stay away from those Sanctuary boys, Bert."

Tina—or *Bertina*, as her misguided parents had named her—bristled. She hated being called Bert, which was exactly why her brothers did so at every opportunity.

"I'll do as I damn well please. And you, you can mind your own business."

"I'm serious."

"So am I. Where the hell have you been anyway? You were supposed to be here hours ago to cover the stand."

Rick knew she had difficulty being on her feet for fourteen hours straight, which meant he'd either conveniently forgotten or he was just being a prick. Again.

His jaw clenched. "Something came up."

"I bet," she said, throwing his own words back at him, but she did sarcasm a whole lot better than he did. "Like what?"

He clamped his lips shut, and she knew she wouldn't get an answer tonight. *Things* had been *coming up* more and more frequently these days. Rick was up to something, and she had a feeling that whatever it was, it wasn't good.

She'd find out sooner or later. Keeping a secret

in Sumneyville was like trying to hold water in your hands. Eventually, it would start trickling out.

She changed the topic. "Climb in. I'll give you a ride back to the farm, and you can help me unload."

"Can't. I'm supposed to meet up with the guys at O'Malley's."

"They can wait. Unless, of course, you want me to call Bonnie and ask if *she* knows why you didn't show today."

Bonnie was Rick's wife and the mother of their two kids. They'd only been married a decade, but they'd already slipped into the phase where they could barely stand to be together in the same room. Tina knew the last thing Rick wanted was another reason for Bonnie to complain.

He scowled but got in, picking up the takeout container so he could sit. "Zook's?"

"Of course."

"Any left?" he asked hopefully.

"Nope." There was no way she was telling him about the second chicken she'd picked up for later in the week. "Maybe if you'd shown up like you were supposed to, you could have gotten one."

"Get off my ass," he grumbled.

CHAPTER TWO

~ *Doc* ~

Doc was still smiling when he returned to the others. The pretty, wholesome-looking blonde who'd caught his eye months earlier was even more attractive up close than she was from afar. Feisty, too.

She had been so focused on her chicken that he'd stood beside her truck for a full minute before she noticed. Should he have rapped on the window like that when, clearly, everything was fine? No, probably not, but he hadn't been able to help himself. It was the first opportunity he'd had to talk to her without half a dozen people around.

"Everything okay?" Brian "Mad Dog" Sheppard finished securing the handcrafted Amish furniture in the back of his truck with a solid tug.

Knowing how much his wife, Kate, admired the craftsmanship, Mad Dog had commissioned a set from one of the families who had a stall at the market. Each week, they picked up a new piece for their custom cabin. Tonight's addition was a stunning corner hutch made of cherry wood.

"Seems to be," Doc answered. "Although I don't think I earned any favor by going over there."

"Why not?"

"She was eating."

Devouring was probably a better word. She'd been attacking that chicken with gusto and single-minded focus. He wondered vaguely if she put that much effort and passion into everything she did.

Kate laughed. "I bet it was a Zook's chicken."

"It was chicken," he confirmed.

"I was never able to make it home without taking a bite either. They're *that* good."

Doc looked back to the older model pickup. A big guy was now leaning against the passenger side, shooting unfriendly glares their way.

Doc's hackles rose, right along with his protective instincts. "Who is that?"

Kate followed his gaze. "Relax. That's her brother Rick."

Doc was sure he'd seen the guy before. It didn't take long to remember where. "He's one of the preppers."

Kate nodded somberly. "All the Obermacher boys are."

That didn't bode well for him or his desire to know more about the woman with the ponytail and a penchant for good chicken. The Obermachers were an old and powerful family in the area, owning hundreds of acres of farmland and dominating the local food supply market.

That they were associated with the survivalist camp bordering Sanctuary property wasn't surprising. Most of the members were of the good ol' local-boy variety. Unfortunately, they also tended *not* to be fans of Sanctuary.

He wasn't interested in getting to know her brothers though. "What about *her*?"

"Tina? She's really nice. Nothing like her brothers."

Tina. Now, he had a name to go with the face. And according to Kate, she was really nice. That was good enough for him. As a member of an old Sumneyville family herself, Kate knew a lot about the locals.

"You know that peach tea you're so fond of?" Kate continued.

Doc nodded. He'd become addicted to the stuff since Sandy—another Sumneyville native now living at Sanctuary—had first introduced him to it.

"You can thank Tina for that. She manages the Obermacher orchards."

Doc looked toward the back of the lot again. The big guy was now getting into the truck, but he didn't look happy about it.

"That guy looks pissed."

"Rick always looks like that," Kate said. "Don't worry. Tina knows how to handle him."

"Hey, do you think she'd be willing to come by and look at the old orchard at the resort, see if it's salvageable?" Mad Dog asked.

"I don't see why not," Kate responded. "I'll call her tomorrow. I bet she'd love to see the greenhouses you designed. From what I remember, she got her degree in agro science."

The more Doc heard about Tina Obermacher, the more interested he was. And if Kate could get her to come to Sanctuary? Even better.

"Great," Mad Dog said. "We can use all the help we can get." He patted the back quarter panel. "All right, everything's secure. We're good to go."

Doc glanced back toward the old pickup, now on its way out the back gate reserved for vendors. With any luck, he'd be seeing Tina Obermacher again soon.

CHAPTER THREE

~ *Tina* ~

Running the orchards was a year-round job, but some seasons were busier than others. Things started ramping up in the spring and then built to a peak in summer and early fall before dropping off again.

March was typically the time to prune existing trees, plant new ones, and fertilize, but exactly when work could be done depended on the weather. This year, winter seemed reluctant to let go of its icy grip on the region, so it was important to make the most of every good day.

Tina had been making her rounds, checking on the state of things and growing angrier with each section she visited. At least half the trees hadn't been pruned yet, and the new trees she'd ordered were still waiting to be put in the ground.

By the time she hit the peach grove, she was fuming.

"Eddie!" she called out, spotting her supervisor hanging around the equipment shed along with several guys. Guys who *should* have been out planting and pruning. Instead, they didn't seem to be doing anything besides shooting the breeze.

Eddie turned and saw her, his face morphing into the expression she knew so well—irritation. He worked the ever-present chew between his teeth and gums before spitting off to the side. "Yeah?"

She waved toward the stationary compact utility tractor and the three dozen newly delivered young peach trees ready to go. "Why aren't those in the ground yet? You know we can't let those roots freeze."

"Tractor's acting up."

The tractor had been fine three days earlier when she hooked up the backhoe attachment and used it to clear debris from blocked drainage channels—something else Eddie should have taken care of but hadn't.

"What's wrong with it?"

He turned his head and spit again. "Ain't a mechanic, am I?"

Some of the guys behind him smirked.

"You sure as hell aren't," she agreed, earning a glower.

Eddie had spent enough time around equipment that he *should* know how to diagnose and fix common problems, but he was more likely to stand back and offer his unsolicited—and often incorrect—opinion rather than actually *do* something. Letting Rick talk her into putting Eddie on her team had been a decided lack of judgment on her part. She wished Fritz's arthritis hadn't forced him to retire. She'd never had to worry about things getting done with Fritz in charge.

Regardless, it didn't matter. They had jobs to do. Growing superior peaches in the upper regions of Pennsylvania was hard enough. She didn't need Eddie's crap, too.

She offered a tight smile and asked the obvious, "Did you remember to put it in neutral and close the choke?"

His shoulders stiffened. "Now, look here—"

"No, *you* look. I'll check out the tractor. *You* grab some shovels and wheelbarrows and get started on those trees."

"By hand?"

"Yes, by hand."

"The ground's frozen."

Oh, for Pete's sake. She took a shovel from the shed and drove it through the light covering of snow and into the soil. Then, she put her booted foot on the edge and gave it a good shove, putting her weight into it. A lift and twist brought up dirt along with the snow.

"It's workable enough. And those trees need to go in today."

"All of them?"

Lord, give me patience. "Yes, all of them."

Getting thirty-six trees into the ground shouldn't be a problem with everyone she had working even if she couldn't get the backhoe operational right away. She scanned the work crew now shuffling into the shed, counting four behind Eddie. There should have been seven.

"Where's the rest?"

Head turn, spit. A dribble of spittle hung on his bottom lip. It was no wonder the guy was still single.

"With Kief."

Her brother Kiefer was in charge of the vegetable fields, and as far as she knew, there was nothing pressing going on there. "Doing what?"

He shrugged. "I don't know. Rick said he needed them."

Tina's ire increased. Unless it was an emergency, she needed them working on the orchards more than whatever her brother had them doing. She'd deal with Rick later—after she took a look at the tractor. Hopefully, it was a quick fix and something that could be handled on-site. Two other machines were already in the shop, and she couldn't afford to go without for the week or more it would take to have someone else fix it.

"More work for you then, huh? Better get started."

They grumbled, Eddie in particular, but she stared them down until they started moving. She'd learned early on not to back down, or they'd walk all over her.

They didn't like taking orders from a woman.

She got that. She didn't care. She was an Obermacher first, a female second. As long as she ran the orchards, they worked for her.

Only when they went into the shed to grab shovels and pickaxes and wheelbarrows did she pull the toolbox from the back of her truck. When she was younger, she'd spent hours tinkering in the garage with her grandfather while her father and brothers were out in the fields, and she had picked up a thing or two about improvisational repair.

As she was passing the door, she heard one of the crew say, "Man, I feel sorry for any man who has to deal with her every day."

Another laughed. "Yeah, well, we won't have to deal with her for much longer from what I heard."

Tina paused and listened, but they said no more before they moved away.

What did they know—or *think* they knew—that she didn't?

She shook her head and chalked it up to pure speculation. Everyone knew there'd been offers to buy up their farmland; that was nothing new. Developers had been wanting to strip the fertile soil and sell it off, turning their rolling fields into residential complexes with luxury townhomes and single-family mansions. One of them had even gone as far as to design an entire community village with restaurants and shops and God knew what else and present it to the township board—or so she'd heard.

Apparently, it was the new thing among rich folk looking to get out of the congested city.

Those offers were just offers, and those rumors, just rumors. Tina wasn't overly concerned. Obermachers had been working their land since the late 1600s and would continue to do so for the next four hundred years. Farming was in their blood.

Even if they *were* inclined to sell off a few parcels, the citizens of Sumneyville wouldn't stand for it. They disliked outsiders and would be especially unaccepting of city folk coming in and building multimillion-dollar homes and golf courses, driving up the tax base and looking down their noses at everyone.

Plus, the township board would never approve the kind of rezoning necessary to allow any of that to happen. Not even the greedy ones.

At least, she didn't *think* they would. Things were changing around Sumneyville, and not all of it was good. The old guard, as she called them—men like her father and grandfather along with Sam Winston and others—were slowly disappearing, and those rising up to fill in the gaps weren't made of the same honorable stuff.

The moment Tina started up the tractor, she knew what the problem was. The machine was rolling coal—shooting black smoke out of the exhaust—which often indicated a faulty glow plug.

Tina dug down into the bottom of her toolbox, grabbed a spare, and swapped out the bad one. It was an easy fix, one that anyone with even a minimal working knowledge should be able to diagnose and repair.

She drove the compact over to where the guys were digging and got to work right along with them despite the cold, damp air seeping into her joints and making them ache. Once the new trees were in and she was satisfied with the way the pruning was going, Tina went in search of her older brother to wrangle back her workers while there was still some daylight.

She found Rick in the office with her brother Gunther, leaning over a large table covered in site maps.

"What the hell, Rick?" she said by way of greeting.

Both men looked up.

Rick's brow rose in question as he straightened and allowed the map to curl in toward the center. "Got a problem, Bert?"

"Yeah, I have a problem." She glared at him. "Why'd you pull my guys off orchards today?"

"Fence repair in the northern border."

"I need them on peaches and apricots."

"Eddie didn't seem to think it would be an issue."

"Eddie doesn't run the orchards. I do. Next time, check with me before you poach my crew. Call them now and send them back."

He shook his head. "The fence takes priority.

The fruit trees can wait."

"Seriously?"

"You've got plenty of time."

"I'll remember that when planting season rolls around."

Tina left the barn in a huff and drove back to the orchards, only to find that the guys had already left. A quick check confirmed her suspicions—they hadn't gotten nearly as much done as she'd hoped.

Eddie needed to go. Rick's best friend or not, he'd gotten too big for his britches, and his piss-poor attitude was affecting the whole crew. Rick could put him on *his* team if he had a problem with that.

She needed someone she could trust. Someone who cared about the success of the orchards and would have her back. Eddie was *not* that guy.

Darkness wasn't far off, but there was no sense in wasting the little bit of daylight remaining by chasing the guys down. She grabbed a handsaw and some telescoping loppers and went out herself, using the headlights from her truck when it got too dark to see with natural light.

By the time she made it back to her place, she was hungry, tired, and *hurting*.

One thing was becoming increasingly clear: things could not continue as they were.

Tina turned on the oven and popped her backup Zook's chicken in. While that warmed, she went to take a long, hot shower to ease some of the stiffness in her upper body and fished out the prescription pain pills she tried so desperately *not* to use.

She curled up on the couch in front of her television with her chicken and a mug of tea—made with herbs known for their anti-inflammatory properties—when her landline phone rang. She glanced at the number on the display; it wasn't familiar.

"No, I don't want to extend my vehicle's warranty," she grumbled to no one and let the answering machine pick up.

"Hi, Tina? It's Kate Handelmann—well, Kate Sheppard now." Even on the machine, Tina could hear the smile in her voice. "Can you call me back when you have a chance? There's something I'd like to talk to you about."

The soft click signaled the end of the call, leaving Tina staring at the now-blinking new message light, bemused.

Tina had always liked Kate. She didn't know her very well, but she knew enough to know Kate was friendly, down-to-earth, and kind of a tomboy, like Tina. Plus, Kate was active in the community and always doing for others. Or at least, she had been before the whole kerfuffle with her family. What exactly had transpired varied based on who was doing the telling. All Tina knew was that Kate had quit her job in the family store—Handelmann's Hardware—and was now married and living at Sanctuary.

What Kate wanted to talk to her about, Tina had no idea. Her curiosity continued to grow, and by the time she finished her dinner, she decided to find out.

CHAPTER FOUR

~ Doc ~

Kate's phone chimed in the semi-darkness, a melodic overlay on the dialogue taking place on the screen. She quickly muted it and looked down at the screen. "Sorry, everyone. It's Tina."

As Kate got to her feet and prepared to leave the room, Sam aimed the remote at the screen and paused the movie. "No problem. I need more popcorn anyway. Anyone else want something from the kitchen?"

When a chorus of requests rang out, Sandy laughed and rose as well, saying she and Sam would return with a full snack bar.

Movie night was Doc's favorite night. Besides meals, it was one of the few times many of them were in the same space at the same time, and he enjoyed the socialization. Invitations were open to everyone on-site, and the event had become a popular thing, even among the newbies.

Anyone interested gathered in what had become known as the decompression chamber to

Sandy would know. Until she and Heff had hooked up, she'd been good friends with Freed's nephew, Lenny Petraski, who also happened to work for his uncle and was one of his biggest supporters outside the police station as well as in it.

Kate nodded. "That's true, but I don't think Tina's the type to believe everything she hears. She's more likely to see for herself and form her own opinion."

"Let's hope so," Nick "Cage" Fumanti said somberly. "But it's in our best interest to be cautious until we have a better feel for what we're dealing with here. Her brothers are firmly in Freed's camp."

"Are we providing an opportunity for a soft recon here?" Smoke mused.

Kate looked to Church for support. "You know Tina, don't you? From school? She's not like that."

"She wasn't then," Church agreed, "but that was a long time ago. Things change."

There was a heaviness to his tone that spoke volumes. Church rarely talked about the negative reaction he'd received upon his return to his hometown, but that had to have struck a nerve. These were people he'd grown up with, people he'd known his whole life. To have them openly bad-mouthing him and the good he was trying to do with Sanctuary must have felt like a betrayal.

"Yes, they do," Kate said quietly. Her family had turned their backs on her when she took up with

Mad Dog.

Her husband wrapped his arm around her shoulders and kissed her temple in a touching show of support.

Hugh "Heff" Bradley shrugged. "It's simple. Keep her tour to the public areas. If she starts asking questions, don't divulge what we know about the preppers, the ongoing federal investigation into Luther Renninger, or the eyes we have on the mines."

"None of us would do that," Sam said firmly, settling back in between her husband's legs. "We protect our own. Now, are we going to watch the rest of the movie or not?"

Sam's question was met by murmurs and grunts of agreement. But as the lights went down and the movie resumed, Doc couldn't help thinking about Tina Obermacher and her upcoming visit.

CHAPTER FIVE

~ Tina ~

Tina felt a tingle of anticipation as she laced up her walking boots.

It had been a hell of a week. An unpredicted ice storm had done some damage, particularly in the cherry grove. One of the guys on her team got hurt and would probably be out for a month at least. Some kids broke into an equipment sheds and vandalized the place. And Eddie was being more irascible than ever. All attempts to pin Rick down and talk to him about it had been unsuccessful.

So, yeah, she was looking forward to getting away for the day to visit Sanctuary, see Kate, and check out what they were doing with the place. From what she remembered, the Winston resort was a gorgeous place with plenty of scenic vistas.

And maybe, just maybe, she'd catch a glimpse of the mysterious men—one hazel-eyed Good Samaritan in particular—who had chosen to make the place their new home.

It was important to keep her expectations

realistic, however. A lot had happened since she'd last been there. She'd been in high school then, the summer before a horrific fire claimed the lives of the entire Winston family—except for Matt, who'd been serving in the military at the time.

Her stomach tightened at the thought of it. The tragedy had gutted their small, tight-knit community. Like the Obermachers, the Winstons were an old, established family, and in the blink of an eye, they were no more.

For a long time afterward, Tina had had nightmares about the same thing happening to her family. Of coming home to find everyone she loved just … gone.

Thankfully, that hadn't happened, but the last decade hadn't been without loss. Tina's grandfather was the first to go. Then, her father had a sudden and massive heart attack while harvesting feed corn one day. Not long after, her mother took an accidental overdose—at least, that was the official story—and was gone too. That had left just the Obermacher matriarch—Tina's grandmother—and her siblings to carry on.

The family business had been divided evenly between Tina and her brothers. Gunther, who didn't like getting his hands dirty, handled the business end of things. Kiefer took over the vegetable crops, Rick handled grains, and Tina did fruits.

They didn't always agree. Rick and Gunther could be pigheaded and often shared the same mind.

Kiefer *could* be reasonable at times, but he was more likely to go along with whatever Rick and Gunther wanted.

There was no doubt in her mind that they would be opposed to her decision to go to Sanctuary alone, which was exactly why she hadn't told anyone about her plans.

She'd heard the same rumors everyone else had, of course. If Rick and some of his drinking buddies were to be believed, Matt Winston was turning his family legacy into a veritable fortress, amassing guns and weapons and building a small army of mentally unstable former servicepeople.

Tina didn't believe that for a minute. For one thing, she knew Matt Winston—or at least, the man he used to be. Sure, serving in the military could change a lot of things about a person but not who they were at their core, and Matt Winston was good people.

Nor did she believe that Matt's purpose in restoring the old place was a dark one. Both he and his family had always been very community-minded. Why people tended to forget that was beyond her. Either they had short memories or they were allowing Daryl Freed and his ilk to rewrite local history.

Dressed in layers, Tina locked up the small caretaker's cottage she called home and set off. The Winston place wasn't far as the crow flies, but there was no road that led directly there from where she was, which meant she had to go down toward the town to get to the road that led back up.

Thirty minutes later, she reached her destination. The long driveway with its overarching branches brought back pleasant memories. Soon, those trees and the abundant mountain laurel behind them would be loaded with blossoms, filling the mountain air with the scents of yet another spring.

She pulled into a parking spot just off the circular drive and gazed approvingly at the half-wall and steps. Both had recently been redone by the look of things, and they'd done a really good job, using the same local stone that had been used in the original manor house and the subsequent additions they'd put on when the place became a resort.

That, too, had been skillfully redone. It bore no resemblance to the charred, blackened ruins that had been splashed across the front page of the *Sumneyville Times* for weeks.

Nor did it look remotely close to a military bunker.

"Tina Obermacher. It's good to see you."

Tina turned around to find Matt Winston offering a friendly, familiar smile. He'd filled out since she'd last seen him, but there was no mistaking that angled, masculine face and those soulful golden-brown eyes. He, like her, was dressed in layers, which did absolutely nothing to hide the fact that he was in great physical condition.

In high school, Matt had been gorgeous. As a man, he was devastating. It was no wonder some women sighed when his name came up, even as their tongues were wagging with the latest hearsay.

"Matt Winston. Good to see you, too. It's been a long minute, huh?"

"That it has. Welcome to Sanctuary. Do you want to come in and have some coffee before we head out to the orchard?"

Since they were both dressed for outdoor exploration, it made sense to get business out of the way. "How about we see what you've got first?"

"Sounds like a plan."

They walked down to the orchard. The grove was small, taking up less than ten acres, so they were able to cover it all in under an hour. There was a nice mix of apple, cherry, pear, and—her personal favorite—peach trees. Unfortunately, the years of neglect had left their mark.

Even in the starkness of almost-spring, it was obvious that nothing had been done in years. Invasive weeds and poison ivy had been allowed to grow unchecked. There'd been no pruning, no pest control, no proper fertilization, and deer had done quite a bit of damage to the trunks with their antlers.

"So, what do you think?" he asked as they were making their way back to the main building.

"I hate to say it, Matt, but I think most of it's too far gone to salvage. You can try, of course, but if it were me, I'd start fresh."

He nodded, unsurprised. "That's what I thought. Wanted to check with an expert first though. What would we have to do to rebuild?"

"Well, the site is ideal. Eastern-facing, rolling land, and a mild slope are exactly what you want, so I don't think you need to relocate unless you really want to. In general, you want to avoid exposed tops and ridges. They get too windy, and the soil erodes easily."

"Makes sense."

"You also want to avoid planting anything in the dips and valleys. The soil there tends to be overly fertile."

His brow furrowed. "Isn't that a good thing?"

"For tree growth, yes. For fruit production, no." She grinned. "That's the short answer. I can give you the scientific reasoning behind it, if you'd like."

"I'll take your word for it."

Yeah, that's what she thought he'd say. While she found the finer points of agricultural science fascinating, most people tended to zone out fairly quickly.

"The first thing I would do is pick up a soil map. You can get one from the local county extension or soil conservation office. That'll tell you a lot about the type of soil you're dealing with and what will grow best for you. At the very least, it'll tell you what you need to do to get stuff to grow for you."

He nodded. "Soil map. Will do."

"Second thing, do a nematode test *before* you take out the old trees."

"What's that?"

"Nematodes? They're microscopic plant parasites. One square yard of soil can hold millions of the little suckers, and they can be devastating. Also, you'll need to get rid of the multiflora, thistle, and poison ivy that have taken over. Two or three treatments over the summer should do it. You can use glyphosate, but I prefer an organic alternative myself. It requires a bit more persistence, but it's worth it in the long run. I can share the formula I use, if you'd like."

"That'd be great, thanks."

"Once you do that, you'll want to remove the trees that aren't salvageable, plow to mix up the subsoil, and do more soil testing."

He laughed. "Is that all?"

"Not even close. You'll need to clear some of those trees at the bottom of the slope to create channels for the cold-air flow. Cold air is heavier and tends to travel downward. Dense woods at the bottom can have a damming effect, and you don't want that cold air backing up, especially during budding season.

"*Then*, if you do all that," Tina continued, "you could see viable fruit in two or three years."

"That long?"

She nodded. "Starting a new orchard doesn't provide the same short-term gratification as, say, planting tomatoes or cucumbers. It takes time, commitment, and year-round care. Don't get me wrong; I'm not trying to discourage you. With a parcel this small, you could do it easily, but you do need to keep up with it."

"I knew asking you was a good idea."

Tina shrugged and grinned widely. "I'm a tenth-generation Obermacher with a master's degree. What did you expect?"

"Fair point. I appreciate you taking the time to come out and have a look. I know you're busy."

"It's my pleasure. I'm glad you asked when you did. In another couple of weeks, I might not have had the time. Plus, I'll admit, I've been curious. You and your guys sure have Sumneyville's tongues wagging, you know."

His smile faded. "Yes, I know."

"It's not all bad," Tina assured him. "You've got a lot of support, too."

Matt said nothing to that. "Can you stay for a bit? I know Kate would love to see you."

Tina looked at her watch. "Sure. Gram's not expecting me for a few hours yet."

"How is your grandmother?"

"Feisty as ever."

His smile returned. "Glad to hear it."

"She'll be thrilled when I tell her I saw you. She's one of your biggest supporters, you know."

"I bet that creates some interesting family dynamics at the dinner table."

Tina laughed, her eyes sparkling. Clearly, Matt knew her brothers didn't count themselves among the pro-Sanctuary locals, but he didn't seem to hold that against her.

"That it does."

Tina followed Matt inside. The lobby had changed somewhat from the last time she'd been here. It was simpler, less ostentatious than it once had been, but still quite beautiful.

After offering to take her jacket and vest, he led her toward the dining area. It, too, had been modernized and upgraded, much more in tune with the twenty-first century.

"Kate!" Matt called out. "Someone's here to see you."

Kate emerged from the kitchen, wiping her hands on her apron. The moment she saw Tina, a huge smile lit up her face. "Tina! I'm so glad you came."

"Me, too."

"Want some coffee?"

"I'd love some, thanks."

"Ladies, if you'll excuse me, I've got some things to take care of. Tina, thanks again for coming today."

"You are very welcome. It was great to see you."

Kate ushered Tina to a table in the dining room in front of the floor-to-ceiling tinted windows. "Have a seat. I'll get us some coffee and snacks and be right back."

Tina settled into the chair and took the opportunity to look around. The room was open and airy, the outer wall of mostly glass panels providing a stunning view of the grounds.

Kate returned shortly with a carafe of coffee, sugar, cream, and a plate of pastries that looked delicious.

"We have the place to ourselves for a while," Kate told her, pouring them each a mug. "People won't start wandering in until it gets closer to dinnertime."

"This place is gorgeous."

"It is, isn't it?" Kate agreed.

Tina took a sip of her coffee and hummed. "This is fantastic. Reminds me of the stuff I used to get at Santori's before it burned down."

"That's because it is. It's Sam Appelhoff's special blend. She used to work at Santori's, remember?"

"I didn't realize she was working here now."

Kate laughed. "Someone clearly hasn't been keeping up with the Sumneyville gossip vine. Sam not only works here; she lives here. She's married to one of Matt's partners."

"I admit, I don't pay much attention to local scuttlebutt. If you ask me, some people would be better off taking a closer look at their own lives instead of paying attention to everyone else's."

"Amen to that," Kate agreed. "So, tell me how

things are going with you."

They talked for a while. The conversation was as pleasant as the company. Kate told her how impressed she was with Tina's management of the orchards as well as how much she enjoyed the products—especially the peach tea in summer, adding that it was a favorite among those at Sanctuary.

For her part, Kate told her that she now ran the Sanctuary kitchen.

"Must be a lot of work," Tina commented.

"It's not work if you love what you do, and I love what I do."

Tina understood because she felt the same way. She liked being out in the fresh air every day, getting her hands dirty, and providing the best produce around. Unfortunately, her health issues prevented her from taking as physical a role as she would like, so she'd turned some of her passion into the food-science aspect. It was the best of both worlds.

The coffee and conversation were Tina's first purely social interaction outside the family in a long time, and she thoroughly enjoyed every minute of it. It felt good, talking to someone who got it and wasn't questioning her judgment at every turn. Kate was definitely a kindred spirit.

"I believe congratulations are in order, too," Tina said. "You got married, right?"

"I did." Kate beamed and extended her left

hand to show off the stunning diamond and wedding band set. "Chris is, well, he's everything I ever hoped for. He's so kind, loving, supportive, and smart. He designed our hydroponic greenhouses …" Kate's eyes grew huge. "Oh! I should show you the greenhouses! Do you have time?"

Tina checked her watch, surprised to see how much time had gone by. "I wish I did, but I don't. I'm sorry. I've got to pick up my grandmother in less than an hour. I would like to see them sometime though."

"I guess you'll just have to come back next Sunday."

A warm feeling spread through Tina's chest. "I'd like that."

"Great!"

"Thanks for the coffee and the pastries. They were really good."

"They should be. Sam made them with your peach preserves. I'll let her know you enjoyed them and the coffee."

"Maybe she can join us next time? I'd love to say hi."

"I'm sure she'd like that, too. Next week then. Same time?"

"Sounds good."

Kate looked at someone over Tina's shoulder and gave a wave. "Hey, Doc. Got a sec?"

Tina's heart sped up at the name. She turned around, and sure enough, it was the same guy she'd seen in the parking lot at Ziegler's. Heat crept into her cheeks when she remembered that the last time she'd seen him, she'd been stuffing her face with Zook's.

"Sure," he said, changing course to join them. "What's up?"

He looked just as good as he had last time, dressed in a flannel shirt, jeans, and work boots. In the daylight, his hazel eyes were even more striking. Rimmed in an almost-vibrant green, the centers were a glowing amber with gold and dark mahogany flecks scattered throughout. For a moment, Tina felt like she was falling into them.

"This is Tina Obermacher. Tina, this is Doc, one of the partners here."

"Nice to meet you, Tina," he said, his lips curling into an easy smile that made him even more attractive.

She wondered if he was remembering the last time they'd met, while at the same time hoping he wasn't.

"You, too," she replied.

"Kate tells me you're responsible for the peach tea I'm now addicted to."

He liked her tea? "Thanks. It's based on my great-grandmother's recipe."

"Tina is also the source of all the jams, jellies, and preserves we have every morning," Kate said proudly.

"Then, I am doubly glad to meet you," he said

smoothly. His eyes crinkled at the corners, leading her to believe he wasn't quite as young as his boyish features suggested.

Tina felt another wave of warmth wash over her. That was twice in the same afternoon.

"Are you staying for dinner?" he asked.

"I can't," she told him, wishing she could. "I've got other plans."

Was that a flicker of disappointment in his eyes?

"That's too bad. Kate's a phenomenal cook."

"Oh, I know. Fire hall fundraisers aren't the same without her."

Kate blushed at the praise, but it was true. From what Tina had heard, ticket sales had gone way down after people figured out Kate wasn't cooking.

"Tina's promised to come back next Sunday," Kate told Doc.

He smiled, and she felt it right behind her breastbone. "Excellent."

"Speaking of dinner, I'd better get back to it. Doc, would you mind walking Tina out?"

Before Tina could tell them that she could find her own way, his eyes met hers, and he said, "It would be my pleasure."

CHAPTER SIX

~ Doc ~

Doc felt Tina's surreptitious side-eye glances and guessed she was thinking about the chicken incident, wondering if he'd connected that woman with the one now walking beside him. It was the slight hint of color suffusing those lovely high cheekbones that clued him in.

Of course, he knew it was her. But he was too gentlemanly to bring it up and possibly embarrass her even if the rosy-golden hue *did* make her light-blue eyes sparkle.

"So, you run Obermacher's, huh?" he said instead.

"Just the orchards." Her reply was accompanied by a shrug, as if it were some small task instead of a major operation.

They reached the foyer. She lifted a sleeveless vest and slim fleece jacket from the hook. He smoothly relieved her of both and held them out for her. She seemed surprised and for a moment, she looked as if she was going to snatch it right back.

Then she realized what he was doing and slipped her arms into the sleeves.

"What about you?" she asked. "What do you do?"

"Nothing quite as impressive."

Her slight smile resembled a smirk. "Somehow, I don't believe you."

It was his turn to shrug. "I do whatever needs to be done."

"Why do they call you Doc?"

"It's a nickname I picked up in the service," he admitted. "My last name's Watson, so …"

"Ah, a Sherlock Holmes reference. Here I thought, you were an actual doctor."

Her tone was light, the gleam in her eyes suggesting that she *might* have been teasing him.

"Not quite. But I am a medic and a huge Holmes fan."

They stepped outside. The air was brisk but pleasant and not nearly as frigid as it had been a few weeks earlier. Spring was definitely on the way, and he was ready to spend more time outside in the fresh air. He hoped they would be moving ahead with the plans for redoing the old orchard because he'd love to get out there and get his hands dirty.

"Close enough for me. Can you tell me your real first name, Doc, or is that against the rules?"

"What rules?"

She waved her hand around in a vague circle. "Sanctuary rules."

Again, he had the feeling she was teasing him. "Ah, *those* rules. Well, I suppose it'd be okay since Matt vouched for you and all. And the full background check we ran on you didn't raise any red flags."

Her eyes widened, and then she laughed. "I stepped right into that one, didn't I?"

"My name. It's Cole."

"Hmm. I like it. It suits you."

An unexpected spark went off in his chest, even as he told himself not to take her words too seriously. She was just being friendly—that was all. He could do friendly.

"And I like a woman who knows what she likes."

That pretty blush colored her cheeks again. It was enchanting.

He opened the door to her truck, and again, she looked at him as if a man opening a door for a woman was an unusual occurrence. She didn't seem to mind though, so he would continue to exercise those traditional courtesies every chance he got.

"So, I'll see you next week?" he asked.

"Barring any unforeseen difficulties, yes."

"I look forward to it."

Just to yank her chain a little and because he *liked* doing friendly with her, he lifted one hand to his ear and said, "Copy that." He looked to her and nodded somberly. "You've been cleared to leave. You have about three minutes before the booby traps reset."

She wasn't fooled this time. Her rich, throaty laughter set off more sparks, not all of them in his chest. "You're all right, Doc."

He watched as she backed her truck out of the space, swung around, and drove away. When he could no longer see her taillights, he shoved his hands in his pockets and went back inside. Unsurprisingly, he found Church and a few of the others waiting for him in the war room.

Church gave them a quick rundown of what Tina had told him.

"So? What's the verdict?" Doc asked. "Are we putting in a new orchard or not?"

"Jury's still out," Church answered. "It's more work than we anticipated, and like Tina said, it's a commitment."

"We've never shied away from work before." Heff sat back, crossing one leg over the other so his right ankle sat atop his left knee.

"No," Church agreed. "But is it worth it?"

Mad Dog nodded. "I think so. Interior renovations are nearly complete, and the more self-sufficient we are, the better."

"Especially if Doc here can find *some* way to get his hands on Tina Obermacher … uh, I mean, her secret peach tea recipe." Heff grinned unrepentantly, and a few of the others smirked.

That was when Doc knew for sure they'd been watching his exchange with Tina on the security cameras.

"Dicks," Doc said, earning some chuckles. He supposed he'd deserved it. He'd done plenty of surveillance himself.

"If Doc here gets a-friendly with the lovely Miss Obermacher, it's going to make some waves for sure," Cage said, putting up his hands when Doc shot him a *what the hell* look. "Hey, I'm not saying you *shouldn't*. I'm just saying, we need to be prepared to deal with the fallout if you do."

"It's not like we haven't dealt with it before."

Mad Dog was right. They'd played out similar scenarios, inciting the ire of some locals before. First, when Smoke got involved with Sam. Then when Heff started seeing Sandy, and again with Mad Dog and Kate. Cage had had it easy with Bree, comparatively speaking, since she hadn't been a Sumneyville resident, but even that had raised a few hackles.

"I'd also like to point out—and I think everyone here would agree—that in each case, it was totally worth it," Heff said.

The others murmured agreement. That was all fine and good but also completely different from his current situation.

"Don't you think you're getting a little ahead of yourselves?" Doc asked. "I walked her out to her car. Big fucking deal."

"Yeah, but we know that look," Cage said, grinning. "You *like* her."

What wasn't there to like? She was an attractive, strong, intelligent woman. Not that he was going to tell them that and throw gasoline on the fire. Nor would he dignify their blatant fishing expedition by taking a bite of that bait they were dangling.

"I'm with Mad Dog," Doc said. "My vote is to move forward with the orchard. Now, anything else? I've got shit to do."

"No, I think that's it," Church said. He, like the others, was trying—unsuccessfully—not to smile.

Except Heff, of course. Heff was grinning like the master baiter he was.

CHAPTER SEVEN

~ Tina ~

"What's his name?" Lottie Obermacher asked, peering over her spectacles at her granddaughter.

"What's whose name?" Tina asked. She stopped absently stirring her bowl of hearty beef stew and reached for the buttery rolls.

These late Sunday afternoon dinners with her grandmother had become one of Tina's favorite times of the week. Not only was Lottie a hoot, but she was also a good source of info.

"The young man who's got you woolgathering."

"I'm not woolgathering."

The old woman snorted. "Don't you lie to me, young lady. I might be old, but my nose is working just fine, and that manure you're spreading is pretty pungent right about now."

"He's no one, really," Tina said lightly. "Just a guy I met when I was at Sanctuary today."

As expected, her grandmother leaned forward in her chair, her eyes clear and sharp. "What were you doing at Sanctuary?"

"Matt Winston wanted my opinion on whether or not the old orchard could be saved."

"My grandfather started that orchard," Lottie said, nodding wistfully. "I remember going there with him as a child. I imagine it's gone to pot since the fire."

"It was in bad shape," Tina confirmed. "A few of the apple trees might be salvageable, but mostly, they'll need to start fresh."

"So, Matt Winston is the man on your mind?" Lottie mused. "I always did think he was a handsome young buck. Takes after his grandfather. That man inspired some lusty thoughts in many a young girl's head, let me tell you. Including mine."

"TMI, Gram."

"Yes, well, I wasn't always this old, you know. The body might be weak, but the spirit is still willing, if you know what I mean."

"Yes, I know," Tina said, unwilling to wade too deeply into those waters. "To answer your question, no, I wasn't thinking of Matt, though I will admit, he probably inspires at least as many lusty thoughts as his grandfather did."

"That's my girl," Lottie said approvingly. "But if it wasn't him, who was it?"

"His name is Cole Watson, but he goes by Doc."

"Dr. Watson. Cute. Proceed."

"He's one of the Sanctuary partners, but he told

me he was a medic in the service. I'm guessing he was a Navy SEAL, like Matt."

"Hmm," Lottie hummed. "Tell me more."

"There's not much to tell. We only spoke for a few minutes."

"And yet he seems to have made quite an impression on you."

"He held my coat for me and opened my door."

"A gentleman then."

Yes, he is. "He told me he thought running the orchards was impressive."

"It is, especially for you."

But Doc didn't know about that, and if Tina had her way, he never would. It was hard enough dealing with the misogynistic views still held by many in their small community. Sadly, most of the men she knew had trouble accepting the fact that a woman could run a successful operation in a typically male-dominated field, her own brothers included. She told her grandmother as much.

Lottie sighed. "It takes a strong, confident man to accept and support a strong, confident woman."

"I think Doc is that. But he's not over-the-top macho, you know? He comes across as laid-back and easygoing."

"He sounds wonderful, dear, but how does he make you feel between the legs?"

Tina nearly did a spit take. "Gram!"

"Don't *Gram* me. It's a valid question. If he doesn't do it for you, he's not going to *do it for you*, if you know what I mean."

"Nobody is doing anything to anyone."

"How else are you going to know if he's worth your time?"

"I don't have time for a social life." Not only did she oversee the Obermacher orchards, but she also ran a successful business of her own. Known simply as The Mill, it was an outlet store specializing in unique orchard-based products, which had been gaining popularity among locals and tourists alike.

"That's part of your problem," Lottie said, shaking an arthritic finger at her. "You work too much, and your only social interaction is a weekly dinner with your feeble, old grandmother."

Tina snorted. Of all the words one could use to describe Lottie Obermacher, *feeble* wasn't among them. Feisty? Definitely. Feeble? Never.

"I *like* having dinner with you. You're the only person in this family I can spend time with and not want to hit myself in the head with a bag of hammers while doing so. Plus, you have all the good dirt."

It was true. Lottie lived in the main farmhouse with Rick, Bonnie, and their brood, which meant Lottie was in the center of everything family-related. Gunther and his wife had had the adjacent carriage house completely renovated and lived there while Kiefer had an apartment above the garage. Tina was the outcast, preferring her quiet, quaint caretaker's cottage, away from the chaos and bedlam of the homestead.

Lottie went on as if Tina hadn't spoken. "When are you seeing him again?"

"Kate invited me back next Sunday for coffee and mentioned something about dinner."

"Will your Dr. Watson be there?"

"I suppose."

"You must go," Lottie said, nodding emphatically.

"But Sundays are our time."

"Well, that's something I've been wanting to talk to you about. You know I love spending time with you, but Mr. O'Farrell has asked me to call on him several times, and I've been putting him off. I think I've played hard to get long enough."

"Mr. O'Farrell?" Tina asked, choking again on her iced tea.

"Yes. We've been … corresponding via text for quite some time."

Tina didn't know what was more surprising—that her eighty-something grandmother was talking about going out on a date or that she'd been *texting* said potential beau. "Really?"

"Really. So, if you wouldn't mind, I'd like you to drive me down to his place before you go to Sanctuary next Sunday. You can pick me up afterward, and we can compare stud stories over tea and bourbon."

Tina gaped at her grandmother, waiting for the

just kidding that didn't come. "You're serious?"

"Absolutely. Of course, this must all be done on the QT. You know Bonnie won't give me a moment's peace, and, Lord Almighty, that woman is a pain in my wrinkled backside. I'll keep your confidence as well."

When Tina raised an eyebrow, Lottie narrowed her eyes and said, "Don't play innocent with me, dear. If your brothers knew you'd gone to Sanctuary today, they would have raised holy hell by now."

Lottie wasn't wrong. While Tina didn't really care what her brothers thought, she felt it was important to pick her battles. She wanted to explore the possibilities before deciding whether or not waging a war with her siblings was worth it.

"Deal," Tina agreed. "Now, enough about that. Have you heard any more rumblings about selling off parcels to developers?"

Lottie's lips turned down at the corners. "Not specifically, no, but something is definitely going on. I overheard Giselle telling Bonnie she was heading into the city—something about needing a new dress for an important dinner."

Giselle was Gunther's wife, the socialite in the family. She served on various community boards and made sure her picture was in the *Sumneyville Times* every week for one thing or another, whether or not she'd actively contributed.

"What important dinner?"

"I don't know. They clammed up when they

realized I was in the sunroom, having my tea. But I do know that she and Gunther have gone out to dinner several times over the past six months, all gussied up, but without the usual name-dropping."

Tina didn't like the sound of that.

"Why?" Lottie asked. "Did you hear something?"

Tina relayed what she'd overheard one of the men say about working for Tina not being a problem much longer.

"Sounds like sour grapes to me." Lottie shook her head. "The male ego is a fragile thing, isn't it? I wouldn't worry too much about it, dear, but I'll keep my eyes and ears open, and you do the same."

"Thanks, Gram."

"Now, call Kate and tell her you'll be there for dinner next Sunday while I start these dishes. It's my turn to choose the movie, and I've already picked one out."

"What did you pick?" Tina asked, carrying plates over to the sink.

Lottie's pale blue eyes, so much like Tina's, twinkled mischievously. "*Magic Mike*."

CHAPTER EIGHT

~ Doc ~

Doc pulled into Mr. O'Farrell's driveway, happy to see colorful crocuses pushing up through the dirt in the pristine flower beds—another sure sign that spring was on the way.

These weekly visits had become a regular thing ever since Kate had suggested Doc talk to the old man about the mines in and around the Sumneyville area. Each time he did, Doc came bearing gifts in the form of meals made by Kate.

At one time, Mr. O'Farrell had been on Kate's Meals on Wheels delivery route, but that was before the Ladies Auxiliary decided they didn't want to get on the bad side of the fire chief—who allowed them to use the fire hall kitchen—and informed Kate that her volunteer services were no longer required.

When Mr. O'Farrell found out what had happened, he canceled his participation and gave the Ladies Auxiliary a severe tongue-lashing. Kate had been so moved that she'd been cooking him special meals ever since, even going as far as purchasing a box freezer for his garage so she could ensure he always had enough meals on hand.

"Want these in the usual place?" Doc asked, nodding to the box of premade meals in his hands.

The old man nodded and stepped back, opening the door wider. At a sprightly one hundred and three, Mr. O'Farrell was an unending source of fascinating local history and a gifted storyteller.

He closed the door behind Doc and nodded. "Yes, please. Did Kate make that special dinner I asked for?"

"She did," Doc confirmed with a grin. "She said to tell you it's in the container with the heart drawn in red Sharpie on top."

"Kate's a good lass. Put that one near the front, so I don't need to dig it out."

"What are you up to, Mr. O?"

The old man grinned and rubbed his hands together. "Got a hot date tomorrow with a classy woman, and I want to impress her."

Doc chuckled. "Nice. Anyone I know?"

"Lottie Obermacher. She's a little young for me—only eighty-six—but I reckon she's old enough, eh?" The old man winked.

The name piqued Doc's interest since he'd been thinking a lot about a different Obermacher female lately.

"Obermacher, huh? Same family that has the produce outlet?"

"That's the one. Lottie's widowed, going on ten

years now. I figured I've waited long enough to be respectful. Neither one of us is getting any younger, you know."

Doc unloaded what he could fit into Mr. O'Farrell's refrigerator and put the rest into the nearly-full chest freezer in his garage. Doc would have to remember to tell Kate to cut back on the extras for next time. Not everyone ate as much as her tank-sized husband.

Once everything was put away, Doc turned to Mr. O'Farrell to ask him which of the delicious meals he'd like for lunch, only to find the older man waiting patiently by the door with his jacket on, his "fancy" cane in hand, and a dapper tweed flat cap atop his snowy-white hair.

"I guess we're running errands today?"

"If you don't mind, son. Like I said, Lottie's a classy woman. She's going to want flowers and chocolates."

As much as he enjoyed simply visiting with Mr. O'Farrell and listening to his stories, driving around town while running errands with him was both a learning experience and an adventure. There wasn't a spot in town that didn't have one or more stories associated with it, and the old man knew them *all*.

It was a beautiful day to do it, too. The sun was shining. The temperature had risen above the freezing mark and was hovering at a respectable forty-five. Plenty of people were out and about, which only added to Mr. O's running commentary.

"They finally got around to leveling Santori's, huh?" he noted as they drove past the spot of the café where Sam used to work. "About time. Sure do miss their coffee though. There was a girl who worked there—made the best damn cup of joe I ever had."

Doc knew exactly who he was talking about. "Sam."

"Yeah, that's right. Sammy Appelhoff. Do you know her?"

"Sam's married, and she lives at Sanctuary now."

"I think Kate did tell me that once, now that you mention it," Mr. O'Farrell mused with a nod. "Her grandpa was a good man but an old-school, fire-and-brimstone type. Couldn't handle it when his only daughter came home pregnant and demanded she give the baby up for adoption."

He paused, as if allowing the memories to funnel back to him. "She ran away shortly after that, if I recall, and he was never the same. He didn't even know about Sammy until family services showed up on his door years later. Not sure what happened to the boy."

Doc knew that Sam's mother had had mental problems and died by her own hand. Cage had dug up that information as part of their covert investigation when Sam was kidnapped by a deranged psycho several years earlier, but the identity of Sam's father remained a mystery.

Did Mr. O know who Sam's father was? And if he did, would Sam want to know? Doc made a mental note to mention something to Smoke about it later.

"Park in the free lot," Mr. O'Farrell directed when Doc was about to make a second pass along Main Street, looking for a good spot along the curb.

The old penny meters were still in place, but no one had been checking them for years as far as Doc knew.

"Are you sure?"

"Everything I need is within a few blocks, and the walk will do these old legs good."

They went to Hoffmeier's Florist first, where a cheerful woman named Penny promised Mr. O'Farrell she'd design a special bouquet and have it delivered the next day. She also inquired about Kate and asked Doc to pass along a hello, which he was happy to do.

Next was the candy shop, Lindström's. The moment they walked in, they were hit with the scents of melted chocolate and freshly roasted nuts. While Mr. O'Farrell hand-selected an assortment of candies, Doc picked up boxes of caramel cashew clusters and chocolate-covered raisins with their next movie night in mind.

As they were walking back to the car, two elderly women in puffy pastel coats were coming toward them on the sidewalk. Mr. O'Farrell grabbed

Doc's arm in a surprisingly strong grip and tugged him into the nearest shop.

Once inside, the older man peered out the window from behind Doc's much bigger frame. He exhaled in relief when the two women passed by.

"The Schaeffer twins," Mr. O'Farrell said in explanation. "If they see me with a box of Lindström's, they'll want to know who it's for. Especially Lydia. She's had the hots for me for fifty years. Not my type though. Too skinny and proper. I like a woman with a little meat on her bones and fire in her soul."

Doc chuckled as an image of white-blonde hair and sparkling pale blue eyes came to mind. He couldn't agree more.

"Can I help you with something?"

Doc turned at the male voice to find Kate's father glaring their way from behind the counter of Handelmann's Hardware. His scowl deepened when he recognized Doc.

Mr. O'Farrell either didn't notice or didn't care. "Eric, my boy," the old man said jovially. "Good to see you, lad. How's the ticker? Heard it was giving you some trouble a while back."

Mr. Handelmann's eyes moved to the older man, his jaw unclenching slightly. "Better than ever, Mr. O'Farrell."

"Good, good. Glad to hear it. Don't mind us. Just taking port in a storm, and then we're going back to enjoy some of Kate's cooking."

Eric Handelmann stiffened at the mention of his daughter's name.

"Fine, fine girl you raised there, Eric. You should be proud." The old man tapped Doc on the arm. "Okay, son, I think the coast is clear. Good day, Eric. Tell Beth I said hello, will you?"

Without waiting for a response, Mr. O'Farrell pushed out the door, leaving Doc to follow.

"The man's a damn fool," Mr. O muttered as they continued down the sidewalk. "Never would have believed he'd treat his own daughter that way, especially Kate, but there it is. Everyone has their priorities, I suppose, and if you ask me, his are grossly misplaced."

Yet another thing they were in full agreement on.

Errands completed, Doc drove them back to Mr. O'Farrell's place and warmed a bowl of pot pie for each of them.

"No one makes pot pie like Kate," Mr. O'Farrell commented after humming in approval.

Doc agreed wholeheartedly and said so. Kate was an excellent cook, and her efforts were very much enjoyed by everyone at Sanctuary.

"Is her young man treating her well? Is she happy?"

"He is, and she is," Doc confirmed.

Mad Dog's whole world revolved around his wife, and there was no question that Kate felt the same way about him. Still, her family's shunning must have hurt, especially when it was so pointless.

"She's a good girl with a big heart. I'm glad she found someone who appreciates her. What about you?"

Doc stopped chewing. "What about me?"

"Got any special ladies in your sights?"

Once again, an image of Tina Obermacher came to mind, but that didn't really count, not the way Mr. O'Farrell meant anyway.

Doc continued to chew, then swallowed, and took a drink of water. "Not particularly."

"Why not? You're a handsome fella with a good head on your shoulders and a kind soul. Shouldn't be that hard to find a decent woman. How old are you now?"

"Thirty-one."

"Thirty-one!" Mr. O'Farrell chuckled. "By the time I was your age, I'd already served my time in the Navy, gotten married, and had three kids."

Well, thought Doc, *one out of three isn't too bad.*

"You know, Lottie's got a granddaughter. Quite a looker, too. If things work out, maybe I could introduce you. We could double-date sometime."

CHAPTER NINE

~ Tina ~

"Good, you're here. She's in a mood today," Bonnie said by way of greeting when Tina arrived at the house to pick up her grandmother.

According to Bonnie, Lottie was always *in a mood*, but Tina believed it was more of a clash of personalities than anything. Lottie made it clear she didn't think much of Rick's wife, and Bonnie had suggested on several occasions that the Obermacher matriarch would be happier living in the retirement village in town.

"Are you wearing makeup?" Bonnie narrowed her eyes and peered suspiciously at Tina. "You look different."

Tina *had* spent extra time on her appearance that morning. As a result, her freshly plucked eyebrows were on point, her skin was properly moisturized and glowing, and her hair had some flattering new layers, thanks to a long-overdue visit to the salon.

"New lip balm," Tina replied.

"Huh. Listen," Bonnie said, lowering her voice, "do you think you could keep her a little later than usual tonight?"

"Sure. Why?"

"Because we're having people over."

Tina took in the state of the kitchen and winced inwardly. Dirty dishes littered the sink and counter. Cereal boxes sat open on the table next to half-full bowls of milk, peppered with soggy floaters—no doubt the remains of that morning's breakfast.

Bonnie wasn't looking much better. Though past noon, she was still wearing a robe over pajama pants and Rick's torn football practice jersey, now stretched to the max across Bonnie's expanding frame. Her hair looked as if it hadn't seen a brush in days.

There was a time when Bonnie, former head cheerleader and queen of both her junior and senior proms, had refused to be seen in public without perfect hair, perfect makeup, perfect nails, but that had started changing not long after their first child was born.

"Anyone I know?" Tina asked half-jokingly, because everyone knew everyone in Sumneyville.

Her sister-in-law shrugged, but didn't answer.

Bonnie and Rick's second child came racing into the room, screaming like a banshee. Their oldest followed closely on her heels, brandishing his junior hockey stick. The younger one stopped behind Tina, grabbed both of her legs, and peered through at her older brother.

"Aunt Tina! Aunt Tina! Save me! Ricky's going to hit me with his stick!"

The little boy's face screwed up with rage. He definitely had his father's temper. "She stole my pucks and hid them, so now, I'm going to use *her* as a puck!"

Tina looked to Bonnie, who exhaled and said wearily, "Both of you, stop right now, or I'll take your games away for the rest of the day."

The kids ignored her completely. They, like Tina, knew their mother wouldn't follow through. If Bonnie took their games away, she would have to find some other way to occupy them, and everyone knew that wasn't going to happen.

Ricky continued jabbing his hockey stick at his sister. One or two solid whacks against Tina's legs was enough to justify an intervention, in Tina's opinion. Bonnie might not believe in discipline, but Tina did.

She reached down and plucked the stick from him with one hand while grabbing the shell of his ear with the other and twisting.

"Give it back," he howled. "Ow! Ow! Ow! Stop it!"

"Hush. Adelle," Tina said firmly to the little girl, "did you take your brother's pucks?"

"Yes."

"Why?"

Her chin quivered. "Because he's going down

to the pond to play and he won't let me go, too."

"She can't go!" Ricky protested. "She's a *girl*."

"So?" Tina asked. "I played hockey with your dad and uncles. Kicked their butts quite a few times, too."

"Yeah, but you're not a *real* girl," her nephew protested. "You drive tractors and stuff. Delle doesn't know how to do *anything*, except play with her stupid dolls."

"Then, maybe you should teach her. That's what big brothers do. What they *don't* do is chase their little sisters around the house with hockey sticks. If it happens again, I'm going to introduce *my* hockey stick to your backside, and mine's a lot bigger than yours."

His eyes got wide.

Tina looked at Adelle, who was now standing beside Tina instead of behind her. "And you—you can't take things from someone just because they make you mad."

"But—"

"No buts. Apologize to Ricky and give him back his pucks. Then ask him *nicely* if he'll show you some of his power moves."

She thought about that for a moment and then said, "I'm sorry, Ricky. Will you?"

Ricky looked at Tina, who nodded. "All right. But I'm not happy about it."

The two kids left the kitchen, and Bonnie poured herself another coffee. "Threatening physical violence? Was that really necessary?"

In Tina's mind, it had been. Those kids were out of control, and if someone didn't do something, they were going to grow up to be bullying, horrible adults. Kind of like their parents.

Thankfully, Lottie appeared and answered for her, "Children need a firm hand, and yours could do with some discipline."

There was a reason Tina and her grandmother got along so well.

Bonnie's lips thinned, but wisely, she held her tongue. Not only was Lottie the matriarch of the family and deserving of respect, but this was also technically Lottie's house, and Lottie was allowing Rick and Bonnie and their kids to live there rent-free, no matter how much Bonnie liked to believe otherwise.

Leaving Bonnie to do whatever it was Bonnie did on Sundays, Tina and Lottie went out through the back door and climbed into Tina's pickup.

"Thanks for having my back," Tina said as she pulled away from the farmhouse.

"That woman," Lottie said on an exhale, shaking her head. "She's a lazy, selfish, disrespectful cow."

Tina's lips quirked. "Tell me how you really feel, Gram."

"It's shameful. She takes no pride in herself, her kids, or her house. No wonder her husband's on the prowl and her kids are running amok."

"Rick's having an affair?"

"I don't know for certain," Lottie said carefully, "but the signs are there. He's around less and less, and when he *is* around, things are tense. Seems like they can't be in the same room for more than a few minutes without arguing about one thing or another. It's no wonder he spends most evenings at the bar these days. Or at least, that's where he *says* he is. Mona Delvecchio told me last month that she saw him driving out of the parking lot of Franco's with Marietta Buschetti, and it wasn't the first time."

"Marietta Buschetti! I don't believe it. She's at least ten years younger than he is."

"She's old enough. Twenty-two now, according to Mona, and just as wild as ever." Lottie exhaled. "But enough about them. Are you ready to put our plan into action?"

The tingles of anticipation Tina had been feeling earlier made a dramatic reappearance. "It feels like we're doing something illicit."

"Not illicit. Thrilling. I haven't been this excited about something since Elvis ground his pelvis onstage right in front of me at *The Ed Sullivan Show*."

Tina turned to gape at her grandmother. "You were there?"

"Not only was I there, I *met* him," Lottie said smugly.

"You did not!"

"I did! He even signed a record for me. Of course, I have no idea where it is now. I had to hide it from my parents. I didn't want them to know that Gertie Handelmann and I'd hopped a bus to New York City. My father would've tanned my backside."

"Gertie Handelmann … Kate's grandmother?"

"We were inseparable," Lottie said with a wistful smile. "She was my best friend right up until the end. Not a day goes by when I don't think about her. Everyone should have a friend like Gertie. I hear Kate's just like her. Not too sure about the other two girls though. The older one hightailed it out to California—not that I blame her—and the younger one went and got herself knocked up by that Renninger boy."

Tina didn't know what to say to that, so she kept her mouth closed and drove to the retirement community where Mr. O'Farrell lived. Like the homes around it, Mr. O'Farrell's place was newer construction, a small rancher with neat flower beds and a front porch where a rocker would surely sit come warmer weather.

He must have been watching for them because she'd no sooner pulled in the driveway than the front door opened.

"Last chance to change your mind. Are you sure about this?" Tina asked.

"Very sure." Lottie's blue eyes were bright and sparkling.

"All right. I'll plan to pick you up around seven, but I can be here sooner if you need me."

"I won't need you," Lottie told her confidently. As she opened her door, she looked back over her shoulder. "By the way, I love what you've done with your hair."

"Thanks, Gram. Have fun."

"Oh, I will." Lottie laughed.

Tina waited until Lottie reached the front door. Mr. O'Farrell's smile was genuine as he welcomed her inside. After returning Mr. O'Farrell's wave with one of her own, Tina backed out of the driveway to set off on her own adventure.

CHAPTER TEN

~ Doc ~

Doc was in the dining room bright and early Sunday morning, fully aware that Smoke accompanied Sam when she came over to get the coffee on and start breakfast around dawn. Sure enough, Doc found him sitting in one of the booths, scrolling through the morning news with a cup of Sam's magical brew in front of him.

Doc got a cup of coffee for himself and slid in across from him. When Smoke set down his tablet and raised an eyebrow in silent question, Doc relayed part of his conversation with Mr. O'Farrell.

"Do you think he knows who Sam's father is?" Smoke asked quietly, shooting a glance toward the kitchen.

"I don't know. He seemed to know a lot about her grandparents, so maybe. Has Sam ever said anything to you about wanting to find out who her father is?"

Smoke shook his head. From the little Doc knew about Sam's situation, that wasn't surprising.

Her mother had had issues, and her grandparents weren't the cuddle-and-coddle type.

"Let's just keep this between us for the time being," Smoke said finally. "Sam's happy, and I don't want to do anything that's going to bring bad memories to the surface, yeah?"

"You got it." Doc leaned back and sipped his coffee. "So … did Sam or Kate say what time Tina Obermacher is coming by today?"

"This afternoon sometime. Why?"

Doc shrugged. "Just curious."

Smoke's eyes lasered into him. When Doc said nothing, Smoke grunted. Smoke was a man of few words, but his glares and grunts were a complete language of their own.

Doc interpreted that last combo as, *No shit. You and Tina Obermacher? Have you lost your goddamn mind?*

That was a loose translation, of course.

Sam emerged from the kitchen with a plate of muffins fresh from the oven, smiling brightly when she saw Doc sitting there. "Oh, hey, Doc! I didn't know you were here. Want some?"

"Absolutely. They smell fantastic."

"Thanks! I made extra today with Tina coming and all. Be right back." Sam beamed and went back toward the kitchen.

Smoke waited until she was out of sight before he said, "Hope you know what you're doing, man."

"Me?" Doc asked innocently. "I'm not doing

anything."

Another grunt, this one clearly expressing disbelief.

Sam returned with a second plate of muffins. "Here you go. Oh, and by the way, we're expecting Tina around one. You know, just in case you were interested." Her eyes sparkled, leading Doc to believe he wasn't nearly as good at hiding his interest as he'd thought he was.

* * *

Despite the fact that he'd kept busy doing something he enjoyed, the morning dragged by. None of that mattered once Doc saw Tina's truck pull into the lot on the security camera.

She looked even prettier than the last time he'd seen her. Her blonde hair was once again pulled back into a practical ponytail, the tip of which extended past her shoulders. Like before, she wore a light, long-sleeved fleece with a down vest, jeans, and combat-style boots. And, also like before, the sight of her set off a series of sparks in his chest. He was about to go out and greet her when he saw Kate open the door and beckon her inside.

Doc tracked their progress through the lobby and into the dining room on the grid of security monitor feeds. The war room was not only for team meetings, but it had also become their command center of sorts. From it, they had eyes and ears on nearly every part of Sanctuary, inside and out.

While some might have considered that overkill, the slew of incidents involving trespassing, vandalism, and threats of physical harm had more than justified the precaution.

Knowing that Tina was just down the hall made it hard for him to keep his ass in the chair and continue with his task of plotting out the labyrinth of mine tunnels beneath the surface even though he found the work fascinating. Ever since they'd discovered that Daryl Freed and his inner circle were using the now-defunct anthracite mines to store weapons, ammunition, and fuel, they'd been creating a map of the underground network. Church's main concern—beyond the obvious—was that some of those old passageways came dangerously close to Sanctuary property and made them vulnerable, especially since Sanctuary had some underground secrets of its own. One or two well-placed explosions could have catastrophic consequences.

Thanks to the Callaghans in nearby Pine Ridge—a group of former SEALs they'd befriended—they had access to some very sweet hardware and software to aid them in their task. Regular ventures on foot were helpful in identifying and marking off cave-ins and blockages as well. But since the coal-rich mountains were chock-full of mines, both documented and undocumented, it could take years to explore them all.

Doc finished one particularly complex section and looked up to the screen, his eyes immediately searching for their guest. He'd been doing so on and off for the last two hours, each time taking comfort in the fact that Tina seemed to be having a good visit with Kate, Sam, Sandy, and Bree. But this time, she wasn't there. The table where they'd been sitting was now unoccupied.

He pushed to his feet, out the door before he realized what he was doing. Tina couldn't have left already. He hadn't even had a chance to talk to her.

He nearly collided with Sandy in the hallway.

"Whoa. Where's the fire?" she asked.

"Sorry, Sandy. Did Tina leave?"

Her brows pulled together. "No. Kate said she had to do something with dinner, so Mad Dog's giving her a tour of the greenhouses."

"Ah." Doc's relief turned to slight embarrassment when Sandy's lips quirked.

"Relax. You didn't miss her. She's staying for dinner."

"Oh. Good to know."

Sandy's quirk turned into a knowing grin. "You like her, huh?"

"What? No. I mean, yeah, she seems nice enough."

Her grin grew. "She is."

"Right. Well … I promised Justin I'd help him

with the dogs. I should get to it."

"Uh-huh. See you at dinner?"

"Yeah, maybe." *Definitely*.

CHAPTER ELEVEN

~ Tina ~

The greenhouses were incredible. Kate's husband, Chris—who had come up with the design—said he had started with a prototype and was expanding from there.

"I'm really impressed," she told him honestly, breathing deep to inhale the heady scents of soil and water and fresh growth. It was like spring but inside.

The massive hexagonal structure was cutting edge with hinged sections on the sloped ceiling that opened with the touch of a button. Sliding Plexiglas panels worked similarly along outer and inner walls, partitioning the massive space into smaller sections, allowing each to have its own ideal growing environment.

What really impressed her, however, was the advanced hydroponic system. Not only did it collect rain and snow melt, but it also brought in water from the nutrient-rich stock pond and recycled it back through a complex gravity-based drainage network. Even better, everything was powered using solar panels and small-scale wind turbines.

"About twenty percent of our fresh produce comes from here," Chris told her proudly as they walked past the raised beds holding an assortment of fruit and vegetable plants. "We're still figuring things out."

Tina had been dreaming of doing something like this for years, but each time she brought up the idea of bringing their greenhouses into the twenty-first century, her brothers would shoot it down, citing the cost as too prohibitive to be feasible. While disappointing, she understood where they were coming from. Obermacher Farms could never produce crops on their current scale using such methods, but Sanctuary could. They needed only to sustain themselves, and that was more than doable.

"I think you've done a phenomenal job," Tina told him honestly. "How did you come up with all this?"

He grinned. "It's amazing what you can find on the internet when you know what to look for. The state university has a great agriculture program with plenty of information on sustainability and renewable resources."

Tina knew they did because that was where she'd earned her degree. In fact, she'd written quite a few articles for the site herself. "I might be able to help. Maybe offer some suggestions. I have some practical experience with sustainable farming."

"You do?"

Tina nodded. "I did work-study programs through my undergrad and grad years."

Those programs had put her in her family's bad graces more than once, but the experience and knowledge gained had been invaluable. "Each year, a team of us would go into a region, usually a poor one with unsuitable natural resources for farming, and build systems that would work for them. In one particularly dry climate, we created a completely soil-free growing environment using suspension and a recycling hydroponic system similar to the one you have here."

"Now, I'm the one impressed."

She felt the heat rise in her cheeks and looked away. The praise was unexpected but welcome all the same.

"We can talk with Church about it over dinner, see what he thinks," Kate's husband said.

"Church?"

"Sorry, Matt," he clarified. "I'm so used to calling him Church that I forget not everyone does."

"It's a call name, I take it?" *Like Doc.*

He nodded.

"What's yours?"

For a moment, she didn't think he'd answer and wondered if maybe she'd made some kind of faux pas by asking. Doc hadn't seemed to mind, but maybe others did.

"Mad Dog," he said finally.

Tina eyed him skeptically. He was a large, muscular guy but clearly soft-spoken and intelligent. Not once had the image of a rabid canine crossed her mind over the course of the afternoon.

"Do I want to know?"

"Probably not."

"Fair enough."

They stepped outside and walked down a path to the stock pond, which was actually an offshoot of the small lake on the property. Chris explained that a depression beneath the surface had created a natural aquarium-like environment. However, it didn't look deep enough to withstand winter temperatures and still function.

"How do you keep it from freezing?" Tina asked, fascinated.

"Filtered pumps and continuous recirculation of warmer water from the greenhouses with pipes below the frostline. We've had some hiccups, but we're making progress."

A sharp whistle had them both looking to the side, where a massive pit bull was running their way. The dog was big and beefy and completely bypassed Chris, making a beeline straight for *her*.

Tina remained perfectly still as the dog reached her and began to circle her slowly.

"It's okay," Chris told her. "He's one of ours."

Tina breathed a sigh of relief and let the dog sniff the back of her hand.

"Duke!" a sharp voice commanded, and

instantly, the dog turned and retreated to the man who joined them.

Doc. He was looking as good as always, his flannel shirt flapping open to hint at the form-fitting thermal beneath it.

The pit bull instantly sat at his feet, regarding her with curious interest.

"Sorry about that. Duke gets a little overexcited sometimes when he sees someone new. We're still working on that, aren't we, bud?" He reached down and scratched the dog's head.

"No problem. I love dogs."

Doc's eyes appeared to shine with approval, but it might have been a trick of the light. Or wishful thinking.

"Kate said to let you know dinner will be ready in about half an hour," Doc told them.

"Good timing. We're just about done," Chris said.

"Mind if I walk up with you?" Doc asked.

Tina could have sworn the two men exchanged a brief glance, but again, it might have been a trick of the light.

"Actually, I've got something I have to do before dinner, so you two go ahead," Chris told them. "See you in thirty."

Chris walked into the tree line and disappeared, leaving Tina and Doc to make the trek back to the resort with Duke trotting along beside them.

"So, how many guard dogs do you have here?"

she asked.

"Nine, including Duke, but they're not guard dogs," Doc told her. "Duke's a stray that Kate took in a few years ago, along with Duke's baby mama and their seven pups. Well, they're not pups anymore, I guess."

Tina laughed. "That sounds exactly like something Kate would do. So, they're pets?"

"We're training them to be therapy dogs."

Tina hadn't considered that. But given Sanctuary's mission, it made perfect sense. "Very cool."

They walked for a while in companionable silence before she said, "You're doing some good things here."

He smiled, unknowingly setting off butterflies in her chest. Or at least, that was what that fluttering felt like to her.

"That's the idea."

When they neared the main building, Doc veered off to the right. When Tina hesitated, he encouraged her to join him, an offer she gladly accepted. He led them to a large, fenced-in area, where they were greeted with quite a few wagging tails.

After taking a few minutes to pet them all, they left Duke with his doggy family and went inside, using a side entrance. The moment they did, delicious aromas assaulted them. Tina hadn't realized how hungry she was until then.

She asked to use the restroom to wash up. As she washed her hands, she looked at herself in the mirror. Her skin was lightly flushed from being outside, but it was the sheer pleasure of the afternoon that made her feel as if she was glowing.

Dinner was no less enjoyable. Kate had cooked a fabulous meal, but it was the easy camaraderie among the residents that Tina enjoyed the most. They felt like a family—or what a family *should* feel like.

She was genuinely sad when it was time to go.

She thanked them and said her good-byes. Once again, it was Doc who walked her out.

"I had a wonderful time today," she told him.

"Glad to hear it. I hope that means you'll come back and visit us again."

"I'd like that."

She'd enjoyed the girl time, the tour, the dinner, seeing Doc—all of it—and she wouldn't be opposed to doing it again. Hopefully, she would, too. Chris had seemed receptive of her offer to collaborate on the greenhouses, just as Matt had with the orchard.

Once again, Doc opened her truck door for her in a gentlemanly gesture. It didn't surprise her as much as it had the last time.

"Listen, Tina, do you think you might like to go out sometime? Maybe grab some dinner or a cup of coffee or something?"

His words thrilled her, but reality came

crashing in hard. It was one thing to see him at Sanctuary. Quite another to be seen with him in town.

"Oh, I'm not sure I can," she hedged. "Things are ramping up at the orchards. There's always so much to do this time of year."

"I understand," he said easily. "You have a good night. Drive safe."

CHAPTER TWELVE

~ Doc ~

No matter how old a man got, rejection was still a hard pill to swallow. Perhaps what made it worse was, he so rarely asked that when he did, it felt like it cut deeper.

Clearly, he'd misread the signals because for a while there, he'd thought that Tina felt the same attraction that he did.

He kept the smile on his face and waved toward her departing vehicle, then went back into the main building, still smiling for the benefit of those watching on the security cameras. He'd done the same himself often enough, so when he'd asked Tina out, he'd known exactly where and how to stand, so he wouldn't be heard, and Heff, the nosy fucker, wouldn't be able to read his lips.

He expected to find them in the war room, and he did. He took a seat and waited for the inevitable discussion to begin.

"Did you see the lovely Miss Obermacher off?" Heff asked.

Doc flicked his gaze to the monitors, specifically the one at the main entrance. "You know I did."

"And?"

"*And* she said she had a great time and would enjoy visiting again."

"That's all?"

Doc shrugged. "Yeah. What else were you expecting?"

Heff blinked, his way of expressing surprise. Kate didn't even try to hide her disappointment. It looked as if they'd misread the situation, too.

"Thoughts?" Church asked.

"She knows her stuff," Cage said. "She did her master's thesis on sustainable farming, and that stuff she told Mad Dog about working in poverty-stricken areas checks out."

"And she's certainly got the experience," Mad Dog chimed in. "Bringing her on board as a consultant would save us time, money, and effort. Not just for the orchard, but the greenhouses as well."

"What about her connections to Freed and company?" asked Smoke.

"I doubt her brothers know about her coming up here," Church said.

Doc silently agreed with that.

"But if this becomes a regular thing, they will," Heff said, looking directly at Doc. "And Tina Obermacher might be forced to choose."

Doc shrugged and kept his expression neutral, though he was pretty sure he knew which side of the fence Tina would choose to stand on, and it wasn't good news for him. "She's an adult. She knows actions have consequences and that by offering to help us, she might be putting herself in the crosshairs. If she's willing to do that, then I vote we should take her up on her offer."

Heff's eyes narrowed. Doc met his challenging stare with one of his own.

"I understand your concerns," Sandy said carefully, her eyes flicking toward Smoke, "but is it possible you're overthinking this? I mean, it's not like she came here to gather intel. We asked her to come and share her thoughts on the orchard, and that's exactly what she did."

"And we were the ones who asked her to come back," Kate agreed, picking up the thread. "It's not like she invited herself."

"What about when you were having coffee? Was she asking a lot of questions?" asked Cage.

"Not really. Mostly, we just caught up with each other," Sam said. "Sorry, guys, but you and Sanctuary really didn't even factor into the conversation."

"In fact, we were talking about making it a regular Sunday afternoon thing," said Kate. "It seems like a win-win for everyone. We get to have some girl time, and all of us get to benefit from her knowledge and experience."

“Fair enough,” Church said, nodding. “We’ll play it by ear for now, and if the situation changes, we’ll adapt.”

As their impromptu meeting broke up and people started to leave, Church said, “Doc, got a minute?”

“Sure.” He hung back until the others filed out. “What’s up?”

“Make sure you know what you’re doing where Tina’s concerned.”

“I’m not doing anything.”

When Church opened his mouth to speak again, Doc put his hand up to stop him. “Seriously. I get it, and I’m telling you, you’ve got nothing to worry about there. Anything else?”

Church looked like he wanted to say more, but he didn’t. “No.”

“Cool. Good talk, Dad. I’ll be in my room if you need me.”

CHAPTER THIRTEEN

~ *Tina* ~

"Judging by the smile on your face, you had a good time today," Tina said to her grandmother as they drove away from Mr. O'Farrell's.

"Ah, it was lovely. The man knows a thing or two about how to treat a lady."

"Do tell."

"He plied me with chocolates and flowers, and we talked for hours."

"And? That's a pretty powerful glow you've got going for someone who spent the afternoon *talking*."

Lottie's face flushed, and her eyes sparkled. "Never underestimate the power of a good *talk*, my dear, especially if it's been a long time since you've had one."

Tina laughed. "Right. I'll mind my own business."

"What about you? How was your day?"

"It was great." On the ride home, Tina told her grandmother how much she'd enjoyed coffee with

Kate, Sam, and Sandy.

She'd almost forgotten what it was like to have real girl time with women she liked and connected with. Her sisters-in-law definitely didn't fall into that category. Any hopes she'd had of gaining "sisters" she could talk to and do things with through her brothers' marriages had been dashed pretty quickly.

Tina was still talking as they went inside the caretaker's cottage. Tina grabbed the bottle of bourbon and poured out two shots while Lottie put the kettle on for tea.

"And you should see their greenhouses! Truly amazing, cutting-edge stuff, things I'd love to try myself at some point—*if* I could get Gunther and Rick to see the possibilities, but they're too stubborn."

"They take after your father."

"True, but at least Dad was willing to listen and consider all sides before making a decision. Gunther and Rick treat new ideas like they're personal attacks on their characters or something."

"It's not their characters that are feeling threatened, dear. It's their pride."

Tina exhaled heavily. Yes, she knew they resented the fact that she'd gotten the opportunity to travel the world and get her master's degree—Rick more so than Gunther. He often complained to anyone who would listen that she got special treatment because she was the youngest and the only girl. Within the family, he cited her health issues. That only made her twice as determined to prove herself.

At least Gunther had managed to get his bachelor's degree. Rick had gotten himself kicked out before he finished his freshman year.

"He could have done more, too."

"He could have, but he made bad choices," Lottie said bluntly. "He's just not that smart. You are special. Your father saw that. Unfortunately, your brothers do, too."

"It's pointless and stupid. We should be working together, not against one another." Tina exhaled heavily in frustration. "It's never going to change, is it?"

"Probably not." Lottie reached over and patted her hand in sympathy or empathy—Tina wasn't sure which. "But enough about them. Did you see that young man today? Dr. Watson?"

Just that quickly, the heavy shadows weighing down Tina's thoughts lifted. "I did." She told Lottie about Duke and how she'd caught Doc looking at her during dinner.

"Now, I'm not the only one glowing," her grandmother said with a smile. "Are you going to see him again?"

"When he walked me out to my truck, he asked me if I wanted to go out sometime."

"And? What did you say?"

"And … I told him I was really busy."

Lottie's lips pursed. "Why? I thought you liked him."

"I do like him, but you know spring is a busy time."

Lottie pulled the kettle from the stove and poured them each a cup of tea. She waited until she sat down at the table before saying, "Nonsense. If something's important to you, you make time for it."

Tina added honey to her tea and stirred. "I know, but …"

Seeing Doc beyond Sanctuary would create issues. What if those tingles she felt around him were just some knee-jerk reaction to a good-looking guy giving her some attention? It wasn't as if men were breaking down the door to get her to go out with them. She said as much to her grandmother.

Lottie considered that for a moment and then replied, "I doubt it. Topical interest feels different than a real connection."

That was what Tina thought, too. What she felt around Doc seemed like more than garden-variety attraction, but what did she know? She could count the number of potentially serious relationships she'd had on one hand, less a thumb and three fingers. There'd been that one guy in college, but they'd parted ways soon after graduation, and more importantly, she hadn't minded at all.

But the thought of not seeing Doc again left her feeling strangely bereft.

"Kate said something about making Sunday afternoon coffee a regular thing, so I'll probably see him again."

"I was hoping you'd say that," Lottie said. "Mr. O'Farrell has suggested we make our Sunday afternoon visits a regular thing, too."

"Then, it sounds like our illicit rendezvous will continue."

Lottie held her shot glass up in toast, prompting Tina to clink hers lightly against it. "Sounds like."

* * *

As the week wore on, Tina found herself looking forward to her visit to Sanctuary more and more. To coffee and conversation with Kate, Sam, Sandy, and Bree. To sharing her thoughts on recycling kitchen refuse into organic compost with Chris. Mostly, she was looking forward to seeing Doc again.

Unfortunately, only two of those things actually happened. She did enjoy coffee with the women, and she did get to talk compost with Kate's husband. However, she didn't cross paths with Doc once.

The week after wasn't much better. When she was helping Matt gather a soil sample in the old orchard, she caught a glimpse of Doc walking

Duke. She waved, hoping he'd come by and talk to her, but he just waved back from afar and kept going.

By the third week, she was convinced she'd messed up big time. It bothered her enough that she felt compelled to bring it up to the others.

"Is Doc still around?"

"Yes," Kate replied. "Why do you ask?"

"I haven't seen him around lately. I think he might be avoiding me."

"That doesn't sound like Doc," said Sam. "He's very easygoing and friendly. I've never known him to avoid anyone."

"Maybe he thinks *you* don't want to see *him*. Did something happen we don't know about?" asked Sandy.

After only a brief hesitation, Tina decided to forge ahead and tell them what had happened when Doc walked her to her truck. "We haven't spoken since."

"Ah, that makes sense," Sam said, nodding.

"I screwed up, didn't I?"

"I think that depends," Kate said carefully.

"On what?"

"On what it is you want from him. As far as I know, Doc hasn't shown interest in anyone since he came here. The fact that he asked you out speaks volumes."

"As does the fact that he turns into a ghost whenever you're around," mused Bree.

Tina considered that.

"Let me ask you this," Sam said. "Did you say no to Doc because you're not interested in him in that way or because Doc is part of Sanctuary?"

She *was* interested, so by process of elimination, it was the latter. "It is a consideration," she admitted.

"At least you're honest," Sam said with a quirk of her lips.

"Was it something any of you considered?" Tina asked them.

Sam was the first to answer. "I was already an outcast as far as the town was concerned, so it wasn't really an issue for me."

"Apples and oranges because I'm not a local," Bree said, waving her hand dismissively. "But I will say that I've never really cared much what other people thought."

"When I first met Heff, I thought I was finally on my way out of Sumneyville, and I didn't really care what anyone thought," Sandy said. "By the time I decided to stay, I'd already burned my bridges, so it wasn't an issue for me either."

Tina looked to Kate, anxious to hear what she had to say. Kate's situation was the one most similar to hers.

"I didn't take it seriously at first," Kate said thoughtfully. "I knew there were concerns on both sides, but I was optimistic that I could have it all. Honestly, I never thought I'd be forced to choose. It came down to them or me, and in the end, I chose me."

"Any regrets?"

"Only that I didn't stand up for myself sooner," Kate answered. "I do wish things were different with my family, but I've accepted that I can't control what other people do, only what I can do."

Wise words indeed. Whether or not they applied to Tina's current dilemma remained to be seen.

"Want my opinion?" asked Sandy.

Tina nodded.

"Talk to Doc. Be honest with him. He's a smart guy. He'll understand."

"We've already established there's interest on both sides," said Sam. "Now, you need the chance to get to know each other better and see if it's worth pursuing."

That sounded like a plan. "Do you know where I can find him?"

"He was out with the dogs earlier. If he's not hanging around there, then he's probably back in his trailer."

Sandy's eyes lit up. "What if, instead of having dinner with us, Tina took food out to him?"

"Since he asked her out, it might be nice if she was the one to make the next move," Bree said, nodding thoughtfully.

Kate clasped her hands together. "I like it! What do you think?"

Four pairs of eyes looked at Tina expectantly.
"Why not?"

CHAPTER FOURTEEN

~ *Doc* ~

After rereading the same page for the third time, Doc set the book aside and sighed. It was a good story, a mystery/thriller that had received rave reviews, but he couldn't stay focused. His thoughts were elsewhere.

He looked at the clock. Again. Sunday afternoons had officially become the longest couple of hours of the week—his own personal, in-depth study on the slowing of time.

Because Sunday afternoon was when Tina Obermacher visited Sanctuary.

Is she still around? he wondered. Had she chosen to stay for dinner this week, or had she opted to leave after coffee with the girls, as she had the week before?

It wasn't as if he could ask. Heff had already given him shit, convinced that Doc's recent scarcity on Sundays was one hundred percent the wrong thing to do. Heff's unsolicited advice involved ensuring that Tina saw him often, thus keeping him in the forefront of her thoughts and thus a constant reminder of what she was missing.

Doc's answer was to remind Heff how *he* had gone full hermit when Sandy decided to move to New York City. However, instead of getting Heff off his ass, as he'd intended, it had the opposite effect. Heff had argued that Doc's analogy was only relevant if Doc's feelings for Tina were similar to the ones Heff had for Sandy.

Which, of course, was a ridiculous comparison. By the time Sandy had gone to New York, she and Heff had already created a bond. They'd spent time together. Gotten to know each other. *Slept* together.

Doc had spoken to Tina three times. Three extremely limited, topical exchanges. Nothing on par with the level of *sharing* Heff and Sandy had engaged in. In fact, Doc had had longer, more revealing conversations with the checker at the grocery store in town than he'd had with Tina.

More importantly, when Doc had suggested something more, something as innocuous as coffee or dinner beyond the Sanctuary property line, she'd shut him down.

So … yeah, he was steering clear of the dining room, the greenhouses, and the orchard on Sundays, hoping to avoid any further awkwardness.

Keeping Tina out of his sights was easy. Keeping her out of his mind? Not so much. Just knowing she was nearby was like a siren's call, and *that* bothered him, not that he'd admit that to Heff or anyone else. How had she managed to get under his skin so quickly and with such minimal effort?

He stood and stretched, welcoming the tiny pops of pain as he attempted to get his spine and neck back into proper alignment. Perhaps he'd just go for a walk, see if her truck was still parked in front of the main building. He'd stick to the trees, nothing but a shadow among shadows. If anyone *did* happen to see him on the security cams, he could just say he was doing a routine perimeter check.

If he spotted Tina's truck in the front lot, he'd continue on his way, maybe head over to the new weight room and get in a quick workout. If he didn't, he'd go inside the main building and see what kind of progress Cage was making on that 3-D mine map. They'd explored several offshoots the prior week, one of which seemed to lead dangerously close to the small lake on Sanctuary property. After that, maybe he'd see if anyone was up for a game of pool or something.

Doc grabbed a flannel shirt from the half-dozen or so hanging just inside the door, prepared to do just that. But when he opened the door, the object of his current obsession was standing there, hand raised, poised to knock.

"Hey," she said, stepping back off the wooden stoop in surprise.

Naturally, he reached out to keep her from

falling. “Hey. What’s up?”

“I thought we could talk.” She held up a box, one of those reusable takeout containers Kate sent him back to his trailer with sometimes. “I brought food. Can I come in?”

His first thought was to say no because being alone in a trailer in the woods with Tina didn’t seem like such a good idea. It was his personal space and decidedly more intimate than the public diner he’d considered taking her to.

And yet … she was looking up at him with those pale blue eyes, and curiosity won out over good judgment.

He stepped back, giving her room to enter. “Sure. Come on in.”

She wiped her feet on the mat and stepped up into the trailer, stopping just far enough inside for him to close the door behind her.

“How’d you find this place?” he asked.

“Sandy walked me out.”

He would be having a word with Sandy about that later. Heff, too.

“Nice,” she said, taking in the space. “So, this is where you live, huh?”

He nodded, wondering what she really thought. It was a modest trailer, nothing like the main building or the custom cabins Smoke, Heff, Mad Dog, and Cage had built for themselves and their women. And probably nothing like she was accustomed to. “It’s not much, but it works for me.”

"I like it. It's cozy. I like cozy. I live in a caretaker's cottage myself."

That was news to him. When analyzing the satellite scans, he *might* have zoomed in on the Obermacher farm homestead. It was practically a mansion with numerous outbuildings. Naturally, he'd assumed Tina lived in one of them.

"Why a caretaker's cottage?"

Her lips curled upward as she tossed his own words back at him. "It works for me."

He gestured toward the table and remembered his manners. "Please, sit down. May I take your coat?"

"Yes, thanks." She put the box on the table, then peeled off her jacket and vest, and handed them to him.

He hung them up next to his shirts, quietly appreciating the clean, fresh, feminine scent that clung to them.

As before, she wore jeans and a top that accentuated her fit, athletic physique. He willed himself not to think about that. Whatever unusual energy he'd felt around her before seemed even more potent in the enclosed space, making his heart beat a little faster, his blood run a little warmer. That didn't happen around anyone else. Only her.

She made no move to unpack the food, which suggested that she was more interested in talking than she was in eating. That was fine with him. He'd take his cues from her, especially since he had no idea what this unexpected visit was about.

"You said you wanted to talk to me about something?" he prompted.

"Yes." She seemed almost as nervous as he'd been when he first asked her out. "I've been thinking about what you said. About going out, I mean. I don't think I gave you a proper answer."

"You said you were busy," he reminded her, careful to keep any hint of disappointment out of his voice.

"I am. Running The Mill and the orchards is more than a full-time job; it's my life. I don't have a lot of free time, so I tend to be protective about the little bit I do."

If she was trying to lessen the sting of rejection, telling him he wasn't worth a thin slice of her limited free time was a piss-poor way to do it. "It's okay. I get it. You don't have to explain."

"I think I do," she said, her face twisting in frustration. "Be patient with me, okay? I'm not used to second-guessing myself, and that's exactly what I've been doing for the last three weeks."

His chest loosened at her admission. A *little.* "Would you like something to drink?"

"Yes, please. Water would be great, thanks."

He rose and got them each a glass. When he returned to the table, she seemed surer of herself.

"The thing is, by not going out with you, I feel like I'm missing out on an opportunity. I'm not saying anything *will* come of it, but the possibility is there, you know? And that sense of possibility is not something I feel often, so it's important I pay attention when I do." Tina blew out a breath and shook her head. "I'm sorry. I'm explaining this badly. You probably think I'm a few peaches short of a bushel, huh?"

His lips quirked. Her awkwardness was endearing. He understood because he'd had similar thoughts. "No, I don't think that. I understand exactly what you're saying."

She seemed relieved. "Good. So … maybe we can start over?" She extended her hand across the table. "Hi, I'm Tina. Want to have dinner with me?"

He laughed and wrapped his hand around hers. The moment he did, an odd energy seemed to coalesce at the point of contact, race up his arm, and spread across his chest. "Doc. Or Cole. Whichever you prefer. And, yes, I would like very much to have dinner with you."

Her smile was brilliant. "Excellent. Now, I feel like I can actually eat something. Got some plates and silverware? Despite prior evidence to the contrary, I *can* be a civilized dinner companion."

He rose and took three steps into the kitchen area, appreciating her self-effacing humor. "According to Kate, Zook's is good enough to warrant a bit of savagery."

"She's not wrong." Her eyes widened in realization as he placed dinnerware and utensils on the table and sat back down. "Don't tell me you've never had a Zook's chicken."

"I haven't," he admitted. "They're usually sold out by the time we get there."

"Next week, I'll pick one up for you."

"That would be great, thanks. If it's even half as good as your peach iced tea, I'm sold."

A lovely rose hue painted her cheeks as she smiled and looked downward. She'd done something similar when Kate mentioned how much he enjoyed Tina's tea. Was she not used to receiving compliments?

"So, your family's been around for a while, huh?"

"More than four hundred years," she said with a touch of pride. "We're one of the original founding families along with the Winstons and the Sumneys."

"The Sumneys? I haven't heard of them, but I'm guessing that's who the town is named after."

Tina nodded. "Efigenia Sumney was the last. She died in the 1800s. It's a tragically romantic story. The man she was supposed to marry was killed in the Civil War, and she was so heartbroken that she died herself shortly after. But something of the bloodline continues. One of Effie's sisters, Emilia, married an Obermacher, and another, Eva, married a Winston."

"You know your local history."

"It's kind of a requirement around here—to know where you came from. Family pride's a big thing. I bet if you asked Matt, he'd tell you the same." She lifted a spoon to her mouth and hummed. "Mmm. I can't tell you how much I missed Kate's pot pie."

"It is good," he agreed, but her words had something else floating to the forefront of his mind. "Tina, can I ask you something?"

"Sure. That's the idea, right? To get to know each other better?"

"Right. Do your brothers know you've been coming up here?"

Tina finished chewing and then took a drink of water. "No."

The answer wasn't unexpected, and yet he'd hoped it would be. "I see."

She set her spoon down, her expression more serious than it was earlier. "Okay. This is good. Let's talk about this because while it shouldn't be an issue, it clearly is." She took a deep breath and seemed to be considering her next words carefully. "You know there are those in town who are not fans of Sanctuary."

"Yes, I'm aware."

"Then you probably also know that my brothers are among them."

He nodded.

"Well, I'm not my brothers. I make my own decisions and form my own opinions, which differ from theirs quite often. We butt heads a lot, and honestly, it's exhausting and a waste of time and energy. Because of that, I prefer to pick my battles for those who are worth it. They're going to find out I'm helping Matt eventually, and when they do, shit's gonna hit the fan. But I think it's worth it."

"And having dinner with me?" he asked.

"That's where that second-guessing comes in," she said, her lips curling slightly upward. "And why I'm here now. Something tells me, Cole Watson, that you are worth fighting for."

CHAPTER FIFTEEN

~ Tina ~

Tina clamped her lips together. While she tended to speak her mind, she wasn't usually *that* honest, especially with someone she didn't know well.

The thing was, she *did* feel like she knew him. Maybe not in a detailed history sort of way. She didn't know where he'd grown up or if he had any brothers or sisters or what he liked to do in his spare time.

But below the surface nervousness, there was this … pull—for lack of a better word—drawing her in and making her want to know more, a simmering sense of anticipation laced with a calming familiarity she couldn't explain. She wasn't even sure how to label it. Whatever it was, it made her feel comfortable enough to say what was on her mind.

She held her breath and chanced a look right into his gorgeous hazel eyes. The green hues seemed more vibrant than they had been, the gold flecks more prominent. Behind them, she sensed more going on than his easy, casual demeanor let on.

Verbally, he wasn't saying anything, and yet her body seemed to think that look said *a lot*. Warmth began to pool in her core and radiate outward. No man had been able to make her feel like that with just a *look*.

He smiled, a slow, sexy smile that kicked that inner simmer up a notch or ten. She discreetly shifted in her seat to alleviate some of the building pressure.

"Too much too soon?" she prompted in an attempt to lighten the mood.

He blinked, and the intensity lessened considerably. The heat was still there, but it was now banked.

"No," he replied. "In fact, I feel the same way."

Relief flooded through her along with the thrill of hearing that he thought she was worth the inevitable stink her brothers would raise. Not many men were willing to go up against Rick, Gunther, and Kiefer—and especially not for her.

Her brothers might not be the only opposition either. Tension was rarely one-sided, and while everyone at Sanctuary had been outwardly friendly and welcoming, she'd detected a low-key wariness, too. They might be okay with her coming up for consultations and coffee, but getting personally involved with one of them could push a few boundaries and make things more complicated for everyone.

"Is this"—she waved her hand back and forth between the two of them—"going to cause you problems?"

He hesitated slightly before shaking his head. "Not me, no."

"But Sanctuary?"

"It's nothing we haven't dealt with before," he said, most likely referring to prior experiences with Sam, Sandy, and Kate. "And nothing that would make me think that this isn't a good idea. But it could make things difficult for you, and that's what bothers me."

That warmth she'd felt earlier blossomed again. When was the last time someone had been genuinely concerned about her? Not the farm, not the bottom line, not the effect it would have on them, but on *her*?

"I can handle it. And like I said, I think it's worth seeing where it goes."

His smile alone made taking the chance worthwhile. "Fair enough."

"You do raise a good point, however," she told him. Thoughts of what she would have to deal with once word got out didn't fill her with the warm and fuzzies. She was already battling her brothers on multiple fronts—pushing for newer, earth-friendlier techniques and equipment; pricier but healthier alternatives; staff issues. Getting involved with Doc would make those pale in comparison.

"Perhaps we can do our getting to know each other here at Sanctuary and away from prying eyes. At least at first."

He considered that and then nodded. "All right. Are we limited to Sunday afternoons?"

"That works best for me," she told him. "Everyone already knows I'm not available then because that's when I spend time with my grandmother."

"You don't think she'll mind?" Doc asked with a frown.

Tina laughed. "No. She has a secret beau she's been seeing while I've been coming up here. We've been covering for each other."

He grinned knowingly. "Mr. O'Farrell."

"How did you know that?"

"Because he told me. I go down to see him every week with care packages from Kate, and a few weeks ago, he asked me to drive him around town and get stuff because he had a hot date with a classy lady."

"You didn't say anything!"

"He swore me to secrecy. He did tell me that his new lady friend had a cute granddaughter and offered to put in a good word for me. Even suggested a double date." Doc winked.

"I'm not sure I'm ready for that," she said on a laugh. "I'm still trying to wrap my mind around the fact that my eighty-something grandmother is getting more than I am."

Doc choked on his drink. "Now, *that's* TMI."

"Sorry." She wasn't sorry. "But how do you think I feel? When I pick her up and take her back to my place for tea and bourbon, she's *glowing*. I mean, I'm happy for her but a little jealous, too."

There was that look again. Intensity mixed with hunger, simmering just beneath the surface. As if he was leashing his baser instincts.

The thought thrilled her. Perhaps one of these days, she'd be glowing at teatime too—and not because of the shot of bourbon. Her body heated instantly, totally on board with that plan.

"Anyway," she said, clearing her throat and pulling her thoughts back to the present, "what do you think about doing it up old school? We could start with good old-fashioned phone calls in the evening?" That way, she might actually be able to concentrate on his words and stop fantasizing about those eyes gazing into hers as he slid into her body …

"That'll work."

By the time they finished dinner, Tina was even more convinced she wanted to know more about the fascinating man sitting across from her. They'd kept the conversation light and not delved into deep details, which was probably good for a first "date."

Among other things, she'd discovered they shared a mutual love for the outdoors, eating healthy—most of the time—and gripping mystery thrillers. He seemed fascinated by local history too—something which she knew a lot about.

All too soon, her phone vibrated with a message from Lottie. When she saw the time, Tina couldn't believe the afternoon had gone so quickly and offered her apologies.

"I'm sorry. I've got to go pick up my grandmother."

He helped her with her jacket and then donned a flannel shirt before walking her back to her truck.

"I had a good time today," she told him as he opened her door.

"I did, too."

"Same time next week?"

"I'll be here."

"And you'll call?" she asked, hoping she didn't sound *too* anxious.

He smiled. "I'll definitely call. You can always call me, too."

She could. But since she was the one driving up to see him, she wanted him to take the lead on phone calls. It felt more equitable if each of them was making an effort. She told him as much. Again, he seemed perfectly okay with that.

"Have a safe drive, Tina."

"I will, thanks."

As Tina drove away, she looked back in the rearview mirror and caught a glimpse of her face in the process. If she didn't know better, she'd swear she saw the beginnings of a glow.

CHAPTER SIXTEEN

~ Doc ~

Once Tina's vehicle was out of view, Doc went inside the main building to return the takeout containers and hopefully find something to keep him occupied for the next several hours.

The afternoon had gone extremely well, in his opinion. Much better than it had started. Tina was a strong, capable woman as well as smart and funny and down-to-earth. She said what was on her mind, and he found that as attractive as he did refreshing.

They shared similar tastes as well. She liked eating healthy and staying active, which were two things he felt fairly strongly about. In fact, everything about the last several hours had confirmed that his initial interest was warranted and that, extraneous influences aside, there was definite potential for something more. He was already imagining long hikes and summer swims and rediscovering simple pleasures.

Some complicated ones, too. He couldn't help but wonder if she was as confident and adventurous in all aspects of her life. Just the thought of what they might explore together filled his mind with possibilities.

After returning the containers to the kitchen, he found the women in the decompression chamber. Some of the dogs were there, too, but none of the guys, which was unusual for a Sunday evening. Either couples tended to head back to their cabins or they gathered to watch a movie or play cards or something after dinner.

Kate was the first to spot him. She sat up and muted the TV. "Well? How'd it go? Did you guys talk?"

"It went well," he answered honestly. "And, yes, we did."

"So, no more hiding on Sundays?" Sam asked with a grin.

"I wasn't hiding," he protested.

He'd simply been avoiding a potentially awkward situation and making things easier on everyone involved. That had been the plan anyway. As it turned out, it hadn't worked, not for him and not for Tina. He was much happier with their new plan.

Sam's grin widened. "Right. You were just keeping a low profile."

"Something like that. Where are your better halves?"

"Better halves?" Bree exclaimed in mock outrage and tossed a throw pillow his way, which he caught easily.

He did enjoy teasing the ladies. They reminded him a lot of his sisters.

"In the war room," Sandy answered. "One of the Callaghans called and said they had some new information. They're on the secure line. Church said to send you over after Tina left."

"Thanks."

Doc made his way down the corridor, his mind wondering what new intel the Callaghans had managed to discover. He didn't know how they got half the information they did, but it smacked of high-level security and black ops.

He knew the brothers had a family tradition of serving in the teams, but like him and the rest of the Sanctuary partners, they were *officially* out. Doc believed, as did the others, that either the Callaghans were still active or they were awfully tight with those who were. Either way, he was glad they were on the same side.

When he walked into the war room, Ian and Jake were on the flat screen. Church was leaning against one of the desks, arms crossed, and glanced his way. Doc offered a nod and quietly took a seat among the others.

"They tried doing something similar with Maggie's land years ago," Ian said. "Suffice it to say, Dumas was not happy when we got involved. He lost millions."

"All right. Thanks for the heads-up," Church

said. "We'll keep you posted."

"Do that," said Jake. "We'll flip a few rocks on our end, too, see what crawls out. If it's legit, there'll be plenty of ripples in the pond."

"Will do. Thanks," Church said and disconnected the call.

"What did I miss?" Doc asked once the screen blinked off.

It was Cage who answered first. "You know those offshore accounts Luther Renninger has been using to funnel funds? Well, Ian's DOJ contact says one of them has been pretty active lately, and they've linked it back to one local business in particular."

If the bad feeling in his gut hadn't tipped him off, the look in Church's eyes would have. "Let me guess. Obermacher Farms."

Church nodded.

Luther Renninger was a local who'd stepped into his father's respectable and established accounting business but didn't have the same sense of integrity his father had had. He was currently under investigation by the IRS, among other agencies, including the Department of Justice. That intel, however, was not public knowledge.

Closer to home, Renninger was on Sanctuary's radar, too. They'd already established that he was using legitimate local business accounts to launder money and siphon funds into international cartels. To complicate matters, one of those cartels was

from Smoke.

"I thought Friedrich was the oldest."

Church snorted. "He is, but Rick Obermacher isn't smart enough to run the business. Gunther is, and unlike Rick, Gunther has the cunning to make things happen. He's also tight with Renninger."

"Based on his credit card activity—all of which are maxed out, by the way—Gunther has been wining and dining some bigshots lately, including Phillip Dumas," Cage said.

"Who is Phillip Dumas, and why do we care?" Doc asked.

"Phillip Dumas is the current CEO of Dumas Industries, located just outside of Pine Ridge. They're a multibillion-dollar company with both domestic and foreign interests."

"Why would the CEO of a multibillion-dollar company be wining and dining a local farmer?" asked Smoke.

"That's the question, isn't it?" commented Heff.

"Do you think they're part of Renninger's illegal arms deals?" Mad Dog asked. "If they've got a global presence, they'd have the connections and the means to move contraband."

Church considered that for a moment and then shook his head. "No. That's not their style. The Dumases are known for being ruthless in the corporate world, but they're not terrorists."

"All right. So what's the angle?"

"Ian thinks Dumas might be trying to get his hands on Obermachers' land. They tried the same thing years ago with Maggie Callaghan's farm. Word got out that Maggie was talking with Aidan Harrison about contracting with the Celtic Goddess to provide fresh, organic produce for their restaurant. It was a novel concept for the area then—a corporate enterprise sourcing from a small-scale local farm—but there was a lot of potential there, and Dumas wanted a piece of the action. Plus, I think Dumas was feeling territorial. He was the only billionaire on the block until Harrison decided to move to Pine Ridge. Ian said Dumas considered it a done deal after paying off the local politicians, thinking he'd send Maggie into bankruptcy and pick up the land for a song. Clearly, it didn't quite pan out that way."

"I bet that's a story," Heff mused.

Doc's brows pulled together. "So … Dumas missed the boat on Maggie's land. He gets wind that Obermachers might be in financial trouble and sees it as another opportunity to get into the organic food business?"

Cage shook his head. "Not exactly. He just wants the land. It's prime property. The Dumas Industries real estate division could make a killing on the topsoil alone."

Mad Dog nodded. "It happens. They strip the land of the fertile topsoil to sell at top dollar and then sell off parcels to developers looking to build high-end homes. Around here, they'd probably start at a cool half-mil, and that's just for a base model."

"In Sumneyville?" Smoke asked doubtfully.

"Read the news, man," Cage said. "The real estate market is booming right now. People who can afford it are leaving cities in droves in search of fresh air, clean water, and low crime rates."

"And million-dollar mansions?" Heff added with a smirk.

"Exactly." Cage nodded. "Bree said our modest cabin would probably cost around two million in SoCal. Imagine what that kind of money could buy around here."

Doc shook his head. "Obermachers won't sell. Tina told me their land has been in their family for over four centuries. It's a pride thing."

"Unfortunately, pride isn't going to pull them out of the deep financial hole Renninger's dug for them," Mad Dog said soberly. "Selling out might be their only option."

Yeah. That was what Doc was afraid of.

CHAPTER SEVENTEEN

~ Tina ~

"You can't fire him, Bert," Rick said heavily.

"I can, and I did. If you want him so bad, you hire him to work with you. I'm done."

Rick exhaled with exaggerated patience. "Tell me what he did again."

"He shows up late and leaves early. When he *is* there, it's like pulling teeth to get him to actually do anything. I've been out there late every night, doing things that should have been done during the day." Her voice was getting louder because every time she thought about it, she got angrier. "And today I caught him changing purchase orders without my consent."

Tina took a moment to take a deep breath and calm down.

"I'm sure he had a good reason for changing the order. What are you out there in the field for anyway? Aren't you supposed to be concentrating on your precious mill and leaving the heavy lifting to someone else?" Rick didn't even try to hide the derision in his tone. He'd been pissed ever since he'd learned The Mill was solely in Tina's name and not the family's.

And why shouldn't it be in her name? He and Gunther had laughed when she suggested buying the old mill, saying it was a complete waste of time and money. She'd used her inheritance to purchase the place on her own, fix it up, and turn it into a profitable business.

"It's not like I have a choice. Ultimately, the orchards are my responsibility, remember?"

Rick scowled. He didn't like being reminded of that either. He'd suggested more than once that she should turn orchard operations over to someone else *in the interest of her health.* She didn't buy that for a minute. Her brothers wanted complete autonomy over Obermacher Farms, and that wasn't going to happen, not in her lifetime.

"Look, it's simple. I can't be in two places at once. I need someone I can trust to get things done out in the field while I'm in The Mill."

He sat back, a calculating gleam in his eye. "You could bring someone in to help with The Mill."

"Not a chance."

The Mill outlet was her baby. Overseeing the making of jams, jellies, ciders, teas, and other fruit-based products they sold was her job. Plus, there was no way she was going to risk her patented recipes in anyone's hands but her own. No one knew what went into her secret formulas, not even her brothers. *Especially* not her brothers.

Rick scowled and exhaled again. “All right, Bert. I’ll talk to Eddie.”

“You do that. Just make sure you’re at O’Malley’s when you do because if he steps foot in my orchards again, I’ll have him arrested for trespassing. The only question is, whether or not his ass will be full of buckshot when the cops arrive.”

Tina left the office, letting the spring-loaded door slam shut behind her. She was nearly vibrating with barely repressed anger. It wasn’t even three o’clock, but she already felt as if she’d put in a full day.

She rubbed her forearms through the soft cotton of her long-sleeved tee, resisting the urge to scratch. Sun and stress, both of which she’d had a lot of lately, exacerbated the itchiness. When she got to her truck, she pushed up her sleeves and reapplied the cooling aloe gel she was now taking with her everywhere.

It helped somewhat. Then, she headed back to her trees, cheering herself up slightly with the knowledge that Eddie wouldn’t be there.

* * *

“It’s so frustrating,” she told Doc later that

evening.

"What can I do?"

"This," she told him truthfully.

Doc *listened.* Even better, he did so without offering useless platitudes or telling her she was overreacting, like her brothers often did. *They* were allowed to gripe and grumble, but whenever *she* did it, they accused her of being thin-skinned or hormonal.

"Thanks for letting me vent."

"Anytime." His voice was smooth and deep and soothing.

Talking with him had the same calming effect as sipping a cup of hot cocoa while wrapped in a fleecy blanket. She closed her eyes and willed him to say something else, trying and failing to stifle the yawns that were becoming increasingly frequent.

"You sound tired."

"I am tired. Mentally and physically."

The long hours she was putting in were hard, and dealing with Rick and Eddie was exhausting. A dull ache had taken up at the base of her skull earlier and spread throughout the rest of her body. It had been an effort just to warm up some soup, take a hot shower, and pull on her comfortable pajamas.

"I should let you go."

"Not yet, please. I just want to lie here and talk to you and forget about my crappy day. Tell me something."

"Like what?"

"I don't know. Something that'll make me smile."

He was quiet for a few moments and then said, "My sisters used to dress me up and make me attend tea parties."

She couldn't help it. She laughed. It started as a small bubble of warmth deep in her core and then blossomed. "You're kidding."

"Not even a little. They treated me like one of their dolls. It was awful."

Contrary to his words, she could hear the smile in his voice, as if it was a funny, if slightly humbling, memory.

"They're older than you, I take it."

"Yes."

"You're the baby, huh?"

"Yep, just like you."

"How many sisters do you have?"

"Five." He laughed. "It was a running joke in our house that my dad was determined to keep trying until he had a son." Doc's voice grew richer, warmer.

"Wow. And I thought I had it bad with three older brothers."

A wave of dizziness came out of nowhere and washed over her. Tina's eyes popped open. "Whoa."

"What's wrong?"

She blinked several times until the room stopped spinning. "I don't know. I just got really dizzy there for a second."

"You okay?"

"Yeah, I just …" Her stomach began to roil, even as a cold feeling swept over her. "Uh, scratch that. I'm sorry. I have to go."

Tina disconnected the call and rushed toward the bathroom, stumbling several times as her stiff joints refused to cooperate. She barely made it to the toilet before her dinner made a sudden and violent reappearance.

"Where the hell did that come from?" she moaned into the empty space around her, but she knew. She'd been pushing herself too hard, and her compromised autoimmune system was pushing back.

She remained on the floor until she was certain there was nothing left, then crawled back toward her bed. Her head was now pounding, her entire body ached, and she had a full-blown case of the chills.

Her phone was still lying where she'd tossed it, the blinking light indicating a new message. She picked it up and forced herself to focus.

Doc: *What happened? Are you okay?*

Doc: *Do you need anything?*

Doc: *I can be there in thirty, faster if you need me to be.*

Doc: *TINA. Let me know you're okay. Please.*

Doc: *Thirty seconds more, and I'm driving down there.*

Despite feeling like crap, Doc's texts made her smile.

Tina: *I'm okay. I think I picked up the flu.*

She'd barely hit Send when a message came back.

Doc: *What can I do? Do you need anything?*

Tina: *No, just rest.*

Three dots appeared and then disappeared. This happened several more times before the next text came through.

Doc: *Okay. If you need anything—and I mean, anything—call me.*

Tina: *I will, thanks.*

Doc: *Get some rest. Call me in the morning and let me know how you're doing.*

Tina managed to send him a thumbs-up emoji before the body shakes took hold.

CHAPTER EIGHTEEN

~ Doc ~

Doc waited all of fifteen minutes after Tina's abrupt *gotta go* before he grabbed his go-bag, jumped in his Rubicon, and headed down the mountain. He'd sent several texts, and she hadn't responded to any of them.

Was he overreacting? Maybe.

Did he care? Not particularly.

The only two things that mattered were that Tina was ill and that he might be able to help. More importantly, he needed to know she was okay.

He was quite well aware that he might be pushing a few boundaries. They were still in the early stages of their relationship, but he already felt invested, and from what he'd been able to glean from their nightly convos, she didn't have a lot of people who had her six.

Tina's answering text came through when he was at the town limits. Doc made a sudden hard right into the twenty-four-hour gas station on the corner, his breath coming easier as he read her message twice more and tapped out a response.

Several brief texts later, it was clear that she didn't need his immediate assistance. For now, he would rein in his baser urges, but if she wasn't feeling any better tomorrow, he would be back with supplies and whatever else she needed.

Instead of heading right back to Sanctuary, Doc figured he might as well top off the tank as long as he was there, so he pulled up to one of the open pumps. He was swiping his card when another vehicle pulled in on his right to do the same.

Doc didn't pay much attention to the pickup at first. It looked like half the vehicles in Sumneyville, except that it was newer than most.

The driver, however, did garner his attention. Through his Jeep's rear windows, he caught sight of the same guy he'd seen at Ziegler's—Rick Obermacher. And just like that night, Tina's brother did not look happy. His raised voice a moment later confirmed it.

Doc lowered his head as he put the nozzle into the tank and focused on the conversation taking place twenty feet away.

"I told you I'd take care of it, didn't I?" Tina's brother said irritably.

"Take care of it how?" another male voice pressed. "She fucking fired me, man."

"Because you're an idiot."

"How the hell was I supposed to know she'd double-check the purchase order?"

"It's your job to know. What the fuck am I paying you for?"

"Not to put up with her shit—that's for sure," the other guy grumbled. "She thinks she's so much better than the rest of us because she's got some fancy degrees and shit. Someone oughta bring her down a few pegs—"

Whatever else the guy was going to say was cut off abruptly with a muffled thud and a grunt as Tina's brother slammed him against the side of the truck. Rick Obermacher was probably close to Mad Dog's size—a muscled, broad-shouldered farm boy. The guy he had pinned against the side of the truck was on the shorter side, also beefy but in a *too much beer, not enough work* kind of way. With his scraggly beard, shifty eyes, and a wad of chew making the skin beneath his bottom lip bulge, he looked like most of the guys in Freed's prepper group.

"You don't touch Bert—*ever*," Tina's brother hissed. "It's one thing to fuck with the operation, but she's off-limits. You hear me?"

The guy paled and stuttered out a response, "Yeah, yeah, I hear you. I wasn't going to do anything. I was just saying."

"Well, don't. When I want your opinion, I'll ask for it." Rick eased off.

The guy straightened, regained some of his false bravado, and spit off to the side. "So, what do you want me to do now?"

"Give her a few days to calm down. She can't handle the orchards by herself, no matter what she thinks."

"What if she tries to hire her own crew?"

Rick laughed. "Who's she going to get, huh?"

"I dunno. People like her, man."

"People might like her, but I can guarantee you, they're more concerned about pissing me off than they are helping her."

The other guy laughed. "Yeah, you got that right. Hey, I need more Skoal. Want anything from inside?"

"I'm good."

The shorter guy ambled off toward the store as Doc's pump clicked off, signaling his tank was full. Rick looked over as Doc was getting back into his vehicle, his eyes narrowing in recognition. Doc met his gaze head-on, and then he started up his Jeep and drove away.

His knuckles turned white as he gripped the steering wheel, simmering with anger on Tina's behalf. Pieces were missing from the big picture, but one thing was glaringly obvious—Rick Obermacher was part of something dirty and was willing to pull his sister down with him.

Rather than go to his trailer when he got back to Sanctuary, he went right to the main building. The place was quiet at that hour, though he could hear faint music and the telltale click of billiard balls from the new rec room down the hall.

He passed the office on the way to the war room, unsurprised to see the light still on. Church was often in there until well past midnight.

Doc rapped on the frame and poked his head in. "Got a sec?"

"Sure. What's up?"

"I want you to confirm an ID."

Without providing more information, Doc continued on to the war room. By the time he swiped his card into the digital lock and entered, Church was right on his heels.

Doc immediately went over to one of the computers and pulled up video footage they'd captured from Freed's compound. It didn't take long to find what he was looking for. Doc froze the image and zoomed in. "You know this guy?"

Church peered over his shoulder. "Yes. That's Eddie Schweikert. Why?"

"Because I just overheard a very interesting conversation at the Sumneyville Gas and Guzzle between him and Rick Obermacher."

Church's eyes narrowed. "What were you doing at the Sumneyville Gas and Guzzle?"

Doc gave him a brief rundown, concluding with, "Do you think the operation he mentioned is the arms and ammo they're bringing in or the money laundering?"

"Could be either," Church mused, "but I don't see what that has to do with Tina. Unless they're using the orchards or The Mill somehow without her knowledge."

That was Doc's thought, too. "Whatever they're up to, this is further proof that Tina's not in on it."

"Agreed," Church said.

"The question is, what are we going to do about it?"

"There's not much we can do."

Doc frowned. "You don't think we should warn Tina?"

Church shook his head. "We can't, not without divulging what we know and how we know it. There's too much at stake. If they suspect someone knows what they're up to, it could blow the entire DOJ op."

Doc understood what Church was saying, but he didn't like it. Tina could lose everything. If she had some warning, she might be able to minimize the damage.

"We don't have to tell her anything specific. Kate could casually bring up Renninger and what he did to Handelmann's, just enough to get Tina thinking and connecting the dots."

"That might work," Church said thoughtfully. "But it might already be too late. That hole they're digging is getting deeper, and it's going to suck in everything around it when it eventually caves in on itself. We'll mention something to Kate tomorrow, but I think the best we can do is be there with a lifeline for Tina when it does. Based on the latest intel, that's going to be sooner rather than later."

"You'd do that for her?" Doc asked doubtfully.

Church nodded. "We take care of our own."

"Tina's not one of us."

"Not yet," Church said with a hint of a smirk. "But something tells me she will be."

Doc wasn't about to argue with that. "There's still one thing I don't get though."

"What's that?"

"Why did Rick refer to Tina as Bert?"

Church laughed. "Because that's her name." At Doc's confused look, Church explained, "Tina's real name is Bertina. Her brothers call her that just to piss her off."

CHAPTER NINETEEN

~ *Tina* ~

For Tina, there was no such thing as a sick day or paid time off, especially not for something as trivial as the flu. It didn't matter how crappy she felt. As long as she was physically capable, there were things that had to be done.

That said, if she'd had a field supervisor she could trust and depend on, she would have stayed in bed. Her head was pounding, and her entire body felt as if it'd been run over by one of Rick's combines.

With the help of tried-and-true homeopathic remedies and the maximum dosage of several over-the-counter meds, Tina somehow managed to get up, get dressed, and get out the door.

One thing she wouldn't do was put other people at risk, so going to The Mill was out of the question. She called in, let them know she wouldn't be in for the day, and headed right for the orchards. With proper distance and one of the N95 masks they used while spraying, there was little chance she'd get anyone else sick in the open air.

Also fueling her need to get out there was a concern about what she might find, given what had happened with Eddie the day before. She hadn't fired him in front of the others; she'd called him over to one of the sheds and quietly let him go, not wanting to humiliate him. But chances were, they'd figured out what had happened when Eddie stomped out, gotten into his truck, and proceeded to tear along the access roads like a pissed off bat out of hell.

Hopefully, by eliminating Eddie, she'd also eliminated the primary source of the issues plaguing the orchards lately. If not, she was prepared to tell any other malcontents to follow him right out the gate, though summoning the energy to do so when she felt so lousy could be a challenge.

She found her crew right where they should be, which was a good sign. A quick head count revealed that everyone who was supposed to be there was.

"Hey, boss," one of the younger guys said, approaching her truck.

"Hey, Billy."

Tina liked the guy; he had a good head on his shoulders and didn't mind hard work. Barely out of high school, he was picking up some classes at the county community college, trying to figure out what he wanted to do. Like Tina, he had a knack for science, so she encouraged him whenever she could.

“You okay? You don’t look so good.”

“I’ll be fine,” she assured him. “Just don’t stand too close.”

“If it’s the flu that’s going around, I already had it. Have you tried star anise tea with honey? It helps. My mom swears by it.”

Tina’s grandmother did, too. In fact, she was pretty sure Billy’s mom got the star anise from Lottie’s private stash.

“I haven’t yet, but I will as soon as I get back. Where are we at?”

“Dormant sprays are done on the pears, and we started spreading the fertilizer. I don’t know about that new stuff though,” he said, scratching the back of his neck. “I don’t think it’s meant for stone fruits.”

Tina had ordered the same stuff she always did—a special organic compound developed by the state university, specifically for fruit trees. It was something she was quite familiar with because she’d been part of the research team that created and tested it.

“What new stuff? Show me.”

Keeping a healthy distance, Tina followed Billy into the shed. A brief scan of the ingredients on the label confirmed Billy’s suspicion. The fertilizer was not the organic, ecofriendly stuff she ordered, but a toxic blend she didn’t want anywhere near her peaches.

"Where did it come from?"

Billy shrugged. "Some guy brought it up a few days ago. I didn't recognize him, but I saw him talking to Eddie, so I figured you knew about it."

"How much did you spray with this stuff?"

"Most of the cherries and some of the plums."

"Shit."

"I'm sorry I didn't catch it sooner, boss. Eddie sent me down to Ehrlick's to get some parts."

Ehrlick's was the nearest farm supply store and the only one within fifty miles that sold and serviced equipment.

"Parts for what?"

"The Kubota. It's rolling coal again."

"Did you check the glow plugs?"

"Yep. Blown."

"How many?"

Billy's face was grave. "All of them."

If Tina hadn't suspected sabotage before, she did now. There was no way they should be blowing through glow plugs as quickly as they were. The recent string of equipment failures, order mess-ups, and crew call-ins was too much to chalk up to coincidence and bad luck. The look on Billy's face suggested he knew it, too.

"What's going on, Billy?" she asked quietly.

He looked down at the ground and lowered his voice. "I don't know, boss, but it isn't good. You need to watch your back."

Billy's eyes flicked toward the entrance. Out of

the corner of her eye, Tina saw another guy come in. Billy's eyes met hers, and she knew in that moment that the newcomer was part of the sabotage team.

"Go with it," she said softly before raising her voice loud enough to be heard. "Not good enough, Billy. Get the *right* fertilizer and do it today. No more spraying until you do."

"On it, boss."

"If we ain't spraying, what are we supposed to do?" the guy asked from behind her. Unsurprisingly, he was a good friend of Eddie's, and judging by the hardness in his eyes, he wasn't happy with the recent staffing change.

"While you're waiting for Billy to get back, get rodent guards up on the new trees."

He scowled. "Rodent guards? Should we be doing pest control?"

"We're not spraying anything until I see what's in the barn. If we got the wrong fertilizer, we might have gotten the wrong pesticides, too."

Tina turned and walked back to her truck. It was only once she drove away that she allowed herself to exhale and slump down against the seat. That show she'd just put on drained what little bit of energy she had.

She went back to her cottage, rationalizing that there wasn't anything that needed her immediate attention. She'd head over to the barn later and check out the remaining shipment of pesticides once everyone else went home for the day, but until then, she was going to grab a blanket or three and take a much-needed nap.

CHAPTER TWENTY

~ Doc ~

Doc knew going to Tina's was a risk, but after nearly twenty-two hours with no response to his texts or calls, it was a risk he was willing to take.

His main objective was exactly what he'd said it was—to see that she was okay. Additionally, he planned on offering to help in any way he could, whether it be giving her the soup Kate had sent along with him or running to the store. The ideal scenario, of course, was that she would allow him to help in other ways, too, but that might be expecting too much, too soon.

When he arrived at Tina's isolated cottage, he found the place dark and quiet. No lights, no sound, and no smoke curling from the chimney, yet her truck was parked at a haphazard angle along the side. Instincts on high alert, he tried calling and texting again. In the muffled silence of the night, he heard her phone ringing from within.

Doc knocked on the door several times and called out to her but to no avail. Convinced something was horribly wrong, he was about to pick the lock when he heard a vehicle approaching.

An old classic car rumbled into view and came to an abrupt stop, narrowly missing the rear bumper of Tina's truck. An old woman got out and menacingly pointed a cane in his direction.

"You there," she called out to him in a surprisingly strong voice. "What do you think you're doing?"

Doc instinctively knew he was looking at Tina's grandmother.

"Checking on Tina, ma'am."

She stepped closer and studied him through narrowed eyes. "You're Tina's Dr. Watson, aren't you?"

Close enough. "Yes, ma'am."

"Well, don't just stand there. Open the door and put some shoulder into it. It sticks."

She shoved a key into his hand and then barged right past him the moment the door was open, turning lights on as she went. "Is that soup you've got there? Good. Put it in the kitchen and get a fire started while I see what we're dealing with."

Doc hadn't even considered not doing exactly what she'd said. Lottie Obermacher was a force of nature and exactly how Tina had described her.

He smiled to himself as he went down on his knee and got to work on the fire. Mr. O'Farrell had his hands full indeed.

"She's had a rough time of it," Lottie said when

she emerged from the bedroom a short time later, “but it looks like her fever has broken. Best thing for her is rest. Let me put a kettle on, then you can tell me what your intentions are where my granddaughter is concerned.”

CHAPTER TWENTY-ONE

~ *Tina* ~

The room was dark when Tina opened her eyes again. She glanced blearily at the ancient digital clock, groaning when she discovered that her short nap had lasted about ten hours.

The good news was, it looked as if her fever had broken. The sleeping shirt she'd hastily thrown on was soaked with sweat, and her hair was plastered to her face and neck.

Tina sat up, immediately sorry she had when the room began to spin. She took a moment and a few deep breaths, vaguely registering the sound of the television coming from the next room. She didn't remember turning it on, but she'd been pretty out of it when she returned from the orchards.

The call of nature grew increasingly insistent, so once the room stopped moving, she got out of bed slowly and with great care. Her headache had lessened considerably, and the racking chills had abated, but she felt as weak as a pup. She leaned heavily on walls and furniture to make it to the bathroom without falling over. By the time she eased down onto the commode, she felt as if she'd run a marathon instead of walked the twenty feet from her bed.

As much as she wanted to take a shower, Tina opted not to tempt fate, even with the extra bars and bench seat she'd had installed. If she got dizzy again and fell, it could be days before anyone came looking. Instead, she splashed some cold water on her face, made liberal use of some mouthwash, and switched out her soaked nightshirt for a dry one.

Her stomach rumbled and cramped, reminding her that it had been running on empty for a while. Tina slipped on a fluffy robe and shuffled out of the bedroom in search of food, her delirious brain cruelly conjuring the mouthwatering aroma of homemade chicken soup on the way.

She made it all the way into the small kitchen before she fully registered the two people sitting in her living room. She turned around slowly, certain she couldn't have seen what she thought she had, but, yep, there they were, staring at her as if she were the oddity.

"Gram? Doc? What are you doing here?"

"I got worried when you didn't answer your phone," Lottie explained, "so I brought out the Buick."

Tina gaped at her. "You *drove*?"

"Rest assured, the citizens of Sumneyville are safe," Lottie said, lifting her chin with a sniff. "I used the private access road. And it wasn't as if I could ask that lazy cow of a granddaughter-in-law of mine to do it. Good thing I did, too, because I found this young fellow skulking around."

Tina turned her questioning gaze to Doc. "And you—what are you doing here?"

He shrugged and looked only slightly contrite. "Same thing. You didn't respond. I wanted to make sure you were okay."

She tried to process that. Lottie's presence made sense because she and Tina looked out for each other. But Doc's?

"Well, now that I see you're up and moving, I should be going," Lottie said, rising.

"You're leaving?"

"It's late, and you don't need me. You're in good hands." Lottie's eyes sparkled. She didn't even try to hide her wink, waving off Doc's offer of assistance. "I can see myself out. Take care of our girl. Just remember what I said, young man."

"I will, ma'am," Doc assured her.

Tina stared, half-convinced she was stuck in some bizarre, fever-induced dream as her grandmother closed the door behind her. If it were a dream, it was a realistic one.

The heavy purr of the Invicta's engine could be heard over the low volume of the television, and the aroma of seasoned chicken, vegetables, and noodles permeated the room.

"How are you feeling?" Doc asked, moving

toward her.

Mortification followed on the heels of the realization that she looked—and probably smelled—like death. “Better.”

“Think you can handle some soup?”

She nodded.

“Good. Please, sit down before you fall over, okay? I’ve got this.”

Tina did as he’d asked, sliding down into one of the two chairs that flanked the ancient table. She watched him as he moved fluidly around her tiny kitchen. Dirty-blond hair framed his masculine profile, long enough to cover the back of his neck and brush over his collared flannel when he moved. Broad shoulders tapered into a trim waist while lean hips and a firm backside flowed into slim but powerful legs.

Had she not been feeling so poorly, watching him would have stirred her desire. That didn’t mean she couldn’t silently appreciate the view.

But it was the sight of him ladling soup into a bowl that had the biggest impact because he was doing it for her. She was usually doing things for others. It’d been a long time since someone had done something just for her.

He brought the bowl over to her along with a glass of electrolyte-infused water—something he must have brought with him because she knew she hadn’t had anything like that in her fridge. After placing both in front of her, he sat down and looked at her expectantly. "Go on now. Small sips."

She dutifully dipped a spoon into the bowl and brought it to her lips. It was every bit as delicious as it smelled. "You made this?"

He chuckled. "Me? No. Kate did."

"I should have guessed. It's the best chicken soup I've ever had." Tina ate another spoonful. "It's so good. She should patent the recipe."

"She says the same thing about your peach tea."

"I did patent it," Tina told him in between sips, "along with about a dozen other recipes. Tell me again what you're doing here."

Doc sat back, his hazel eyes watchful and intense. "I told you. I was worried about you. I hadn't heard from you since last night, and I wanted to make sure you were okay."

"But *why*?"

"Because we're"—he paused, appearing to choose his next word carefully—"friends. Aren't we?"

Friends. Tina rolled the word around in her mind. It felt right while at the same time feeling like an understatement.

"I suppose we are," she agreed. "But to tell you the truth, I'm embarrassed."

His head tilted to the side. "Why?"

"I'm not exactly looking my best, am I?"

His eyes grew more intense. "Do you think that matters to me?"

She shrugged lightly. "It does to most."

"I'm not most."

"Yes, that's becoming increasingly obvious," she said softly, tearing her eyes away from his hazel gaze when she felt herself falling into it. She cleared her throat and changed the topic. "So, you've met my grandmother."

His lips curled into a smile. "That I have. She's exactly as you described her."

"Yeah, she's something all right," Tina agreed. "Did she give you the third degree?"

"And then some. She's one hell of an interrogator."

"Oh no. I'm sorry about that."

"No worries. I've been trained in anti-interrogation techniques." He winked, and she felt a flutter behind her rib cage.

Tina *might* have done some online research into the Navy SEALs to learn more about them when she first heard about the Sanctuary project. It was hard to imagine the soft-spoken, handsome man sitting across from her enduring the kind of harsh training designed to break even the strongest of men. Clearly, there was much more beneath the friendly smile and easygoing nature he showed the world.

She wanted to know all of it. She had a feeling few people did.

Unfortunately, with the soup sitting pleasantly in her belly, fatigue was pulling heavily on her again. She covered her mouth and tried to stifle her yawn but was unsuccessful.

"I'm sorry."

"Don't be. You need your rest."

"I need a shower more."

"Don't take this the wrong way, but I don't think you're up for that yet."

"It's okay. I'll be sitting down the whole time. One of the first things I did when I moved in was replace the old claw-foot tub with a shower kit. The hardest part will be getting in and out."

"I can help with that."

"Let me guess … you're a doctor, and I don't have anything you haven't seen before?"

He laughed. "First of all, I'm not a doctor; I'm a medic. And secondly, you can undress after you're in the shower, so I won't see anything. Same thing when you're done. I'll wait until you're decent to help you out."

"I can't ask you to do that."

"You're not asking. I'm offering. And if you don't let me help, I'll just end up hanging around until I know you're safely back in bed anyway."

The determined look in his eye told her he was serious, and if she was honest with herself, she liked that he cared enough to stand his ground. Beyond that, she didn't have the strength to argue with him.

CHAPTER TWENTY-TWO

~ Doc ~

Doc was certain she was going to refuse with a polite *thanks, but no, thanks*. That would complicate things because he wasn't kidding about sticking around. He was fully prepared to camp out on her doorstep until he knew she was tucked safely back in bed. She looked like she was about to do a header into the table any moment.

But once again, she surprised him.

"In that case, thank you."

He discreetly released the breath he'd been holding. Tina stood slowly, steadying herself against the table. She fussed about letting him get too close—as if he hadn't had to deal with much, much worse in his time as an active SEAL combat medic—but he didn't think she wanted to hear that. He held out his hand to steady her instead, and thankfully, she did accept that.

Her grip was tentative at first, but she leaned on him more heavily with each step as they made the short trip together.

"Thanks," she said.

"You're welcome. Let me know when you're ready to get out."

"You don't have to stay, you know," she told him.

"I know. But I'd like to."

Her expression softened, and she nodded. Once she was safely seated in the shower, he left the door slightly ajar and got to business, keeping his ears open in case she needed him.

He understood her reluctance. She was used to doing things for herself, and it was apparent that she didn't like asking for or accepting help. She would soon learn, however, that doing so wasn't a sign of weakness, especially where he was concerned, and the sooner she did, the easier it would be for both of them.

As per Lottie's instructions, he located the jar of dried star anise and put water on for tea. Then, he stripped her bed and changed the sheets and pillowcases. He threw the dirty ones into the stacked washer-dryer combo he'd found in the tiny mud room off the kitchen when he heard the water go off in the shower.

He waited patiently outside the door until she was ready. The aroma of eucalyptus wafted out with her.

"Feeling better?" he asked.

"So much better. Just weak and tired." She

gave him a small smile. "You must think I'm a real wuss, huh?"

"Not at all. Flus hit harder when your resistance is low."

"I have been working a lot," she admitted, "and not taking care of myself like I should." She looked at the fresh bedding. "Did you change my sheets?"

"Yes."

For a moment, Tina looked like she was going to cry. "Why are you being so nice to me?"

He pulled back the covers for her to get into bed, acutely aware of the way she was staring at him, searching for the truth. "I thought we already covered this."

"Because we're friends?"

He nodded, noting her slight frown as he pulled the covers around her.

"So … you do this for all of your friends?"

He chuckled, imagining Smoke's or Church's reaction if he tried to tend to them with the same care. "Not exactly. In the interest of full disclosure, there's more to it than that."

"How so?"

Doc sat on the edge of the bed and pressed his hand lightly against her forehead, pleased to find her temperature only slightly above normal. "When you came to my trailer, we talked about that sense of possibility we felt around each other. Do you remember?"

She nodded.

"Well, this is that. Think of it as the friendship-plus plan."

A smile graced her lips. "Friendship-plus. I like that. Is that anything like friends with benefits?"

He hoped it would be—eventually. "If I'm lucky," he said with a smile and a wink. "But we'll cross that bridge when we come to it. For now, your benefits are limited to soup delivery and laundry service."

"Fair enough. Hey, Doc?"

"Yes?"

"Do those benefits also include sitting on the couch and watching a movie together?"

He appeared to consider it, but the reality was, he was all for it. "Hmm, I don't know. Friendship-plus is all about give and take. What's in it for me?"

"Probably the flu," she said wryly. "But at this point, it'd be like closing the barn door after the horses got out."

"I'm not worried about it. But throw in a jar of your peach preserves with the Zook's chicken you already promised, and you've got yourself a deal."

Doc helped her back out of bed and got her settled on the couch with a thick blanket and a mug of hot tea. They agreed on an old whodunit. Ten minutes in, Tina was fast asleep.

When the final credits rolled over the screen, Doc knew he could delay no longer. He'd rationalized his way through three full-length features. With dawn only an hour or so away, he knew it would be better to be off Obermacher property when the sun came up.

Tina barely stirred as he carried her into her bedroom and put her to bed, tucking the covers around her. After ensuring she had everything she might need within reach, he scribbled a quick note, pressed a light kiss to her forehead, and slipped out into the early morning darkness.

CHAPTER TWENTY-THREE

~ Tina ~

Tina woke, feeling better than she had in days. She still wasn't one hundred percent, but there was a definite improvement.

Doc was gone, having slipped out at some point. She had a vague memory of him carrying her to bed sometime in the wee hours of the morning. She wasn't sure when exactly, but it must have been pretty late—or pretty early, depending on how she looked at it. All she knew was, each time she'd woken on the couch, it had been to find herself snuggled against him with a different movie playing.

She wasn't complaining. Doc's presence had been unexpected but very much appreciated. Sure, it had been humbling for her to have him see her at her worst, but on the plus side, if he could handle that, he could probably handle anything.

As she fixed herself a cup of tea, the thought made her smile, as did the clean dishes drying in the rack and the neatly folded sheets he'd left on the table. Unexpected bonus: he knew how to fold a fitted sheet to perfection—a skill she had never quite mastered.

A girl could get used to that kind of pampering.

Tina was sipping her tea and pondering the benefits of the friendship-plus plan when she heard the telltale crunch of gravel outside, indicating an approaching visitor. A moment later, she identified the distinctive roar of her brother's truck, followed shortly thereafter by his beefy hand pounding on the door.

"Bert! Open up."

She took her time in getting up and walking to the door, opening it just a crack. "What do you want?"

Rick pushed open the door and walked in like he owned the place. Technically, she supposed he did since it was on Obermacher property, but it annoyed her more than usual.

His gaze swept over the small interior, coming back to rest on her accusingly. "Is there something you want to tell me?"

Did he know about Doc's visit?

She tightened the sash on her robe and crossed her arms as she pretended to think about it. "No, I don't think so."

"I was just down at The Mill, looking for you. Aggie said you didn't show up the last couple of days. And why the hell are you still in your pajamas?"

"Because I'm sick," she told him. "And I didn't go to The Mill because I didn't want to get anyone *else* sick."

"Yeah, well, just because you're taking it easy doesn't mean your crew should be. I told you firing Eddie was a mistake."

Rick had just blown past the *I'm sick* part. No *how are you.* No *can I do anything* or *how can I help.*

"Firing Eddie was not a mistake," she told him firmly. "The crew's idle because the supplier sent the wrong fertilizer, and I refuse to spray that toxic crap on my trees."

"So, I'm supposed to pay them for hanging around the barn and drinking coffee?"

"Last I checked, their salaries come from the orchard budget, which, if I'm not mistaken, brought in more than any other division last year. But if it bothers you so much, poach them like you usually do until I get this mess straightened out."

When Rick continued to glare at her, she prompted, "Was there something else?"

His mouth twisted into a grimace. "Someone told Bonnie they saw you driving up the mountain last Sunday."

"*And*?" Tina driving around wasn't exactly prime gossip fodder.

"*And*," he said with exaggerated patience, "they saw you heading up the mountain. Alone. And it wasn't the first time. Where'd you go, Bert?"

"Whoever *someone* is, they need to mind their own business. And I'll start telling you my whereabouts when you start telling me yours."

He narrowed his eyes. "You weren't at Sanctuary, were you?"

She lifted her chin defiantly. "What if I was?"

"Goddammit, Bert! I told you to stay away from there."

"First of all, last time I checked, you weren't my keeper. And secondly, get your head out of your ass and stop listening to window lickers like Eddie. You've known Matt Winston all your life. You know he's not the paranoid, unstable guy some people say he is, and neither are the others."

"Jesus. You have been going up there, haven't you?"

Tina had been hoping to put this battle off for as long as possible, but it appeared as if she would be fighting it sooner rather than later.

"Not that it's any of your concern, but Matt asked for my advice on the old orchard, and I gave it to him. And while I was there, I saw Kate Handelmann and Sandy Summers, and they invited me for coffee. It was nice. *They* were nice."

Rick's face darkened even further. "You want girl time? You've got two sisters-in-law. You don't need to go up to Sanctuary for that shit."

She snorted. She had no desire to spend time with either of her brothers' wives. Bonnie was wrapped up in her own issues, and Giselle had her nose too high in the air to be bothered.

"What do you have against them anyway?" she asked. "Because I've heard the rumors, and I can tell you that Sanctuary is nothing like the mercenary stronghold some people make it out to be. In fact, it looks a lot like it did when we used to go up there as kids. Matt's even restoring the—"

"God, you're so gullible. They were just putting on a show for you. Can't you see that?"

"Oh? Where's your proof, huh? Have *you* actually been there? Talked to them?"

His teeth ground together. "You have no idea what you're dealing with."

"And you do?"

His body stiffened. "I'm not going to tell you again. Stay away from Sanctuary."

"Or what?"

"Or you're not going to like the consequences," he said darkly.

"Don't threaten me, Friedrich. You have a hell of a lot more skeletons in your closet than I have in mine."

Rick shot her a look of such rage that she felt a frisson of fear run up and down her spine. But she'd been dealing with his tantrums for a long time, and she stood her ground, knowing that any indication of weakness would be her downfall.

"We're done here. Don't let the door hit you in the ass on the way out."

The standoff lasted for a full minute, maybe

two, before he turned on his heel and stomped out of her cottage. Tina sagged against the door and let out a big exhale. As the sound of his truck faded away, Tina picked up her phone and sank down onto the couch.

The first call she made was to Lottie. "Gram, Rick was just here. He knows I've been going up to Sanctuary."

"How?"

"He didn't say, only that someone told Bonnie."

"Figures. That woman's not happy unless she's ruining someone else's day. Well, I suppose that cat had to get out of the bag sometime," Lottie said on a sigh. "How bad was it?"

"Bad. I can't remember when I've seen Rick so angry."

"I don't like the sound of that."

Tina wasn't crazy about it either.

"I don't think he knows about Mr. O'Farrell."

"Oh, I don't care about that," Lottie said dismissively. "I'm more worried about you. How are you feeling?"

"Much better."

"You sound better. I take it, the good doctor had something to do with that?"

"He's a medic," Tina said with a smile, remembering Doc's correction.

"Close enough. I like him for you."

"I do, too. We'll talk later, okay? I've got to

take care of a few things."

"All right, dear. Don't overdo it."

"I won't."

Tina ended the call and considered her next move. She had planned on visiting the warehouse, but just the thought of getting dressed and driving down there was exhausting, especially when she could accomplish the same thing with a phone call.

Thankfully, Otto answered the phone. Otto had been managing the warehouse for as long as she could remember.

"Otto, it's Tina. Could you do me a favor?"

"Anything for you, Peaches."

She smiled at the familiar nickname. Her grandfather had given it to her a long time ago because of her obsession with them. Otto was the only one who still called her that.

"Would you check the shipment of pesticide that came in for the orchards?"

"Sure thing. Give me an hour. Three tractor trailers just pulled up."

"No problem."

While Tina waited for Otto to call back, she dressed in comfortable lounge pants and made herself some scrambled eggs and toast. She just sat down when a text came through from Doc.

Doc: *How are you feeling?*

Tina: *Much better, thanks. I'm taking it easy today.*

Doc: *Glad to hear it.*

Tina: *I learned my lesson.*

Doc: *Kate's making loaded baked potato soup. Want me to bring you some tonight?*

Tina bit her lip, debating on whether or not to tempt fate, especially after the morning's visit from Rick. However, the desire to see Doc outweighed the potential risk.

Tina: *That depends.*

Doc: *On ...*

Tina: *If you'll share it with me.*

Doc: *That's a given. Anything else you want me to bring?*

Tina: *Just you. Even the soup is optional.*

As had happened before, three dots appeared and then disappeared before his response popped up on the screen. She couldn't help but wonder what he wanted to say but didn't and why.

Doc: *See you tonight—after dark.*

Tina set the phone down, feeling markedly better than she had only a few minutes earlier. Not only had simply exchanging texts with Doc lifted her spirits, but she also wasn't going to have to wait until Sunday to see him again.

She decided to make the most of her rare time off with a bit of pampering. A long, hot shower with moisturizing body wash and sinus-clearing essential oils, followed by an exfoliating scrub and a long-overdue manicure and pedicure. By the time Otto called back, she was almost feeling human again.

"The stuff we got isn't the stuff we ordered," Otto told her, confirming her suspicions. "Not sure where things got messed up."

Tina had a pretty good idea. "Who else has access to place orders?"

"Besides me and Hank? You and the boys, of course, and the field supervisors."

Field supervisors. Like Eddie. "Thanks, Otto."

"No problem. I put a call in to the supplier. He assured me he'll have good stuff here by the end of the week."

"We don't pay you enough."

"You pay me plenty," he said. "But while we're on the subject, any word on when the new checks are getting cut?"

"What new checks?"

"The payroll checks. My last one bounced. Gunther said there was some mix-up with the bank and he'd take care of it."

"I didn't know. I'll look into it, okay?"

"I'd appreciate that."

CHAPTER TWENTY-FOUR

~ Doc ~

Doc found Tina much improved when he arrived on her doorstep later that night. She must have been watching for him because she opened the door before he had a chance to knock.

"Hey," she greeted. Her gaze moved past him. "Where's your car?"

"Behind that copse of maples," he told her. "I parked it out of sight, just in case someone besides your grandmother happens to come by."

Her features softened. "That's very thoughtful of you."

"I'm a thoughtful guy."

"So you are. Come on in. Is that Kate's potato soup?"

"It is."

"Perfect. I've been looking forward to it all day … among other things."

She gave him an almost-shy smile that lit him up from the inside out.

"We should warm this up a bit."

"It's probably just as good cold, but okay. I guess I can wait a few more minutes."

She pulled two ceramic bowls from the cupboard and set them on the counter, but he gently plucked the ladle from her hands before she could fill them.

"Sit. I've got this."

"You're kind of bossy, you know that?" she grumbled, but amusement laced her tone, and she did as he'd asked.

"You just said I was thoughtful."

"You are. Thoughtful *and* bossy."

"Only with stubborn patients." He filled both bowls and popped them into the microwave.

"I'm not stubborn."

When he laughed at that, she added, "Okay, maybe I am. But I'm used to doing things for myself, you know?"

Yeah, he'd already figured that out for himself. That made the fact that she'd allowed him to help her that much more meaningful. "I get that. But it's okay to accept a little help sometimes, especially when it's coming from a good place."

"I'm beginning to realize that," she said softly. "Be patient with me, okay?"

She had no idea how patient he could be.

"I'm not going anywhere."

He brought the soup to the table and then sat down. Rather than digging in like he'd expected, however, she fussed with her napkin.

“You might change your mind about that after I tell you what happened today.”

“I doubt it,” he told her honestly. In fact, the only thing that would stop him from coming around was if she truly wanted him to. Even then, he wouldn’t give up easily. “What happened?”

“My brother stopped by earlier. He knows I’ve been visiting Sanctuary. Needless to say, he’s not happy about it.”

Her tone was light, but concern was evident in her pale eyes.

“And?” he prompted, knowing there was more to the story.

She shrugged and gave him a brief, high-level overview. “He doesn’t know that I’ve been seeing you, only that I’ve been helping with the orchard and having coffee with Kate. He warned me not to go back.”

Doc sat up straight. “He threatened you?”

Tina waved her hand, as if it wasn’t important. “I can handle Rick. I just wanted to make you aware in case you want to rethink things.”

“I don’t,” he said immediately.

“But if you did,” she continued, “I’d understand. He’s going to find out about us sooner or later, and when he does, he could make things difficult. He’s got some powerful friends.”

So did Doc. “Tina, look at me.” Doc reached across the table and wrapped his hand around hers, waiting until her eyes met his. “I’m not afraid of your brother or his friends. As long as *you* want me around, I'm here. Got it?"

Relief was evident in her face as her eyes softened and her lips curled into a hint of a smile. "Got it."

She picked up her spoon and dipped it into the soup, moaning softly when she put it into her mouth. "Mmm. Kate has a gift."

"Things have definitely improved since she moved to Sanctuary. Between Kate's dinners and Sam's coffee and muffins, I think we have it pretty good."

"Sucks for the rest of us though." She finished her bowl and paused to take a drink of water, looking thoughtful. "I'm glad they've found their happiness. It's a shame not everyone sees it that way."

"It is," he agreed.

"Even more so that some people who'll believe anything just because of whose mouth it came out of. Do you know there are those who liken Sanctuary to a cult? They think you guys are shamelessly using your innate sexiness to lure naive women to your lair to build your own secret society?"

Doc choked on his soup. "What?"

Tina nodded. "It's true. They say you target women on the fringes, make them feel wanted and desired, and then ply them with sexual favors to do your bidding."

"You're joking."

"Not even a little. But you have to consider the source. Most of that is coming from men who feel threatened by you. The saddest thing is, it's not even because of anything you've done. It's their own insecurities that are fueling the fire."

His lips quirked. "Are you sure you studied agriculture and not psychology?"

She laughed. "I might have had a gen ed course or two. But it's really more about understanding human nature, I think. Those who are talking the loudest are usually the ones who have the most to hide."

She wasn't wrong about that. Her brothers were fairly high on the list of loud talkers. Doc thought she knew it, too.

He nodded toward her now-empty bowl. "Want more?"

"No, thanks. It was delicious, but my stomach's still getting used to having food in it again." Tina rose, her movements stiff.

"Still feeling achy?" Doc asked.

"Yeah, but not much more than usual."

"How about a massage?"

Her eyes sparkled with mischief. "Uh-oh. Offering a massage to an achy, needy woman sounds like it could be a gateway to those sexual favors we were just talking about."

"I guess you'll just have to take your chances and find out."

"Challenge accepted."

"Put some cushions on the floor in front of the couch while I clean up."

"Bossy," she mumbled, making him chuckle.

It didn't take long to clean up and put the rest of the soup in the refrigerator. Doc used the time to mentally prepare himself for what he was about to do. Other than the night before when she'd snuggled up to him in her sleep, they'd had limited physical contact.

He sat on the floor with his back against the couch and coaxed her onto the cushions between his legs.

"Like this?"

"Exactly like that."

He brushed her hair over her shoulder. It was every bit as silky and soft as it looked.

"Relax," he commanded softly, putting both hands in the tender area between her neck and shoulders and feeling the tension there. "Close your eyes and take a deep breath."

She moaned softly when he began to gently knead the knotted muscles there. He used his thumbs to make small circles on either side of her spine. Before long, she dropped her head and loosened up considerably.

"That feels amazing."

He thought so, too.

"I think I'm really liking this friendship-plus plan," she murmured. "But it seems pretty one-sided so far."

"It's not," he told her. "I'm getting something out of this, too."

"Like what?"

"Spending time with you."

CHAPTER TWENTY-FIVE

~ *Tina* ~

By the time Saturday rolled around, Tina was feeling almost back to normal. She credited much of her quick recovery to Doc and the desire to see him again. He had been so awesome over the past week, so she wanted to do something nice for him.

Kate had let it slip that Doc was a fan of Obermacher's peach products, so she went down to The Mill and put together a basket of goodies, including a few specialty items from her private stash, before she went to the farmers market for the day.

Sunday morning, she gathered everything together, anxious for her trip to Sanctuary. Rick's warning from earlier in the week had been relegated to the back of her mind. She hadn't seen or heard from him since that day. Hopefully, he'd had time to calm down, but regardless, she would do what she wanted to do.

When she walked into the main house, however, it became apparent that a quick in and out was not in the cards. Bonnie wasn't the only one in the kitchen. Rick was there, too, sitting at the table and managing to look both impatient and irritated. The tension in the air was palpable, but that wasn't unusual when Bonnie and Rick were in the same room.

"Well, this is a surprise," Tina told him. "It's Sunday. Don't you have somewhere else to be? O'Malley's? The compound? A lynching?"

He scowled at her. "Sit down, Bert."

"Sorry, I've got plans. I'm feeling much better, by the way. Thanks for asking."

"Cancel them. We need to talk."

"No, and no—unless you're planning on telling me what's going on with payroll because I'm still waiting for an answer on that."

Tina had called Gunther and left several messages inquiring about the bounced paychecks, none of which had been returned.

Rick's face reddened, confirming that he knew all about it. "Nothing you need to worry about."

"Yeah, that's what I thought. Where's Gram?"

"I'm right here," Lottie said, making her way into the room just as a piercing scream rent the air. "And I'm ready to go. Bonnie, Rick, your son is using Adelle's stuffed animals for target practice, and I just saw Adelle heading toward his room with a pair of scissors. I *strongly* suggest you intervene before someone gets hurt."

Bonnie made a noise of irritation and left the

room, reluctant to miss any of the brother-sister showdown.

Lottie put her hands on her hips and glared at Rick. "Well? What are you waiting for? Go disarm your son!"

Rick clearly wasn't happy, but not even he would openly disrespect his grandmother in her own kitchen. He turned to Tina and said, "This isn't over," before stalking out.

"Let's get going, dear," Lottie said to Tina, urging her out the door. "I might have overexaggerated the situation a bit. Give me a boost, will you?"

Tina helped Lottie into the truck, thankful she'd invested in the non-slip, solid running boards, and then she hurried around to the driver's side and climbed in. Only once they were safely on their way toward the main road did Tina ask what was really going on.

"Ricky *was* using Adelle's stuffed animals for target practice but with a Nerf gun. And the scissors I saw Adelle carrying were the safety kind that wouldn't cut through warm butter."

"What was that horrible screech?"

"I'm not sure, but I suspect Ricky booby-trapped his room and Adelle walked right into it."

Tina laughed. "Just like my brothers used to do to keep me out."

Lottie chuckled. "Until you started turning the tables and set a few traps of your own."

"Ah, good times, good times."

"You always were a feisty thing, holding your own against those boys. You still do," Lottie said with warmth, and then her smile faded. "But an ill wind's blowing, Bertina. I can feel it in my bones."

The fact that her grandmother had used her given name spoke volumes. Lottie only did that when something was really important.

"What do you mean?"

Lottie shook her head. "Something is going on. Rick has been in an even fouler mood than usual, and Gunther and Kiefer haven't been much better. They've been to the house every night this week."

"Do you think it's because of me going to Sanctuary?"

"I'm sure that doesn't help," Lottie told her, "but I don't think that's the root of it. No, my intuition tells me it's something much worse than that. I think Gunther has gotten into something pretty bad. What was that you said about bounced paychecks?"

Tina relayed what Otto had told her.

Lottie's expression grew even darker. "I bet it has something to do with that Renninger boy."

"Luther?"

Lottie nodded. "His father was a good man, but he's his mother's son."

Tina didn't know much about Luther's mother. As far as she knew, no one did, except that she'd never really been part of the picture. That was one of those rare, well-kept secrets among the Sumneyville elite.

Luther, Tina knew. He'd been in Gunther's class, and the two were good friends. Like Gunther, Luther was a smooth talker and considered exceptionally good-looking among local females. He was well-off, too—his father had left him an established, prosperous business—and that added to his appeal. But to Tina, he'd always seemed like a snake oil salesman—disingenuous and sneaky. It was one of the primary reasons she'd hired someone outside of Sumneyville to manage The Mill's finances.

Unfortunately, her brothers didn't feel the same way.

If Luther was involved with whatever had Rick vexed, things could get bad indeed. He handled the business accounts for Obermacher Farms. When the farm had been divided equally among them, her suggestion that they have someone else do the finances had been outvoted three to one.

"Do you still have your own private account?" Lottie asked suddenly.

"I do," Tina confirmed. "And my LLC isn't tied to Obermacher Farms. Neither Gunther nor Luther can touch it."

"Good. At least you'll have something to fall back on if things go to hell in a handbasket, which, I suspect, they will."

When they arrived at Mr. O'Farrell's, Tina

helped her grandmother out of the truck. The older man was waiting for them on the porch, his eyes lighting up as they always did when he saw Lottie.

Tina walked with her grandmother to say hello to Mr. O'Farrell.

"Are you by any chance heading up to Sanctuary?" he asked Tina.

"I am."

He lifted a canvas tote filled with meal containers from one of the two rocking chairs there. The second rocker had been added shortly after Lottie began her weekly visits. It appeared that Mr. O'Farrell was just as sweet and thoughtful as Doc.

"Would you mind taking these back to Kate? Doc forgot to take them with him yesterday."

It didn't surprise Tina that Mr. O'Farrell knew about her Sunday trips to Sanctuary, nor did she mind. "Sure, no problem."

"He's a fine young man, you know," he said with a twinkle in his eye.

She grinned. "Yes, I know."

"Kind, smart, generous, honorable, brave. A hero really. He'll make a good husband for the lucky woman who can capture his fancy." The old man winked.

"You think so?"

"Oh, aye."

"Good to know. You two have fun. I'll be back around seven."

Mr. O'Farrell reached out and took Lottie's

hand in his. "No hurry."

Tina was smiling as she backed out of the driveway. She continued to do so all the way to the edge of town—right up until the time she realized she was being followed.

She didn't recognize the vehicle. It stayed far enough back that she couldn't make out the make or model, only that it was a dark pickup similar to hers. That didn't tell her anything since the majority of vehicles in and around town were either trucks or Jeeps.

The driver and passenger were unrecognizable. From what she could see in her rearview, they wore dark hoodies, baseball caps, and sunglasses. She couldn't even say for sure if they were male or female, but her instincts told her they were male.

To confirm that she wasn't just being paranoid, Tina drove past the turnoff to go up the mountain toward Sanctuary and into the gas station on the corner instead. The dark truck cruised past at least twice while she filled up her tank and cleaned her windows.

Once she left the gas station, she noticed the truck a few lengths behind her again. Several turns later, there was no longer any question she was being followed.

Thankfully, traffic was light. Tina gunned the gas pedal and shot forward, taking advantage of all eight cylinders to put a decent amount of distance between her and the cars behind her. When the road opened up to the straight quarter-mile stretch past the town limits, she jammed on the brakes and executed a sliding U-turn any stunt driver would be proud of. Once she was facing the opposite direction, she sped back toward town—and her pursuers.

When she spotted them—the driver was definitely a him, given the visible facial hair—she hung another U-ey, putting *her* behind *him.*

Heart racing, adrenaline pumping, she floored the accelerator, closing the gap between them. A flash of an arm from the passenger side was the only warning before a bottle hit her windshield and exploded, sending golden-colored liquid across the glass.

"You fuckers!" she yelled. She flipped on the wipers, even angrier when she saw the crack in her windshield.

A second bottle came hurtling back, connecting with her front end. A third quickly followed, this one heading for her driver's side. Tina swerved and narrowly avoided it, growing angrier and more determined by the second.

Their narrow back window opened up, and Tina caught sight of the rifle barrel. She might have been angry, but she wasn't stupid. She yanked the wheel hard to the right and decelerated but not before she heard a pop, and the right front end of her truck dropped suddenly.

CHAPTER TWENTY-SIX

~ Doc ~

Doc checked his phone again, frowning when it remained dark and message-free. Tina was late.

His plan was to greet her upon arrival and then occupy himself while the women had their coffee. What happened afterward would depend largely on Tina. If she was feeling up to it, they could take advantage of the beautiful spring day with a slow-paced walk along one of their many trails. If she wasn't, they could hang in his trailer and watch a movie or something.

"She'll be here," Kate told him. "She's probably just running behind."

Maybe, but the growing knot in his gut told him it was more than that. He worried that perhaps Tina had pushed herself too hard, too soon and suffered a mild relapse. Or worse, she'd had another run-in with her brother over her weekly trips to Sanctuary and had a change of heart. Either way, he didn't like it.

He went back inside, silently reciting the

watched pot never boils rule. His scientific side recognized the ridiculousness of his own reasoning. Water would boil when it reached the correct conditions to do so regardless of whether or not anyone was there to witness it, and Tina would arrive when she arrived regardless of whether or not he was waiting on the steps to greet her.

Doc made his way to the rec room, finding only one other there—a relatively new guy who went by Yaz. It wasn't unusual to find it so empty during the middle of the day, especially when the weather was nice.

Most of the residents were in their rooms or off doing something. Part of the Sanctuary philosophy was ensuring that everyone always had something useful to do. Exactly what that was depended on the individual. Some helped out in the kitchen. Others did general carpentry or landscaping, or if they had special skills—like Justin, the dog whisperer—they did whatever suited them best. Church firmly believed that everyone had something useful to contribute and strongly encouraged those around him to utilize their own unique strengths to do so.

Yaz looked up when Doc entered. "Up for a game?"

"Sure."

Doc was a decent pool player, but Yaz was better. It was pure luck that Doc won the first game. Yaz easily won the second, neatly pocketing one ball after another with skill and precision.

They were just about to start the third game for a best *two out of three* match when Mad Dog poked his head into the room.

"Doc. Tina's just arrived. You're going to want to see this."

Something about Mad Dog's tone made Doc's blood run cold.

"Continue this later?" Doc said to Yaz, setting his cue stick back in the rack.

"Sure, man. Just say when."

"What's going on?" Doc asked Mad Dog as they walked toward the front entrance.

"I think it's better if you see it for yourself," was Mad Dog's decidedly unhelpful reply.

Doc understood when they stepped out of the main doors and he got a look at Tina's truck. The windshield was cracked on the passenger side, as if a sizable stone had been thrown at it. A closer inspection revealed bits of broken glass lodged in the wiper cowl between the hood and the windshield, and one front tire was noticeably newer than the others.

The need to see Tina and make sure she was okay was overwhelming. "Where is she?"

"Relax. She's fine. She's inside with Kate and the others."

"Any idea what happened?"

"Not yet. Church saw her come in on the security cam and thought you'd want in."

Damn right he did.

Tina was in the dining room, sitting with a mug between her hands, looking pissed. Other than a smudge of dirt on her forehead, she appeared unharmed.

"Tina." When she saw him, her features softened. He slid into the seat next to her. "You okay?"

She nodded. "I'm fine. Just really, really angry."

Tina proceeded to tell them what had happened, starting with the realization that she was being followed and ending with the shot that took out her tire. His ire grew with each new development. While part of him silently appreciated her spirit, a much larger part of him wanted to wrap her in his arms and insist she never do anything so risky again. As it was, he settled for holding her hand beneath the table.

"Did you recognize them?" Church asked.

"No," Tina told them with obvious frustration. "Both guys were wearing baseball caps with their hoodies pulled up over the top, so I couldn't even tell what color their hair was, except for the driver's beard. It was dark, maybe brown or black. They had on sunglasses, too."

"Why were they following you, do you know?" Sandy asked.

Tina shook her head. "I'm not sure. My first thought was that it had something to do with Rick finding out I've been coming here on the weekends, but it could just as easily be payback."

"Payback for what?" That was from Kate.

"I fired my field supervisor earlier in the week. Let's just say, Eddie wasn't pleased, and it wasn't an amicable parting of ways."

"Eddie Schweikert?" asked Church, shooting a glance at Doc.

"Yes. You know him?"

Church nodded but refrained from saying more.

"Yeah, I guess you would," Tina mused. "For what it's worth, I don't think they meant to do anything more than send a message. Things didn't get nasty until I turned the tables on them."

"It was reckless," Doc said before he could stop himself. "Exactly what were you hoping to accomplish?"

Doc received some surprised looks and several raised eyebrows, probably because he was usually the one sitting back and considering all angles of a situation before imparting his two cents. But this was different. His objectivity took a backseat to his protective instincts when it came to Tina.

As for Tina, icy-white-blue flames flared in her pale eyes. "Send a message of my own—that's what. One that says I don't like people following me around or telling me what I can and can't do and that I definitely don't respond well to intimidation tactics."

"Except what you did was back them into a corner."

Her frown deepened. “Are you suggesting I should have done nothing?”

“No,” Doc said carefully, “but I do think there were better ways of handling it.”

“Oh yeah? What would *you* have done?”

Doc opened his mouth to answer, but a strong nudge on the top of his foot and a glare from Sam made him pause and consider his answer.

“Truthfully? Probably exactly what you did,” Doc admitted. “But that doesn’t mean I like the fact that *you* did it. You could have been seriously hurt.”

Whether it was his logic or the genuine concern in his voice, he didn’t know, but the ire in her eyes faded, and she exhaled. “Fair enough. But after growing up with Rick, Kief, and Gunther for brothers, I learned early on not to take any shit from anyone.”

“Fair enough,” Doc said, echoing her words. “But next time, maybe consider the risks before you put yourself in danger like that again?” He squeezed her hand.

She nodded. “I will.”

Church cleared his throat, reminding Doc that they weren’t alone. “Did you happen to get a plate?”

She shook her head. “No. They started hurling stuff before I could get close enough to make it out. The truck had a rack of spotters across the top. That much I know.”

“Newer model? Older model?” Mad Dog asked

the question casually, but he was clearly thinking the same thing they all were.

A similar-looking truck had forced Kate's Jeep off the road while she was on her way to see Mad Dog one night. They'd identified the driver as Joe Eisenheiser, a local cop who was firmly on Team Freed.

"Newer, but something didn't look quite right about it. Like it had been in an accident and someone had replaced some parts from the U-Pull-It yard."

That made perfect sense because Mad Dog and Smoke had taken it upon themselves to bring a bit of Karma to Eisenheiser's doorstep after Kate's accident, and his expensive pickup hadn't fared well.

"It was black or a dark shade of blue or green or something," Tina continued. "I'm partially color-blind, so I can't say for sure." She sighed. "I know that's not much to go on, but I'll know it again if I see it."

"We're just glad you're okay," Sandy said.

Murmurs of agreement echoed around the table.

Kate got up. "Right, well, sorry, everyone, but I need to get back to getting dinner ready. I'm sorry you had to deal with all that, Tina."

"Me, too. It's been a day."

"Want to head back to my place for a while?" Doc asked.

She nodded. Doc stood and held out his hand, pleased when Tina accepted it without hesitation.

As they stepped out of the main building and into the lot, Doc caught sight of the damage to Tina's truck again and felt another wave of something dark and ugly swell in his chest.

Tina must have picked up on it because she squeezed his hand and said, "It's okay."

"There's *nothing* okay about this. This wouldn't have happened if you hadn't been on your way here."

"We don't know that," she said.

He knew. "Maybe you shouldn't—"

"Doc. *Stop*. I knew what I was getting into," Tina said. "Well, maybe not the *getting shot at* part, but I knew there would be consequences, and I still think it's worth it. In fact, I'm more certain now than ever."

Her words filled him with warmth.

"You are, huh?"

"I am. That reminds me, I've got something for you."

"For me? What?"

Tina carefully climbed into the back of her truck and went to a large wooden crate held in place by a bungee cord. She opened the crate and removed a picnic basket, handing it to him over the side along with a small cooler.

"What's all this?" he asked.

"That," she said, pointing to the cooler, "is the

Zook's chicken I promised you. And that"—she waved her hand toward the picnic basket—"is some new stuff I've been working on as well as some old standbys. Kate said you had a thing for peaches."

"I have a thing for *your* peaches," he corrected.

She laughed, a lovely tint creeping up her neck and coloring her cheeks.

Basket in one hand, Tina's hand in the other, Doc led her to his trailer.

"I was going to suggest a walk along the trail," he told her, "but maybe just chilling at my place would be better."

"I'd prefer that, if you don't mind. My energy level isn't fully back to where it should be, and after this morning's excitement, just chilling sounds good to me."

"Fine by me. How about the joint pain? Any improvement?"

"Some," she said. "You'd think with all the time I spent lying around the past couple of days, it would be better than it is."

They reached his trailer.

Doc unlocked the door and opened it for her, noticing her slight grimace as she stepped up into it. "Are you taking anything for it?"

"Just regular OTCs. That's usually enough to take the edge off, but they haven't been doing the trick lately. I probably built up a tolerance and should switch it up. It happens sometimes."

He wanted to ask her more, but she turned

around and flashed him a smile that made him forget what he was going to say.

"Fair warning: I got inspired this week and am dying to have someone try out my new recipes."

"You mean, no one else has tried these before?"

"Not some of them, no. You'll be the first."

"I'm honored."

She extracted a red-and-white checked picnic blanket from the basket and spread it out on the table. After smoothing out the wrinkles, she lined up a variety of jars and sealed containers.

"You really went all out, didn't you? I thought you were taking it easy."

"I was. Only a few of them are new. The rest are from my private stash." She lifted a small, covered glass dish. "Most of these are good at room temperature, but this one and the Zook's need to be warmed up. Can I use your oven?"

"Knock yourself out. Hopefully, it works. I don't think it's ever been used."

She laughed at that. "Not much of a cook, huh?"

"I *can* cook if I have to, but it's not my forte. Kate and Sam do a much better job than I could."

"I can understand that," she told him. "I don't cook much for myself either. By the time I get home at night, I'm too tired to do anything but pop something into the microwave. Anything more isn't worth the effort, not for one person."

Doc looked skeptically at the items on the table.

"This is different. This isn't me cooking for myself. This is *science* and, if I'm lucky, a sellable product. I installed a small commercial-grade kitchen at The Mill, and I spend a few hours there most days, especially during the summer. The best part is, I have staff that cleans up after me."

She put the baking dish in the oven and managed to get it started.

"Okay, while those are heating up, let's start with some staples."

She opened a mason jar of sliced peaches, then dipped in a fork and held it to his lips.

"Delicious," he said. "What is that?"

"My hybrid Snow Beauties with natural juices and vanilla schnapps. It's one of my favorites."

It was now officially one of his, too. "More, please."

She obliged, spearing another slice. This time, he wrapped his hand around hers and let her take a bite first. A drop of liquid dribbled over her lips, and without conscious thought, he leaned down and pressed his lips to hers.

She stiffened at first, and he feared he'd made a grave error. He pulled away and was about to apologize when her free hand reached up, curled around the back of his neck, and coaxed him for another.

This time, her lips were soft and welcoming,

tasting of peaches and vanilla. The kiss lasted much longer. Not long enough, but longer.

When she released him, he said, "Even better. I think I should sample everything this way."

"Yes to some things," she said with a smile. "But no to others. The chicken, for example. That could get weird."

He appeared to consider it. "I see your point. All right. I'll leave it up to you."

CHAPTER TWENTY-SEVEN

~ Tina ~

There were many things about Doc that Tina liked, but his easygoing manner and ready willingness to cede control over to her were particularly attractive. It balanced nicely with the protective, dangerous SEAL she'd glimpsed earlier. While she appreciated a strong, capable man, she had no use for overbearing he-man types. At the same time, she couldn't be with someone who was passive and deferential by nature.

It was a tough ask, but she refused to settle. Now, it didn't look like she would have to. Doc checked all of her boxes and then some.

Since he was being so agreeable, she decided to press her luck.

"All right then. How about you sit down and let me take care of this?"

For a moment, she thought he was going to refuse, but he surprised her by sliding into the booth seat. "All right."

"Here. You can open this," she said, handing

him a bottle. "It's a peach Riesling I've been working on with a friend I met on one of my summer internships in college. Her family owns vineyards along the Mosel River in Germany. Phenomenal white grapes. I'd love to start a mini vineyard of my own at some point."

"Why don't you?"

"Gunther thinks it's too risky. It would require a prime south-facing slope and several years to achieve anything viable. Still, I think it would be a good investment. Local wineries are becoming more popular every year."

"Does your brother make all the decisions for the business?"

"We each get an equal vote, but Kief and Rick rarely vote against Gunther, so he usually gets his way."

Doc didn't say anything else on the subject, but the slight downturn of his lips suggested he didn't like her answer. She didn't either, but it was what it was.

Under Doc's watchful eyes, Tina pulled the chicken from the oven but left the stuffed peaches in to stay warm. She located dishes, glasses, and silverware with his direction and prepared plates for them both.

"Zook's chicken stands on its own," she told him, "but I made a peach and currant chutney that I think goes well with it."

He took a bite and closed his eyes in bliss.

"This is … I don't even have words for this."

"I know, right? I was thinking of giving a few jars to Eli and Rachael Zook next week, kind of a cross-promotional thing. We did something similar with a hot chow chow last year."

"Chow chow?"

She shook her head and laughed. "We really need to work on your cultural awareness. It's a Dutchie thing—a sweet-and-sour mix of pickled vegetables. Except I used a prototype sweet peach cider instead of the usual sugar and vinegar. It went over well."

"If it's even half as good as this, I can see why."

Doc was already familiar with her peach jam, tarts, and whoopie pies—thanks to Sandy—so she decided to leave those for him to enjoy later.

"Are you ready for the *pièce de résistance*?" she asked when he finished the last of his chicken.

"There's no way you can top this," he insisted, shaking his head.

Oh, she planned on topping it all right. She pulled her latest creation from the oven—baked peaches stuffed with a cookie-cashew filling, topped with a whipped zabaglione.

"I got the idea for this one from Rico Buschetti," Tina explained as she scooped some onto a clean plate and added a generous dollop of her peach-based zabaglione. "He runs the Italian restaurant in town and does this flaming dessert with strawberries that is simply outstanding."

Instead of sitting across from him, she cut a spoonful and held it to his lips. His eyes didn't leave hers as he took the first bite.

"Well?"

"I need another taste to be sure."

Tina held her breath as Doc coaxed her down onto his lap. Then, he dipped his finger into the serving dish and spread the filling and whipped topping over her lips.

She gave herself over to it, quickly deciding that being devoured by Doc was her new favorite thing. He nibbled, he licked, he savored, and she loved every second of it.

"Delicious," he said softly.

He repeated the process, and it was even better the second time. By the time he reached over for a third helping, her heart was racing, and heat was pooling between her legs. The only thing she wanted more was to feel those talented lips working magic on other parts of her body, too.

His hands gripped her hips, those long fingers flexing as if they wanted to explore. She desperately wished they would. Tina scooted up on his lap in an attempt to get closer, but all that did was situate her more solidly over the hard proof that he was enjoying their kisses, too.

"Tina," he warned when she began to rock her hips.

She nibbled his lips. "You're right. This is a

much better way to taste-test. But I need more data."

"What data?" he mumbled.

"Maybe it tastes better on some parts more than others."

She took a page out of his book and swiped her finger in the dish, spreading the sweet mix onto his skin. She licked along the column of his throat. He growled, a low, supremely masculine sound that made her ache.

"Hold on."

It was the only warning she had before Doc was on his feet. Her legs tightened around his hips, her arms around his neck. The next thing she knew, she was on the couch, and he was looming over her with a hungry look in his eyes.

There was nothing easygoing about that look. Gold flecks flashed in vibrant green and deep amber. This was a man with things on his mind. Wild, passionate things. Yet he was keeping them under control. She knew that as surely as she knew her nipples had never been quite so hard, nor her panties quite so wet, from simply kissing.

"Yes," she whispered. Whatever his unspoken question was, the answer was an unequivocal yes.

He grinned, a sexy, predatory grin that thrilled her, and began to raise the hem of her shirt. He smeared the dessert on the exposed skin and then took great time and attention in removing it. When finished, he lifted the material a few more inches and repeated the process.

Before long, her impatience got the best of her, and she yanked the shirt over her head. He chuckled.

Tina loved the way his eyes darkened when he saw the hardened tips clearly through her bra. Even more, she liked the way he wasted no time in slipping the straps over her shoulders to expose her flesh.

The look in his eyes was priceless. An intense mix of hunger and passion and want. In that moment, she felt like the most desirable woman on the planet.

So intent was she on watching him that she didn't notice him reaching over to the plate, but she certainly noticed when he began to swirl the whipped topping around her nipple. Just the light touch of his finger was enough to send her building lust into overdrive.

That was nothing compared to what it felt like when he began to use his tongue.

And *that* paled in comparison to when he wrapped his lips around the hardened peak and sucked. *Hard.*

Her back arched, and a sound she'd never made before rose, unbidden, from deep within, passing over her lips in an unintelligible form of, "Yes, more, please."

Tangling her fingers in his hair, she writhed beneath him, shamelessly and breathlessly encouraging him. Seeing him take so much pleasure in her body, feeling that pleasure amplified everywhere, hearing her moans of enjoyment harmonizing with his, was incredibly hot.

When his hand slipped down into her panties, she vaguely wondered when he'd unfastened her jeans. When his skilled fingers touched her where she ached most, she thought she'd died and gone to heaven.

She was wet. So wet that he glided easily between her folds as she tilted her hips to get him exactly where she needed him. He obliged, and after several strokes, she felt the glorious penetration of one long, talented finger. He plunged and withdrew, using the palm of his hand in a synchronous kind of waving massage motion that was incredible.

Then, he added another finger.

With his lips sucking and nibbling each of her breasts and his fingers and hands doing absolutely magical things down below, she reached her peak quickly. He was right there with her, reading her body, somehow knowing exactly where to touch, exactly how much pressure to use, and when to stroke and flick to give her what she needed.

He took her to the edge and pushed her over, her body exploding in a spectacular climax, complete with bursts of light behind her eyelids and a momentary loss of hearing.

His passionate kisses became tender as he gently guided her back to earth. Eventually, her heartbeat slowed to normal levels, as did her breathing, but Tina wasn't sure the rest of her would ever feel the same again.

"Wow," she said when her ability to speak returned. "That was …"

He lifted his fingers to his lips, licked, grinned, and said, "Best dessert *ever*."

She grinned right back at him. "I don't know. I think I need to sample a few things, too."

His eyes went molten, but then he shook his head as if clearing it. "Not today."

"What? Why not?"

"Because."

"Because why?"

He fastened her jeans and carefully put her back together. "Because I want you to be sure this is what you want."

She reached for the snap on his jeans. "Then, we're good because I'm sure."

He gently but firmly wrapped his hands around her wrists and stopped her. "Tina. Not today."

"This hardly seems fair."

"I know, but humor me, okay?"

It really didn't seem fair. He did so much for her yet seemed reluctant to allow her to do anything for him, food sampling notwithstanding. It was highly inequitable and, in her opinion, contrary to the friendship-plus plan and not a proper way to go about forging a relationship. She told him as much.

"I didn't see it that way," he admitted, "but I

can see your point. Doesn't change my mind though."

"Can you at least give me a better explanation than *because*?"

He considered that and then nodded. "Yes, but I'm not sure I should."

"Why not?"

"Because it might change things, and I like the way things are going."

She did, too, which was why she wanted them to continue. "Try me."

He released her hands and took a deep breath. "All right. I really like you."

So far, so good. "I really like you, too."

"And I like doing things for you, especially things that help you or make you happy. I can walk away from that, feeling good, you know?" When she nodded, he continued, "But if I let you do things for me, I'm afraid I'm not going to be able to walk away, and I don't want to put that kind of pressure on you."

Her heart skipped. She understood exactly what he was saying because each time he did something for her, she lost another tiny piece of herself to him.

"Doc, I'm not going anywhere. And I don't want to feel like I'm the only one who can't walk away."

His eyes darkened. "You can't?"

She shook her head, willing him to see the truth in her eyes. "No. Nor do I want to. Trust me enough to let me in, the same way I'm trusting you. Okay?"

His response was to pull her against him, wrap his arms around her, and kiss her passionately. From the close bodily contact, she could feel that he was still aroused. She reached between them and stroked him through his jeans, eliciting a groan.

"So, in a show of good faith, how about letting me do something about this?"

CHAPTER TWENTY-EIGHT

~ Doc ~

The woman made it damn hard to refuse. Not only had she provided a convincing, logical case, but giving her pleasure had him walking the razor's edge between self-control and the desire to plunge deep into her body and make her his.

She didn't wait for him to answer. Taking full advantage of his hesitation, she quickly undid his jeans. He found himself hissing at the feel of her hands pushing his pants down over his hips. Before he knew it, she was on her knees and humming in approval.

Doc called upon every last thread of discipline he had, looking up at the ceiling and searching for the strength to remain still as she stroked, fondled, and explored. His eyes closed in bliss, then snapped open when he felt her spreading the baked dessert on him.

She grinned wickedly, holding his gaze as she extended her tongue and began to lick at him just as he had done to her. His hands threaded into her hair—something to hold on to while she cast her special brand of magic.

The woman was relentless, doing amazing things with her hands while loving him with her mouth. He was already so worked up that it didn't take long before his thin thread of control was ready to snap.

"Tina." The single word was a strangled warning.

Instead of backing off, she doubled her efforts, sucking harder, grasping firmer, stroking faster. He didn't stand a chance, and before long, he was no longer capable of holding back.

Afterward, she treated him with the same gentle care that he had her—with soft kisses and tender strokes—before pulling up his jeans and tucking him away with a satisfied and triumphant smile. It—*she*—was perfect.

"Well?" she asked smugly.

He pulled her close and touched his forehead to hers. "Woman, you have no idea what you've just done."

Her grin widened. "What have I done?"

He lightly smacked her ass. "You know exactly what you did. You'll never get rid of me now."

She laughed and wrapped her arms around his neck. Her body fit so perfectly against his. "Good. At least now, we're on the same page. But I should be going."

Doc didn't like the idea of her driving around

the back roads alone after what happened. “Are you sure you can’t stay?” He leaned down and pressed kisses to the tender spot below her ear.

“Tempting, but no.” She cupped his face with her hands and said earnestly, “I’ll be fine.”

“Someone *shot* at you.”

“Someone shot at my tire and only after I started chasing them.”

“Yeah, don’t do that again.”

She went up on her toes and kissed him, then stepped out of his embrace. “It’s sweet that you care.”

He grunted and grabbed his keys. She had no idea how much he cared or the lengths he was willing to go to keep her safe.

“Where are you going?” she asked, raising an eyebrow in question.

He was going to make sure she got home safely, that was what he was going to do. What he said was, “I need to pick up a few things in town.”

Her lips quirked. “You do, huh?”

“Yes.”

The quirk grew into a grin. She was so onto him.

* * *

After returning from town with a bag of

groceries he didn't really need, his body was still humming as he made his way over to the main building. He was doing his best to remain cautiously optimistic.

He wasn't a fool. He knew that, in her eyes, he looked pretty good. She was going through some stressful times, and he was there for her, bringing her soup, lending a sympathetic ear, and most recently, giving her pleasure. He was also someone her overbearing brothers didn't approve of, which added the allure of rebellion.

But would it last beyond the novelty?

For him, the answer was yes. Tina was different. She'd captured his instant and immediate attention, and that showed no signs of changing. If anything, he was becoming more invested every day. And after today? Well, he hadn't been kidding about not being able to walk away.

For her? Only time would tell.

In the meantime, he'd take whatever she was willing to give him and hope that the inexplicable force that kept drawing him to her was working on her as well.

He set a course for the war room, his intent to use the slick setup to do some digital recon. He should have known Cage was already on it. Mad Dog, who had gotten up close and personal with Eisenheiser's truck, was there, too.

"How's Tina?" Mad Dog asked.

"She's fine. A little shaken. I think she was

more pissed off than anything."

Cage chuckled. "Yeah, I got that impression. She's pretty tough."

"She has to be with brothers like hers," Mad Dog said. "Cage has been doing a little digging. They're real pieces of work."

"How so?"

"Besides their questionable taste in friends, you mean?"

"Yeah, besides that."

"Friedrich isn't the sharpest tool in the shed. Reached his peak in high school as a star linebacker. He actually got drafted by a Division I school but got himself kicked out after several drunken brawls and half a dozen charges of sexual harassment. Most of it got buried; apparently, the school didn't want the bad publicity. He came back here, citing a knee injury and the need to help with the family business. Oh, and you'll never guess who his BFF was. Dwayne Freed."

"Shocker."

The ne'er-do-well son of the Sumneyville police chief had a reputation for being a troublemaker and was, thanks to some poor choices, now serving time in a federal prison.

"Gunther Obermacher isn't much better. He's not a linebacker like Rick, but what he lacks in brawn, he makes up for in cunning. According to Sandy and Kate, he considers himself quite the ladies' man and likes to hobnob with the big dogs."

When Doc raised his eyebrows, Cage grinned and put up his hands. "Hey, their words, not mine. But it's pretty apparent Gunther likes to live beyond his means. Expensive clothes, expensive dinners, expensive car."

"Where's he getting the funds?" Doc mused.

"That's the question, isn't it?" asked Mad Dog. "On paper, it looks like he doesn't have a pot to piss in, but he and his wife have been racking up some impressive tabs. They're not just wining and dining Phillip Dumas. They're branching out, contacting heavyweight real estate developers, some of whom have known mob ties."

That didn't sound good at all.

"We do know that Gunther is tight with Luther Renninger," Cage said. "He might even be the mastermind behind Renninger's financial schemes. Church always said Renninger didn't have the brains or the stones to pull off something like that on his own."

"If Gunther is pulling the strings, he's damn good at covering his tracks."

"And Ian Callaghan is a damn good tracker. If there's more there, he'll find it. We reached out to him earlier."

"What about the third brother, Kiefer?" asked Doc.

"We don't know a lot about him," admitted Cage. "If we look close enough, he's always there, lurking in the shadows, but his name rarely comes up on the radar."

"That's what worries me," Mad Dog said. "He's a little *too* boring, if you know what I mean. But back to your woman. We're pretty sure Eisenheiser was the one tailing her."

Doc liked the way Mad Dog referred to Tina as his woman even if it wasn't a done deal. Yet.

"It all fits," Cage added. "Tina's description of the vehicle, his alliance with Freed, his propensity for road rage. *And* he just happens to be Eddie Schweikert's cousin."

"Is everyone in this fucking town related?" Mad Dog murmured.

"Apparently. But it's not really surprising, is it?"

"No, I guess not," Doc said on an exhale. "All right. Thanks, guys."

"Oh, one more thing. We managed to extract a few pieces of glass from Tina's grill while she was with you. We're going to hand them over to Ian, see if he can pull any prints."

"Good thinking."

CHAPTER TWENTY-NINE

~ *Tina* ~

After a busy morning in the orchards, Tina left the crew to it. She was anxious to get to The Mill; her time with Doc had provided inspiration for a new project. But first, she took a detour toward the old outbuilding that had been converted into an office way before her time.

"Does your brother make all the decisions for the family business?"

Doc's question kept rolling around in the back of her mind. It wasn't so much the question itself as the way he'd said it. As if he knew something she didn't.

That seemed unlikely. How would he?

Regardless, it continued to bother her until she felt compelled to do something about it.

Gunther was a creature of habit, and lately, one of those habits was taking a particularly long lunch. Tina didn't know where he went, but if the rumors were to be believed, he wasn't heading back to his house to spend time with Giselle.

She waited on the ridge until she saw Gunther drive away in his fancy car. She dawdled a few minutes more, just in case he doubled back for something.

Otto was walking the short distance from the office toward the warehouse. He looked up when she pulled into an empty space in front of the building.

“Hey, Otto.”

“Hi there, Peaches. How are you feeling?”

“Back to normal finally. Thanks for asking.”

“If you’re looking for Gunther, you just missed him.”

“Damn,” she said, hoping she sounded convincing. “I wanted to catch him before he left. He said he has some papers for me. Any idea when he’ll be back?”

“Didn’t say, but I imagine it’ll be around two, as usual. Anything I can help you with?”

“No, I don’t think so. Did everything get straightened out with your paycheck?”

Otto tapped the envelope sticking out of his shirt pocket. “Yep. Going to cash it right now, in fact.”

“Good. I’m glad to hear it.”

“You have a good day now.”

“You, too.”

Tina went back to her truck and pulled out her phone. She waited until Otto was across the lot before she went inside. The outer area was kept unlocked, but it was the inner office where Tina was headed. She knocked first, and after receiving no answer, she tried the knob and found it locked.

After checking the window to ensure the coast was clear, she pulled out her set of rakes and hooks and picked the lock. Her skills were rusty, but thankfully, she hadn't lost her touch.

Tina slipped into the office and closed the door behind her.

The place still smelled slightly of her grandfather's pipe tobacco. Quilted flannels hung on pegs inside the door, most likely Rick's or Kief's. Gunther preferred his high-end designer outerwear. Framed photos of generations of stern-looking Obermachers hung on the walls along with images of the farm over the centuries.

She wasn't sure what she was looking for exactly. The optimist in her hoped she found nothing to warrant her growing sense of concern, but intuition and experience suggested otherwise.

A quick scan of the desk revealed nothing useful. Purchase orders. Work schedules. A bunch of square notes impaled on a round wooden base with a nail-like spike, a relic from the days before Post-it Notes.

The filing cabinet gave up no clues either. While Gunther's filing system left a lot to be desired, she found no evidence to suggest her suspicions were anything more than the product of an overactive imagination.

Her hand was on the door when an image of Otto reaching into his pocket flashed into her mind for no apparent reason. For the hell of it, Tina walked over to the jackets hanging on the wall and started going through the pockets. She found gloves, a half-empty pack of chew, some pocket money … and a key.

It looked old and worn and familiar, as if she *should* know what it went to but the memory eluded her.

At the sound of the outer door opening, Tina shoved the key back into the pocket and quickly pulled out her phone.

Rick entered a moment later, his eyebrows pulling down hard when he spotted her. “Bert. What are you doing here?”

“I was just sending a group text,” she said, slipping her phone into her pocket. “Do you know if we got the results back on those soil samples yet?”

“We didn’t,” he said quickly. Too quickly. “Where’s Gunther?”

She frowned. She’d seen the manila envelope stamped with the university logo in the inbox beneath the latest seed catalogs. However, she couldn’t exactly say so without admitting that she’d been snooping.

“I don’t know. He wasn’t here when I got here. Are you sure about those results? They promised me I’d have them last week. I need those numbers to optimize the fertilizer ratio.”

"I'm sure."

"Shit. All right. I guess I'll call the lab directly. Thanks."

"How'd you get in?"

She pretended to think about it. "Uh, I turned the knob and pushed?"

"Wasn't it locked?"

"Sure it was," she said, crossing her arms over her chest and cocking out her hip. "I waited until everyone left, and then I climbed up the drain pipe, squeezed my fat ass through the ventilation window, and mission-impossibled my way into the office. And *then*, I unlocked it from the inside to make it look as if it had been open the whole time. In retrospect, I suppose I shouldn't have parked my truck right out front in plain sight. That's a dead giveaway, huh?"

"Don't be a smart-ass," he rumbled.

"It's who I am. Let me know when those numbers come in, will you?"

Without waiting for an answer, she turned to leave.

"Bert."

"*Yes*?" she said with exaggerated patience.

"You need to get that windshield fixed."

He didn't ask what had happened, suggesting he already knew.

"I will. I'm still waiting for the auto insurance guy to call me back."

"You need me to spot you some petty cash?"

If she didn't know better, she might think Rick was trying to assuage a guilty conscience.

"No, thanks. I think you've done enough, don't you?"

His eyes widened. "You don't think I had anything to do with that, do you?"

"Well, you did threaten me. Something about"—she made air quotes with her fingers—" 'consequences' if I kept going up to Sanctuary. Sound familiar?" She let that soak in for a moment and then continued, "Look, I know it wasn't you who followed me and shot out my tire. But there's no doubt in my mind that some of your friends did."

He didn't deny it, instead asking, "Why would they do that?"

It might have been retaliation for firing Eddie. Or maybe someone warning her off Sanctuary because if Bonnie knew what she'd been doing, *everyone* knew. Maybe it was both—retaliation and a warning.

It didn't matter what message they had been trying to send. Eddie was never stepping foot in her orchards again, and she was now more determined than ever to continue her weekly trips to Sanctuary. If her pursuers had intended to intimidate her, their plan had backfired spectacularly.

To Rick, she replied, "You could probably answer that better than I can."

His expression hardened. "You know, if you'd gotten off your goddamn high horse and just listened once in a while, none of this would have happened."

"And if you got your head out of your ass and stopped listening to idiots, you'd realize how ridiculous you're being right now."

"*I'm* being ridiculous? I'm not the one cozying up to borderline psychopaths."

She almost laughed. Compared to Rick's temper tantrums and Eddie's half-assed sabotage, the Sanctuary guys were models of rational, adult behavior.

"But they're not the ones shooting at me now, are they? Tell me, Rick, who are the real psychos here?"

Rick's jaw clenched, as did the hands curling into fists at his sides.

"Yeah, that's what I thought."

"You can't even see it, can you?" he asked, shaking his head in disbelief. "They're luring you in, just like they lured in the others. Next thing you know, one of those guys will be hitting on you, if one of them hasn't already." He narrowed his eyes. "Have they?"

"How do you know *I* haven't been the one hitting on one of them?"

"Don't even joke about that."

"Let's face it, Rick. There aren't many keepers in the Sumneyville pond."

"Jesus, Bert."

"I'm done here. Oh, and, Rick? Stay out of my

business—unless you want me poking into yours. Or maybe I'll just follow you to O'Malley's one of these nights. That's where you go, isn't it?"

He ground his teeth and said nothing.

"What's going on? And don't even think of telling me nothing because I know better. Something has you vexed."

"I told you. Nothing you need to worry about."

"Bullshit. Obermacher Farms is as much mine as it is yours."

"You sure about that? Because I'm not the one who went and created my own company now, am I?"

He was still pissed about that—clearly. And she still didn't care. Now more than ever, she was convinced she'd made the right decision.

"If something's going on, I need to know."

"You just worry about your precious mill and leave running the farm to us. Anything else? I've got work to do."

Tina glared at him. There was no point in arguing further, not when his back was already up. But if he thought she was going to stop trying to get answers, he had another thing coming.

On that note, Tina turned around and walked out of the office.

* * *

"I don't want to wait until Sunday to see you again," Tina told Doc over the phone later that night. It had only been three days, but they'd been three very long days. "I could really use one of your magical massages."

"I could drive down and give you one."

"Would you?"

"In a heartbeat. Sooner if those gateway sexual favors are still on the table."

She laughed, taking great pleasure in the fact that he seemed every bit as anxious to see her as she was to see him. Plus, she couldn't stop thinking about the time they'd spent in his trailer. Her body lit up at the thought of what they could do with her new prototype edible body butter and the box of condoms she'd picked up.

"What are you waiting for? Get down here."

"Yes, ma'am."

The crappy mood that had been plaguing her instantly lifted. Doc had that effect on her.

Figuring she had a good thirty minutes before he arrived, she took a quick shower, ensured she was completely stubble-free, and then applied the cocoa, coconut, and orange butter to her skin. It soaked in almost instantly, leaving her skin soft, smooth, and delicious, if she did say so herself.

Doc made good time. She'd barely thrown on leggings and a brushed cotton tee when he knocked on the door.

He took one step inside her cottage, wrapped her in his arms, and told her she smelled fantastic.

"It's a new product I'm working on, and you're the inspiration."

"I am?"

"I enjoyed our taste-testing so much that I decided organic body edibles were the way to go. I did some online research, and the stuff that's available is all chemically—"

She didn't get to finish that statement. The steamy kiss that followed made her especially glad she'd done the extra prep. Judging by the damp ends of his hair and the lingering scent of shaving cream on his skin, he'd done a bit himself.

"You taste as delicious as you smell."

"That's the idea."

The gold flecks in his eyes flashed at her. "Ready for that massage?"

"So ready. But good manners require me to offer you food or a drink first. Do you want anything?"

"Just you."

She grasped his hand and led him to her bedroom.

"What's all this?" he asked, taking in the scented candles and the soft, barely audible ocean sounds coming from her white-noise machine. His eyes widened when his gaze landed on the open jars of body butter in various trial flavors and the foil packets beside them.

"I figured we might as well make it a full sensory experience."

She'd barely gotten the words out before he was using his larger, stronger body to back her toward the bed. Then, suddenly, she was on her back, feet still on the floor, and he was over her, kissing her again.

She pushed her hands up under his shirt, needing the skin-to-skin contact. He stood up and shrugged off his flannel shirt, and just that quickly, he was leaning over her again. One arm suspended him above her, the other reached behind his head and tugged, removing the T-shirt in one smooth move.

Tina took a moment to observe and explore. Taut skin stretched over a toned, sculpted chest dusted with dark golden hair. She ran her fingers over his broad shoulders, along the ridges and dips, and then downward.

Doc sucked in a breath as she skimmed over his abs, reaching for the waistband of his jeans. He captured her hand before she could do anything more than unfasten them.

"Slow down."

"Why?" The one-worded question sounded breathy and impatient.

When she'd imagined the evening, it had been with images of sensual touches and lots of exploring, pushing those self-control boundaries of his, and culminating in great sex. Suddenly, that didn't seem nearly as much fun as taking the edge off quickly and leaving the leisurely exploration for later.

"Because I promised you a massage."

"I don't mind. I can wait."

He chuckled softly, deftly stopped another attempt of hers to get into his pants, and straightened. His gaze dipped to her chest, where her nipples were pressing prominently against her shirt, bidding for attention. If the desire in his eyes was anything to go by, her impromptu decision to go braless had been a good one.

Dipping his head, he wrapped his mouth around one hardened peak through the material. He tongued and then bit lightly, eliciting a moan and a desperate need to tangle her hands in his hair.

He moved to the other and repeated the process. The warm, wet spots cooled quickly, making them even harder.

When he leaned back and admired his handiwork, his eyes were practically glowing.

"Beautiful. But this"—he fingered the collar of her top—"needs to go."

She was totally on board with that plan and wasted no time in grabbing the bottom edge and lifting her shirt over her head. Once again, he chuckled at her enthusiasm and then sucked in a breath when her breasts were revealed.

In that moment, she learned another interesting fact about Doc—he was clearly a breast man.

He lavished the same attention on her without the cloth barrier between them. By the time he pulled away again, the area between her legs was as wet as her nipples.

"Too distracting," he murmured more to himself than to her. Reaching behind her knees, he swung her legs onto the bed, then promptly rolled her onto her stomach and tugged at her leggings.

It all happened so quickly. One moment, she had been pulling his hair and arching her chest into his face. The next, she was facedown and naked. A delighted thrill ran through her.

Now, who was the impatient one?

"Fuck, Tina," he said on an exhale, discovering that she'd gone commando down there, too.

He climbed up onto the bed and straddled the backs of her thighs, the denim of his jeans providing a soft friction against her freshly shaved skin. Then he leaned over and dipped two fingers into the jar.

The cocoa butter–based lotion melted against her skin with the heat of his hands, releasing the rich aromas of chocolate, coconut, and oranges as he applied just the perfect amount of pressure.

"My mouth is watering. This smells good enough to eat."

"It is," she said on a moan.

He started at her neck and worked his way slowly downward. By the time he got to her ass, she was limp, relaxed, and incredibly turned on.

He dipped his fingers in the jar again and slid

them along her natural creases and crevices, and she was the one holding her breath. His finger glided down from her tailbone to the needy area at the juncture of her thighs and back up. It was hard to tell if the slick wetness was the melting body butter or her body's natural lubricant.

He repeated the gliding strokes several more times, adding a finger dip and an artful swirl each time he reached her sex.

Then, it was two fingers.

Then three.

Tina moved her hips in a desperate bid for more, but instead of giving her what she wanted, he stopped entirely.

She was about to voice a complaint when the warm weight of his body pressed against her back—his warm, *naked* weight—and she felt something thicker and stiffer where his fingers had been.

"I wanted to make this last," he grumbled against her ear in a low, sexy growl as his hips rolled, sliding his cock along the outside of her sex.

It felt wonderful, but it wasn't enough.

She slid her hand beneath her body and touched her fingers to the sensitive bundle of nerves, desperate for some contact. When his cock touched her fingers, she included him in her self-stroking action, too.

In another smooth move, demonstrating his strength and mastery of basic leverage, she was on her back, staring up into his beautiful face and lust-filled eyes.

"Say yes or say no, but say something before I lose my fucking mind."

"Yes. One hundred thousand times *yes*."

His sheathed cock teased her entrance with agonizingly shallow strokes, each one going just a hairbreadth deeper than the last. Tina lifted her knees, opening herself to him, needing more.

But he was in no hurry, his thrusts slow and controlled as he lavished her with kisses and rolled her aching nipples between his lips and fingers.

"Doc. *Please*."

He paused his kisses only long enough to gaze into her eyes, a hungry smile dancing over his lips. Had any man ever looked at her with such intensity? As if she belonged to him and him alone?

In that moment, she wanted nothing more.

Without breaking eye contact, he entwined his fingers with hers and raised her hands above her head. He began to push deeper but still not enough to satisfy the need building to a fever pitch inside her.

She stretched to accommodate him, greedy for more, until he filled her completely. He was so far inside her that it was impossible to tell where he left off and she began.

She'd never felt anything so good. She'd never felt so connected to another human being. It wasn't just his body entering hers. It was *him*. And they fit together perfectly.

He began to move, slowly at first, drawing back his hips in a smooth glide. Her inner muscles squeezed around him, desperate to hang on, only to relax and welcome him back a second later.

She wrapped her legs around his hips and moved with him, matching his rhythm, curling her hips to take him even deeper with each thrust as they stared into each other's eyes, saying everything without words.

His strokes became faster, more insistent, stealing her breath away and pushing her toward a peak the likes of which she'd never experienced.

Tina tried to prolong it—she really did—but her traitorous body obeyed only him, and before long, she was clamping down around him in the throes of a powerful orgasm. Just when she thought it couldn't get any more intense, he pushed even further, and she felt the pulsing throb of his own climax deep within her.

Then, he pressed his lips to hers in their most intimate kiss yet.

"I'll be right back," he whispered and withdrew.

Her body protested the loss immediately. He was back a moment later with a warm washcloth, wiping gently between her legs and then pulling the covers up over both of them.

"You okay?" he asked softly, stroking her skin with the back of his hand.

"Perfect," she murmured. "You?"

"Perfect," he echoed. "Though I don't think I'll ever be able to smell chocolate without getting a hard-on again."

* * *

"I should get going. It's going to be dawn soon, and you need some sleep." Doc nuzzled the sensitive spot near her ear. He didn't sound any happier about it than she was.

"I *was* sleeping." Quite soundly in fact.

"I know, but if I stay any longer, I'm going to have you again."

Spooned as they were, she could feel the hard ridge of his cock tucked snugly in the gap at the apex of her thighs. With a slight lift and shift of her hips, he could be inside her. She was certainly wet enough. Something about having his bare skin pressed against her and his arm possessively cupping her breast kept her in a constant state of readiness.

"You say that like it's a bad thing."

He kissed her shoulder and squeezed her hip, withdrawing only long enough to sheathe himself. She moaned in pleasure as he pushed into her again in a slow, deliciously snug glide. She pushed back, taking him even deeper.

"Fuck, Tina. I have no willpower when it

comes to you."

His words gave her a thrill. He slipped his arm under the knee of her upper leg and lifted, opening her and changing the angle of his thrusts. At first, his strokes were slow and deep, but they soon escalated to hard and fast until he took them both over the edge.

"Now, I really have to go," he said regretfully, "or I won't make it to the road while it's still dark."

"I know. Go." She placed her hands around his face and kissed him. "I'll call you later tonight."

She stayed in bed, appreciating the bunch and play of his muscles as he got dressed. It was a nice view indeed. He had the lean build of a healthy, athletic guy who took care of himself and worked out regularly. That, combined with his intelligence, thoughtfulness, and generosity, made him pretty much her ideal man. She'd have to be careful. If he kept being so wonderful, she could easily see herself losing her heart.

"Take care of yourself today," he commanded softly, and with one more quick kiss, he was gone.

Tina snuggled under the blankets and buried her face in the pillow, still warm and scented from the man who was quickly becoming an addiction. She didn't have to get out of bed for a little while yet, and she was going to enjoy the quiet, happy moments while she could.

Her body was still thrumming with the aftereffects of her latest orgasm. Some parts were more tender than others, but she wasn't complaining. The man knew a thing or two about pleasure points. She wondered vaguely if that was a natural talent or something he'd picked up in his medic training.

She allowed her eyes to drift shut, using tactile memory to recall the heat of his skin, the grip of those strong fingers, and the weight of his body atop hers. It was a nice place to be, suspended in between sleep and wakefulness and wrapped in such lovely thoughts.

She drifted deeper, and other happy, cozy memories rose up, too. The way her mother used to brush her hair. Her father lifting her up into the air to pick the plumpest, juiciest peaches. Accompanying her grandfather into the network of underground root cellars …

Tina's eyes popped open, and she sat up abruptly. She remembered where she'd seen the key in Rick's jacket pocket.

CHAPTER THIRTY

~ Tina ~

"Do you have any idea why anyone would need to access the old root cellars?" Tina asked Lottie later that evening.

"No. As far as I know, no one's been down there since your grandfather passed. And even before then, you were the only one who enjoyed spending time there. What makes you ask?"

"I found the key in a jacket pocket. I think it's Rick's."

Tina explained how she had gone snooping around the office, looking for anything that might explain the ever-increasing suspicion that something was afoot. "I need to get that key and find out what, if anything, he's doing down there."

"Whatever it is, I don't imagine it's anything good. What if he catches you?"

"He'll be mad," Tina said matter-of-factly. "But that's par for the course."

Rick was *always* pissed off at her for one reason or another. Sometimes, her mere existence seemed to agitate him.

"The male ego is a fragile thing. He's threatened by you."

"That's ridiculous."

Rick was the eldest son, which meant he had been born with special privileges the rest of them didn't have. He had been blessed with good health and a strong body. Maybe he wasn't the sharpest tool in the shed, but more often than not, his problems came from poor choices and not a lack of intelligence.

"Is it?" Lottie mused. She let the question hang between them for a moment before continuing, "In any event, I agree that your brother's recent behavior suggests he's gotten himself—and possibly all of you—into some real trouble."

That was what Tina was afraid of, too. "Even more reason why I need to find out what's going on."

"I don't like the idea of you sneaking around by yourself."

"I can't just sit idly by and wait for shit to hit the fan, Gram."

"Have you tried talking to Gunther and Kiefer?"

"No," Tina said, shaking her head. "Chances are, if Rick did do something stupid, Gunther was the one who's behind it. I suppose I could try talking to Kief, but you know he doesn't have the stones to stand up to Rick or Gunther."

"What about your young man? He's a SEAL, isn't he? Perhaps he can help. If nothing else, he can have your six."

Despite the seriousness of the conversation, Tina's lips quirked. "You've been watching that show on television again, haven't you? The one about Navy SEALs?"

"Well"—Lottie sniffed—"it's quite educational. You should watch it, too. It could give you some valuable insight in your Dr. Watson. Those boys, they're wired differently."

That Tina already knew. Doc was unlike any man she'd ever met.

But she couldn't involve him in this. It was one thing for *her* to go poking around. If she got caught, the most she'd catch was an earful. But if Doc were involved and Rick found out, tensions between Rick's idiot friends and Sanctuary could escalate exponentially. She'd been keeping her relationship with Doc under wraps for exactly that reason even though she was now convinced her future lay with him.

When she told Lottie as much, the older woman was forced to admit she had a point.

"I still don't like it," Lottie told her.

"I know. But someone has to do it."

"Just be careful, dear."

"I will."

* * *

One thing about older houses, every door had its own key.

Another thing: there was usually a skeleton key that unlocked them all.

And Tina knew where the skeleton key was because her grandfather had given it to her.

Whether it would work on the root cellars, she didn't know. But she was about to find out.

Under the cover of darkness, Tina made her way across the fields on foot toward the hill that housed the underground cellars. The good news was, the entrance wasn't visible from the family farmhouse where she'd grown up and Rick now lived.

The first cellar had been built next to where the original homestead once stood, back in the days when underground springs served as natural refrigerators. That house had been little more than a shack, a humble home for the first Obermacher to settle in the area.

The cellars had a fascinating history. Over the years, generations of Obermachers had expanded on the single-room storage area to a larger network now consisting of several chambers. Not only were the constant cool temperatures ideal for storing root crops throughout the year, but they were also good for crafting and aging wine, mead, and grain-based alcohols—something that had become particularly lucrative for her great-great-grandfather, Ezekiel Obermacher, during the Prohibition era.

According to Tina's grandfather, Ezekiel had expanded his business by employing dozens of local anthracite miners to create secret tunnels and passageways in exchange for free hooch.

By the time Tina had come along, most of those tunnels had been closed off and the stills long since disassembled, but for a little girl who was forced to spend the hottest, sunniest parts of the day inside, it was a magical, secret place. She'd wiled away quite a few hours there with her grandfather, listening to his stories and drinking juice while he experimented.

Tina believed that was where her passion had originated. He had encouraged her to try new things, to keep improving, and to always strive for something better.

A wave of nostalgia and lingering grief washed over her. She missed her grandfather terribly. He'd passed away before she earned her degree, but she thought he would have been proud. At least, she hoped he would have been.

Tina took a deep breath and slid the skeleton key into the ancient lock. She had to jiggle it a little, but a moment later, it settled into place, and with a turn of her wrist, the lock opened with a decisive *snick*.

The scents of cool, damp earth, stone, and

wood filled her nostrils, bringing back a slew of memories. Reaching into her pocket, she extracted a powerful halogen flashlight and turned it on.

At first glance, the entrance looked much the way it always had—a gateway to another time and place. Massive wooden beams and stonework kept the walls and ceiling from collapsing inward. Along the right side was the stone-lined trench, where spring-fed water continued to flow in a gentle trickle. To the left, hand-smithed black metal rods protruded from between the rocks. Their original purpose had been lost to history, but Tina believed they'd once held oil lamps and sacks of foodstuff suspended above the packed dirt floor.

When she directed the beam downward, she spotted several small tire tracks, like those from a hand truck, in the dirt floor and frowned. They looked fresh, too clearly defined to have been there for long. She followed them into one of the interior chambers, where several crates had been shoved against the wall.

Those definitely hadn't been there before.

Curiosity getting the better of her, Tina pried off one of the lids and peered inside, gasping when she saw the contents. Guns. Lots and lots of guns. And not the kind they sold at Jenkins's Sporting Goods.

She lifted one out carefully to take a closer look. It reminded her of those she'd seen armed guards carrying during one of her trips to South

America.

"Bert!"

Tina swung around at the sound of her brother's voice, finding him in a shadowy recess at the far end of the chamber. "Rick! What the actual hell?"

He quickly closed the space between them, removed the automatic weapon from her hands, and returned it to the crate. "You shouldn't be here. You have to leave."

"*These* shouldn't be here," she said, waving her hand toward the crates. "Why are they?"

His mouth twisted into a grimace. "The less you know, the better. And you need to leave. Right now."

"Oh no. You don't get to pull that crap. You're going to tell me what's going on."

"*Tina*"—Rick's large hands closed around her shoulders in a strong grip and shook lightly—"you can't be here."

The sound of footsteps came from deeper within. Rick's eyes were as desperate as she'd ever seen them, and in that moment, she felt his fear.

"*Please*."

"You're going to explain this."

He hesitated. The footsteps were getting closer. His head dipped in a jerky nod.

"I mean it, Rick."

He spun her around. "*Go*!" he hissed with a shove.

She did. She was nearly to the door when she heard the murmur of male voices. As much as she wanted to know who was in there and what they were doing, Rick's desperate plea and the genuine fear she'd seen in his eyes kept her moving.

* * *

It was after midnight when Rick finally showed up at her cottage. She opened the door and waved him in. Without a word, he stepped over the threshold and sank down into one of the two chairs at her small table.

She sat down, too, holding the questions burning on her tongue. She knew from experience that if she laid into him too quickly, he'd get his back up, and things would devolve into a battle.

He sat there in silence for so long that she began to think he wouldn't say anything at all. He continued to stare at the table, looking tired. Tired and despondent.

It unnerved her. The last time she'd seen him look that way, he'd had to explain to their father how he'd lost a full-paid football scholarship and been expelled from the university.

"What's going on, Rick?" she coaxed softly.

"Do you still keep a bottle of bourbon around here?"

Bourbon suddenly sounded like a good idea. Tina got up, got the bottle and two glasses, and then poured them each a few fingers. Rick tossed his back and poured another right away.

"I made some bad investments," he said finally.

"*You* made some bad investments?" she asked skeptically. "Or Gunther did?"

Rick's mouth twisted. "We all did, I guess. It was supposed to be a sure thing. Gunther said Luther had inside info."

Luther. Tina should have known he was involved somehow. The guy was bad news wrapped in a shiny, smooth-talking package.

"But …" she prompted.

"But something went wrong. And before you ask, I don't know what exactly. All I know is, we're fucked."

"How fucked?"

Rick looked miserable. "We leveraged everything. Bet the whole farm."

The true horror of the situation began to dawn on her. "You did *what*?"

"He was so sure," Rick murmured.

"There must be something—"

"There's not," he said abruptly, cutting her off. "We're going to have to sell. Gunther's been talking with some developers. He thinks he can get us a decent deal."

Tina shook her head. "No. No! It's not possible. It can't be that bad."

Rick lifted his eyes and met hers. His gaze said more than words ever could. He believed it was. That didn't mean she wasn't going to try to find a way out. There had to be some recourse. A four-hundred-year-old legacy farm didn't just go belly up overnight.

"What about those guns? What do they have to do with anything?"

Rick exhaled. "I wish you hadn't seen that. I don't want you involved."

"But I did, and apparently, I am involved."

"Luther said he could fix things. He just needed some cash to work with."

"And you thought dealing in illegal arms was the way to do that?" she asked in disbelief.

"It's not like that," he said irritably.

"Oh? You're telling me the weapons in that crate are legal? Should I call Chief Freed to come check them out?"

"Where do you think they came from?" he said with a humorless laugh.

Sadly, Tina should have been more shocked than she was. "Friedrich Elias Obermacher, what the hell is going on? Straight up. No bullshit."

The fact that Rick didn't argue, just exhaled and nodded, told her more than anything that he'd lost all hope.

"Dwayne met a guy when he did time downstate."

Dwayne was the police chief's son and at one

time, Rick's best friend. He'd gotten into some trouble outside his daddy's jurisdiction. Unlike every other time, Daryl hadn't been able to get him out of it, and Dwayne had been sentenced to a prison down around Philly somewhere.

"They got to talking about hunting and shit, and this guy told Dwayne he could get his hands on some quality firearms for cheap. When Dwayne got out, the guy hooked him up, and Dwayne brought a few pieces with him to the compound."

"The hunting camp?" Tina asked.

Everyone knew about the private encampment on the Freed family's mountain parcel. Many of the guys in town were members and used the club as an excuse to drink beer, shoot guns, and get away from their wives and kids on the weekends.

Rick nodded. "They were pretty slick. I'm talking military-grade, black ops shit, like the kind your friends are trained in and probably stockpiling up there at Sanctuary."

Tina was about to protest but held her tongue. She didn't *think* they were doing that, but she couldn't prove that they weren't, and she wanted to stay on topic.

"So … Dwayne brings cool new toys to the playground," she said, moving her hand in a circular motion to get Rick to continue.

"Yeah, well, everyone wanted one. Including me."

Tina had a feeling she knew where this was

going. “Let me guess. Gunther’s eyes turned green.”

It was an inside family joke that Gunther’s blue eyes turned green when he saw an opportunity to make money.

Rick nodded. “At first, we just got enough for us, you know? But Gunther saw the potential and figured other survivalist groups might want in, too. He was right. The demand was there. We even had a waiting list.”

“This was the sure thing you were talking about?” she asked quietly.

“Money was rolling in. Luther said he could double or triple it, so we gave it to him to invest. Everything was fine until those Sanctuary fuckers got Dwayne put back in the slammer,” Rick said with vehemence. “Dwayne’s contact got nervous. He didn’t want to go back to prison and ghosted, leaving us with orders to fill.

“It was just as well. Demand was greater than he was willing or able to supply anyway. Gunther found an alternate supplier, one who could think beyond a couple of crates now and then. But they demanded more—a lot more—up front. Gunther said if we pooled our resources, we’d make bank.”

“And you didn’t even think to question it? You just went along with him?” Tina felt cold and hollow.

“Gunther said it was a good investment. It was risky, sure, but Luther assured us we had plenty to play with,” Rick said again, as if the thought of

Gunther being wrong or Luther being dishonest was incomprehensible. “We weren’t going to do it forever. I thought we could make a few bucks and put it back into the farm, you know? Get some new equipment and bring in some of that eco-friendly shit you’re going on about all the time.”

A pang of guilt went through her. She had been pushing for incorporating wind turbines and solar power and earth-friendly farming techniques for years. Was part of this unknowingly her fault?

“So, what happened?”

“It went too far. Things got out of hand,” Rick said, running his hand over his face. “We’re in too deep.”

“I don’t believe that. There must be something we can do.”

Rick shook his head. “It’s too late, Bert. Our only option is to sell. If we don’t, we’ll wind up in jail.” His eyes met hers. “Or worse. These aren’t the kind of guys who issue idle threats if we don’t hold up our end.”

CHAPTER THIRTY-ONE

~ Doc ~

Doc just sat down to dinner when his phone vibrated with an incoming call. He pulled it out, expecting to see Tina's name pop up, but the number on the screen wasn't one that he recognized.

Since very few people had his private cell number, he figured it was a random telemarketer and let it go to voice mail. When they didn't leave a message, he assumed his guess was correct. But when he received another call from the same number almost immediately, he picked up.

"Hello?"

"Dr. Watson?" asked an older female voice.

"Yes," he answered carefully.

"This is Lottie Obermacher, Tina's grandmother. I got your number from Mr. O'Farrell."

His blood went instantly cold. The only reasons Doc could come up with for why Tina's grandmother was calling him weren't good ones.

"Mrs. Obermacher. Is Tina okay?"

"I'm not sure that she is," the older woman said cryptically. "That's why I'm calling. Can you go to her cottage and check on her?"

Doc was already on his feet. "Of course. Can you tell me what's going on?"

"I'm afraid the shit finally hit the fan," she told him. "She's not answering her phone, and Friedrich hid the keys to the Buick."

"I'm on my way."

"Please call or text me when you get there."

"I will."

"What's up?" Cage asked when Doc disconnected the call and shoved the phone back into his pocket.

"I'm not sure. That was Tina's grandmother. She wants me to go check on Tina."

"Did she say why?"

"Only that 'the shit finally hit the fan.'"

"That doesn't sound good."

No, it didn't. It didn't help that he'd been carrying around a bad feeling all day.

Tina's call the night before had him worried. She'd been distracted. When he asked her about it, she said that she'd been thinking a lot about her grandfather. He hadn't thought too much about it until she mentioned the old root cellars where he used to experiment, crediting him for her desire to try new things and create superior organic products.

Based on her description of the cellars, they

sounded a lot like the networks of old mines and caves used by Freed and his crew. With her brothers being in Freed's inner circle, it seemed a logical step to assume those underground storage areas were being used for nefarious purposes. Freed was showing increasing signs of paranoia, stashing stuff in separate locations around the mountain, including one of the caves on the far end of Sanctuary property. Each time they discovered a new location, they wired it with cameras and listening devices to stay abreast of what was going on.

He hadn't shared what Tina had told him about the root cellars with anyone yet, but perhaps he should have.

"Do you want backup?" asked Cage.

"No. Let me see what's going on first. But there is something you can do."

"Name it," Cage said.

"See if you can get those private satellites to do a sweep over Obermacher Farms, particularly in the hills behind the main house. Tina mentioned something about her grandfather using root cellars back in the day. I'm not sure if it's anything, but …"

Cage nodded, the look in his eyes telling Doc his mind had gone down the same path Doc's had. "Will do. Keep us posted."

Doc wasted no time in getting to Tina's, a sense of urgency riding his ass. Unlike the previous times he'd gone down there, he was less concerned about being spotted and making things difficult for Tina than he was about getting to her and ensuring she was okay.

He had no idea what he would find when he got there. "The shit finally hit the fan" could mean *lots* of things.

One glance at Tina, and it was obvious she was upset. Her skin was pale; her eyes were puffy and red. If her appearance hadn't tipped him off, her greeting would have. The moment she saw him, she wrapped her arms around his waist and buried her face in his neck.

"Hey now," he said soothingly, cupping the back of her head.

She squeezed him tighter.

"How did you know?" she asked, her words muffled.

"Your grandmother called me. She's worried about you."

Tina released him, took his hand, and tugged him inside. "How much did she tell you?"

"Not much. She said the shit hit the fan and Friedrich hid the keys to the Buick."

"More like he auctioned it off behind her back and doesn't have the balls to tell her," Tina practically growled. "Not that it's going to make a difference. They lost everything, Doc. They bet the farm, and they *lost. Everything.*"

"Tell me."

"I will but not here, okay? I'm afraid Rick's

going to show up, and if he does, I might just shoot him."

"All right. Want to come back to Sanctuary with me?"

She looked relieved. "Yes, please. Give me a minute. Don't go anywhere, okay?"

"Take your time. I'm not going anywhere."

With a grateful look, Tina went up on her toes and pressed a kiss to his cheek before disappearing into her bedroom. Moments later, he heard drawers opening. Doc remained by the window, his eyes watching the access road for any sign of her brother, and fired off a text to Lottie.

Doc: *Tina's fine. I'm taking her back to Sanctuary with me.*

Lottie: *Good. Keep her there for a while.*

Doc: *What about you?*

Lottie: *Sweet boy. I'll be fine. Tell Tina to call me later.*

Doc: *Will do.*

Tina emerged from her bedroom with a carry-on bag. "I don't mean to be presumptuous. If this makes you uncomfortable, I can get a hotel room or something."

"It doesn't," he told her honestly. He wanted her with him. If the time he'd spent with her thus far made anything clear, it was that he would much rather be with her than without.

Tina locked up the cottage. Instead of getting into his vehicle, she went to her truck. "I'll follow you, okay? That way, you don't have to bring me back in the morning."

"I don't mind."

"I know."

She didn't take him up on his offer, so he let it go. If it made her feel better to have her truck, so be it.

When they arrived at Sanctuary, Doc drove directly to his trailer. Tina pulled up and parked alongside him. He took her bag and carried it inside, just in case she was serious about going to a hotel.

"Have you eaten?"

She closed her eyes and shook her head. "Not recently. It's been a day."

"How about I go over to the dining room and bring something back?"

She hesitated. "Don't go to any trouble."

"It's no trouble. I haven't eaten yet either. Might as well get something for both of us, right?"

Her eyes softened, and for a moment, it looked like she was going to cry. "I'm sorry."

"Don't be. We have no set schedule here. Kate keeps the kitchen well stocked. There's always something on hand."

She sniffled. "In that case, yes, please."

"Make yourself at home. I'll be back shortly."

Doc hightailed his way to the main building, anxious to pick up some food and get back to Tina as quickly as possible. She looked drained, both physically and emotionally, and the need to take care of her was strong.

First, he'd make sure she had a decent meal. Then, he'd find out what had her so upset and do whatever he could to fix it. Or kill it. Whatever.

Doc looked up at the security camera outside the main entrance and simply said, "Kitchen."

If anyone was in the war room, they'd get the message. If not, he'd catch them up later.

It was Church who came into the kitchen while Doc was raiding the fridge.

"Cage said you got a distress call from Tina's grandmother?"

"Yes. Tina's fine, just upset. She'll be staying with me tonight," Doc told him. Longer, if he had his way.

"Did she tell you what went down?"

"Not yet. Why? Do you know something?"

"Nothing definite. Cage is in the process of getting the eye in the sky in place, but there's been another development that might or might not be related. Luther Renninger is MIA."

CHAPTER THIRTY-TWO

~ *Tina* ~

Tina wasn't particularly hungry, but she was teetering on the edge of control and didn't want Doc to witness a full-blown breakdown. Moments after he left, the floodgates opened, and the tears came.

She was so angry. A trip to Sumneyville First National Bank, a dozen phone calls, and some rudimentary online sleuthing had confirmed that Rick hadn't been exaggerating. Obermacher Farms was indeed on the brink of financial collapse.

They were going to lose everything. The farm. The crops. The houses. The equipment. And for what? Because they'd had to get greedy? Because making an honest living hadn't been enough?

The whole mess sickened her. Worse, it looked as if there was nothing she could do. It had gone too far.

The feeling of helplessness was overwhelming, and she gave herself over to the racking sobs. She wasn't used to feeling so powerless. There were only a few times in her life when she had, and each of those had involved the death of someone she loved. For everything else, there had always been options, other avenues to pursue, a way out.

But not this time.

After several minutes, Tina took a deep breath, got shakily to her feet, and went into the bathroom. She splashed cold water on her face until some of the puffiness abated and the ugly red splotches faded.

"No matter how bad it is, you have to pull yourself together and deal with it," Tina said to her reflection, recalling the words Lottie had said to her at the funeral home at her grandfather's viewing. "You're an Obermacher, and Obermachers are made of strong stuff. We endure because sometimes, that's all we can do."

The words gave her some small comfort, as did the knowledge that for tonight at least, she wouldn't have to endure alone.

That was something else she wasn't accustomed to—the feeling that she could lean on someone even if it was only for a little while. Someone who didn't make her feel weak simply for feeling bad.

Perhaps it was wrong of her to put so much faith in Doc, especially in these early stages of their relationship. Ceding control and exposing vulnerabilities were things she'd learned not to do. Not at home. Not in college. Not in business. There were always those lurking in the shadows, looking for weaknesses and opportunities to take advantage.

But Doc, he wasn't like that. All he wanted was … well, Tina wasn't quite sure what he wanted, but she knew it wasn't her land or her patents or her business, and that was a great start.

Tina heard the trailer door open and close a moment before Doc called out his return. "Tina?"

"In here. I'll be out in a sec." She patted her face, pleased to see that she looked slightly better than she had when she came in, and stepped out.

"Are you okay?" The look of concern in his eyes was like a balm to her ragged soul.

"Not yet, but I will be. What do you have there?"

He started removing items from the bag and laid them out on the table. "Broccoli cheese soup and some sandwich fixings. I wasn't sure if you preferred turkey or ham, so I—"

Tina cut him off, wrapping her arms around his neck and pulling him into a kiss.

He returned the kiss with equal fervor and then asked, "What was that for?"

"For being you," she said simply.

Over soup and sandwiches, she gave him a condensed version of what had happened. She hadn't planned on telling him everything, especially not about the guns, but once she started talking, she couldn't seem to stop.

"I was so angry after I got back from the bank. I went to the office and found Gunther and Kiefer there, discussing offers with Rick. I got even angrier when Gunther started shoving papers in my face and told me I needed to sign them. Like I would ever trust him after this! I told him I wasn't signing anything until I had a lawyer look over it and that it sure as hell wasn't going to be anyone from Sumneyville. Gunther didn't like that at all, which made me think he was trying to slide something else shady through. Rick would sign anything if Gunther told him to. He'd never take the time to read through the fine print, and neither would Kief."

Doc listened quietly and patiently while she got everything off her chest. It was only after she'd talked for an hour that she realized he didn't seem shocked by any of it.

"Did you know about any of this?" she asked suddenly.

In the few heartbeats it took for him to answer, her blood turned cold, and a shiver ran the length of her spine.

"Did you?" she pressed.

"I'm not shocked because this isn't the first time Renninger's name has come up in connection with sketchy business practices," he said slowly, as if choosing his words carefully.

Tina's brows pulled together. She couldn't help feeling that what he *wasn't* saying was every bit as important as what he was. It didn't take long to connect the dots. "He handled Handelmann's accounts, didn't he?"

Doc nodded.

The pieces began falling into place. Tina hadn't understood how Kate had been shunned by her family and certain members of the community after she did so much for them. In an unexpected plot twist, Kate's younger sister had gotten pregnant and ended up marrying Luther—Kate's ex—shortly after Kate moved to Sanctuary.

Tina had believed there had to be more to the story than simply the fact that Kate had taken up with one of the Sanctuary guys. Now, she knew there was. Kate had probably discovered—or at least suspected—that Luther was up to no good, and no one had listened, just as Rick and Gunther and Kiefer had refused to listen to Tina whenever she raised concerns about Luther handling the Obermacher Farms' accounts.

Which might also explain why Kate hadn't said anything publicly. If she had bad-mouthed Luther, everyone would have believed it was just sour grapes.

But why wouldn't Kate have said anything to Tina during their coffee time? Maybe she assumed that Tina wouldn't believe her either. Or that because Luther and Gunther were such good friends, Luther wouldn't screw them like he'd screwed Kate's family.

Or maybe Kate *had* said something. Kate had been asking Tina about The Mill and seemed relieved when Tina told her she'd created her own business entity, separate from Obermacher Farms and handled by a professional accounting firm outside of Sumneyville. At the time, Tina hadn't thought much of it other than a shared mutual dislike of Luther.

"Enough," Doc said, carrying the bowls and plates to the sink. "You look beat. What do you say we call it a night?"

"I am tired," she admitted.

"I can take the couch," he offered.

"Doc, the only reason I'm here is because of you. If I wanted to sleep alone, I would've gone to a hotel."

His lips quirked. "Well, in that case …"

Tina was only slightly disappointed when Doc slipped into bed, wearing pajama bottoms. As much as she'd enjoyed their sexy times thus far, what she really wanted was just to be held. Doc seemed to understand that, which proved once again how amazing he was.

She snuggled against him, instantly feeling calmer.

"Doc?"

"Hmm?"

"Thanks."

He kissed her forehead. "My pleasure."

* * *

Despite Doc's presence, Tina didn't sleep well. She tossed and turned and woke throughout the night, but she was certain she wouldn't have gotten any sleep had she remained alone and in her cottage. At least when she was tucked up against Doc, listening to his strong, steady heartbeat with his arm wrapped protectively around her, she was able to stay the panic and think semi-rationally.

When the call of nature became impossible to resist, Tina attempted to slip out of bed. Doc was having none of it.

"Where do you think you're going?" he grumbled sleepily.

"To the bathroom. Got a problem with that?"

"Not as long as you come right back."

She made no promises. After doing what she needed to do, Tina checked on Doc and found him fast asleep. Not wanting to disturb him, she crept quietly toward the front of the trailer, closing the partition behind her. Dawn was nigh, and her body was programmed to rise with it. Besides, her mind was too active, her thoughts too scattered to sleep.

First and foremost, she needed to find a good lawyer, preferably one who didn't know her brothers and practiced outside of Sumneyville. If she was going to sign away her share in the farm, she wanted to make one hundred percent certain they were getting the best deal they could.

The next thing she had to do was face her crew,

though chances were, they already knew. News—especially bad news—traveled quickly, and it probably wouldn't come as a complete surprise. Those murmurings she'd overheard now made a lot more sense.

That morning in the orchards seemed like a lifetime ago. She wondered how long this had been going on and why she hadn't been aware of any of it.

Regardless, she needed to talk to them. Once she knew what to tell them, that was.

Doc emerged from the bedroom, naked from the waist up and looking incredibly sexy. His hair was sleep-tousled and his jaw dusted in dark golden shadow, but his eyes were vibrant and alert.

"You didn't come back," he said accusingly.

She shifted slightly, crossing her arms to hide the sudden pebbling of her nipples.

"I can't help it. I'm an early riser."

CHAPTER THIRTY-THREE

~ *Doc* ~

So was he, apparently, especially since Tina had been moving and shifting against him all night. His body didn't care that she was dealing with life-altering issues. It only remembered what it felt like to be deep inside her and wanted desperately to do so again.

Thankfully, his big head held more sway over what happened than his little one. "Get dressed."

"Why?"

"Because if I'm going to be functional at this hour, I'm going to need some of Sam's crack coffee."

"I should get back to town."

"Not without breakfast," he said firmly. "It's still early. You have time."

He turned and went back into the bedroom area, fully intending to get dressed and do exactly that—namely, head over to the dining room, get some coffee and breakfast, and then do whatever Tina needed him to do.

What he was *not* going to do was bend her over the bed and fuck her into orgasmic bliss.

The sneak attack from behind came without warning. One second, Doc was willing himself to calm down and consider Tina's emotional needs above his physical ones. The next, she was launching herself onto his back.

The unexpected blow caught him off guard, the forward momentum making him stumble until his legs hit the bed and his upper body went down on top of it. Her thighs settled on either side of his waist, and it was then he realized that at some point, she'd gone commando.

His noble intentions fled instantly in a mass exodus of epic proportions.

"What if I counteroffer with an alternate eye-opener?" she asked, her mouth close to his ear.

He used his training and his bigger, stronger body to execute a swift, smooth move, one that put her beneath him. He was forced to question the wisdom of such a move when the maneuver placed his now-granite cock against her panty-less sex and only the thin layer of his cotton pajama pants between them.

"What did you have in mind?"

She reached between them and slid her hand into his waistband. She wrapped her fingers around him and did a pulling, stroking move that made his balls ache and his eyes cross. The woman simply had to touch him, and he was walking a razor's edge.

"You're not making it easy to do the honorable thing here."

"Honorable thing?"

She kept stroking, which required him to pull upon the same self-discipline that had gotten him through BUD/s all those years ago.

"I don't want to take advantage of you when you're feeling vulnerable."

Her wicked smile sharpened the ache. "Last night, I was feeling vulnerable. This morning, I'm feeling something entirely different."

"What's that?" he said through clenched teeth.

She reached down further between his legs, cupped his balls, and fondled him while gazing into his eyes. "*Empty.*"

He muttered several curses. He was a strong man, but he had no defense for this. He withdrew only long enough to shuck his bottoms and wrap his cock. Checking her readiness, he slid his fingers along her folds, finding her wet and oh-so ready.

Before long, he was pushing into her, savoring the feel of her tight sheath taking all of him, pausing only when his balls rested against her. "Okay?" he asked.

"Perfect," she whispered.

He began to move, impaling her with slow, thorough strokes. She arched up, countering his movements with a rhythmic clench and release while gripping his ass and curling her nails into his skin.

They'd had sex before, but this felt different. As if she was inviting him into more than just her body.

Afterward, as they lay in each other's arms, Tina placed her hands around his face and kissed him tenderly. "Thank you. *Now*, I'm ready for coffee."

* * *

It felt natural to be walking into the dining room hand in hand with Tina. He was going to see about getting a coffeemaker though for those occasions when one early morning eye-opener wasn't enough. Because there *would* be more of them.

"Something smells fantastic," Tina said.

"Sam's making muffins, most likely," Doc told her. "They're almost as addictive as her coffee."

Smoke was sitting in his usual spot and looked up when they entered.

"Morning," he said, which Doc knew was for Tina's benefit. Had it just been him, Smoke would have offered a brisk nod, if that.

"Good morning," Tina responded.

Doc got them both coffee, but it was still early enough that a hot breakfast wasn't yet available.

Instead of sitting down at the table, Tina asked if she could go into the kitchen and see if Sam needed or wanted help.

"How's she doing?" Smoke asked when Tina disappeared into the kitchen.

"She was pretty pissed off last night, but I think the gravity of the situation is sinking in," Doc answered.

"How much does she know?"

"She knows the farm is deep in debt. She's also now aware that her brothers have been dealing in illegal weapons, thanks to the cache she discovered in the family's root cellars."

Smoke's eyebrows rose. "They admitted it?"

"Not in so many words. Rick said he was—" Doc made quotes with his fingers "—holding them for a friend."

Smoke snorted.

"Yeah, Tina didn't buy it either, though she believes that Luther and Gunther are behind everything. But she doesn't know the full scope of the operation. I don't think Rick does either, honestly. He believes it's a lucrative side hustle Gunther and Renninger came up with, one that caters to a niche market of survivalist groups, and they pulled him along for the ride."

Smoke snorted again. He had a low tolerance for idiots. "He didn't happen to provide a good origin story, did he?"

"As a matter of fact, he did." Doc shared what

Tina had told him about Dwayne Freed's prison buddy contact and how he bailed when things started getting out of hand, leaving them to find a new supplier.

"It's pretty sad when a convicted felon dealing in illegal arms has a higher moral code than a pair of local boys," Smoke said, shaking his head.

"It also explains how they managed to get in over their heads. Chances are, if they hadn't gotten greedy, they wouldn't be in the mess they're in now. Rick basically came right out and told her that losing the farm was preferable to what'll happen if they don't come up with the money to pay off some of those debts."

Smoke chewed on that for a moment and then said, "You do realize that she's got a target on her back now, too, right?"

Doc did realize that, and it scared the hell out of him.

"As long as she's here, she's safe."

The problem was keeping her there. She was determined to keep the orchards running for as long as possible, as well as her mill.

"And when she's not?"

"I'm still working on that part."

"We've got your six, which means we've got hers, too."

A sense of relief washed over him. He hadn't thought it would be any other way, but it was nice to have Smoke's confirmation just the same.

Sam and Tina came out of the kitchen, rolling a cart with trays of fresh muffins and thermal carafes, presumably filled with Sam's secret coffee blend. Just in time, too, because Doc's mug was empty.

They brought one of each over to the table and sat down.

Doc snatched a muffin for himself and offered one to Tina.

She waved him off. "I've already had *six*."

Sam laughed. "It's true. She did."

"I can't help it. They're even better than the ones you used to make at Santori's."

"That's because I use better ingredients," Sam said matter-of-factly. "Straight from The Mill in fact."

Tina smiled, but Doc was watching her closely and saw the sadness in her eyes.

"Do you have any idea what's going to happen?"

Clearly, Tina had shared at least some of what had happened with Sam.

Tina shook her head. "No. I guess that depends on who the buyer is and how fast they tear down the orchards. If there's something you're particularly fond of, let me know, and it's yours."

"I don't think you realize what you're offering," Doc said with a smile.

"Yes, I do. The Mill is still mine—for now at least—and once word gets out, I imagine we'll sell out quickly. I'd much rather give it away to people who have supported me over the years than make a few bucks. Even if I sold everything, it wouldn't make a dent in what we owe."

Doc hated the undercurrent of defeat in her voice.

"Have you told anyone yet?" asked Sam.

Tina shook her head. "Not officially, no. I keep thinking there has to be a way out of this, but if there is, I haven't found it. In any event, I need to head back this morning and talk to my crew, so they can prepare. Some of them have families and might want to start looking for other jobs. That's the least I can do."

She looked at the cheap but functional watch on her left wrist. "In fact, I should go. Thanks for the coffee and the muffins."

"Anytime."

"Want company?" Doc asked as they walked back to his trailer.

"Thanks for the offer, but no. It would complicate things."

He understood, but he didn't have to like it. "Will you come back here afterward?"

"I don't know. Let's see how the day goes and take it from there."

* * *

Doc watched her drive away, fighting the powerful urge to jump in his Jeep and follow her. He got as far as extracting the keys from his pocket before Heff's disembodied voice called out from somewhere off to his left.

"Don't do it."

Doc sighed and shook his head. He wondered how long Heff had been eavesdropping.

"Seriously, don't do it," Heff told him, stepping out of the woods. "You'll lose your sensitive, supportive guy cred and, more importantly, you'll piss her off."

"And you know this because?"

"Because I know *women.* Tina isn't some fragile flower. She's a strong, independent female, capable of taking care of herself, and if you go in there, trying to fight her battles for her, she'll resent you for it."

"So, what am I supposed to do? Sit back and wait for her to ask for help?"

"That's exactly what you're supposed to do. Stand on the sidelines and let her know you're ready to step in at a moment's notice, but it's got to be *her* call, feel me?"

"Is that what you did with Sandy?"

"Yes, and it damn near killed me," Heff said cheerfully. "But it all worked out in the end, so it was worth every agonizing moment. It'll work out for you, too. I've seen the way she looks at you."

"Yeah? How does she look at me?"

"Like you're the cream to her peaches. The whoopie to her pie. The—"

"Enough," Doc said, holding back a laugh.

Once Heff got on a roll, he kept going, and the last thing Doc wanted to do was encourage him.

Heff did have a point though. And while Doc would never feed the guy's ego by admitting it, Heff did know a lot about the fairer sex.

Doc changed topics. "Is there a reason you're skulking around my trailer? Besides channeling your inner love guru, I mean?"

"As a matter of fact, yes. We're doing a conference call with the Callaghans, and Smoke said you had some info to share with the rest of the class."

"You could've just texted me."

"I did."

Doc reached into his pocket and realized he didn't have his phone on him. "I must have left it in the trailer when we went for breakfast this morning."

"Good sex will do that to you," Heff said with a knowing smirk. "Shorts the circuits. It's how you know you've found the right one."

Doc chose not to respond to that, but he agreed wholeheartedly. He and Tina fit in every way that mattered.

"When is this meeting?"

"As soon as everyone gets there. Cage and Mad Dog are on their way."

The two men started walking toward the main building when Heff shook his head and muttered, "After we get you situated, we need to get Church a woman."

"Why's that?"

"So he stops calling these early morning meetings. Some of us have better ways to start the day, if you know what I mean."

Doc laughed. Yeah, he knew, especially since his day had started off pretty damn good.

* * *

Once they were all assembled in the war room, Cage started a video call.

Doc shared what Tina had told him, feeling only a slight pang of guilt. Tina hadn't explicitly asked him *not* to say anything, but she probably assumed confidentiality was implicit. However, he couldn't exactly ask for her permission, not without explaining why he wanted to share and with whom.

He rationalized his decision by reminding himself that Tina had no idea how dangerous the men were that Renninger and her brothers were involved with. Sure, Tina was angry with them for what they'd done, but he didn't think she'd want to see them made an example of by international cartel assassins.

"Renninger is in hiding," Ian confirmed. "But we'll find him. We've got flags on all of his accounts, and we're combing through his list of contacts. If he so much as sticks his nose out from beneath whatever rock he's crawled under, we'll know it."

His eyes found Doc. "How's your woman holding up? She seemed pretty pissed off when she showed up at Renninger's office in town yesterday."

"How did you know about that?" Doc asked.

Ian's grin was devilish. "Renninger's office is under twenty-four-hour surveillance."

Translation: Ian had hacked the feed.

"She's got a colorful vocabulary," Jake chimed in. "She'd get along well with my wife."

"It sucks that she got sucked up in this," Ian said, becoming serious once again. "If there's anything we can do to help, let us know."

"Thanks. I'm not sure what anyone can do at this point."

Ian's gaze turned thoughtful. "You might want to talk to Maggie."

Doc remembered an earlier meeting where they'd mentioned something similar happening to one of their own. He didn't know if that would help, but he filed it away for later.

"In the meantime, try to keep her as far removed from the situation as possible," said Jake. "It's not going to be long before people notice Renninger's absence, and when they do, they're going to start looking at who he was doing business with."

CHAPTER THIRTY-FOUR

~ *Tina* ~

Leaving Sanctuary—leaving *Doc*—was hard, and it wasn't just because she was dreading what she had to do. She liked his soothing presence and the fact that when she was with him, she didn't feel so alone.

She wasn't a damsel in distress, nor would she ever be. But it sure was nice to be able to feel like she could let go and have someone else take the reins for a little while.

Tina stopped at The Mill first. These were the people who she felt closest to, the ones who had been with her the longest and supported her when she first took over the orchards.

As expected, they'd heard the rumblings. She would have given anything to be able to look them in the eye and squash those ugly rumors, but that wasn't possible. Instead, she did the only thing she could do. She told them the truth. Not the horrible, gory details, but the gist. That Obermacher Farms was in financial straits and would probably be sold to developers sooner rather than later, and when it did, The Mill was going to lose its primary source of fresh produce from which its products were based.

If there was a bright spot, it was that The Mill operated as a separate business entity from the rest of the farm.

Around the time Tina had started applying for patents, she'd tried to talk Gunther into buying the old mill and turning it into a cider mill. She'd seen similar places do well in upstate New York, particularly in the fall, and envisioned Obermachers doing something similar.

He declined.

Rather than be deterred, she became even more determined. A college friend suggested she create her own small business and incorporate. She did, and shortly after, she used her inheritance to buy the old mill and fix it up herself.

At the time, the mill had been in bad shape. Gunther laughed at her business plan, saying that he fully expected to be buying it from her within the year. Tina resolved to prove him wrong.

She got business loans and hired Amish craftsmen to bring the place up to par. She put in sixteen-hour days between the orchards and the mill, using her degrees to grow the highest-quality produce possible and then create superior and one-of-a-kind products.

It had taken nearly five years before Tina was

able to pay off the loans and start making a decent profit, but she had *done* it, and as word spread, the demand for her unique products had grown substantially.

The bad news was, The Mill couldn't continue to operate without Obermacher Farms providing the produce—at least not at its current capacity. There were other smaller farms in the area she might be able to source from but nothing on the scale she would need. For centuries, Obermachers had been the dominant force in the local fresh-produce industry.

Still, Tina would keep the place up and running and would continue to provide her employees with a paycheck as long as possible. However, she was also honest about what the future might bring and said she wouldn't blame anyone who wanted to look elsewhere.

After that, Tina drove out to the orchards and had a talk with her crew. That didn't go nearly as well. The orchards fell under the Obermacher Farms umbrella, which meant that they would be sold along with everything else to whoever bought the land, so there was little Tina could offer them.

Also, since their paychecks came from the OF corporate account, she couldn't guarantee them a wage like she could her mill workers. They were understandably upset and had lots of questions. How long would Obermacher Farms continue to operate? Could they count on at least one more paycheck? What were they supposed to do once the farm was sold?

Unfortunately, Tina didn't have answers. The best she could do was promise to keep them informed, and if that wasn't sufficient, she encouraged them to speak directly with Gunther, who was lying almost as low as Luther these days.

Many of them probably would or already had. Despite the fact that she'd been running the orchards for years, they treated her as if she were simply her brothers' mouthpiece.

She drove over to the office to let them know she'd addressed her crews and to talk—hopefully more calmly and rationally—about the situation, only to find it locked and dark. Calls to Rick, Gunther, and Kiefer went right to voice mail. She drove up to Rick's house, but it was her grandmother who greeted her with a warning.

"Watch where you step," Lottie told her. "There's broken glass everywhere, and I'm sure as hell not going to clean it up."

The kitchen looked as if a cyclone had torn through it. Pieces of broken dishes and glasses littered the floor and surfaces. Stains dotted the walls where bottles had been thrown at them.

"What happened?" Tina asked.

"Bonnie and Rick got into it, and things got rather heated, I'm afraid. Probably would have been worse if I hadn't grabbed your grandfather's old air gun and threatened to pump BB shot into both their backsides if they didn't calm down."

"Where are they now?"

"Bonnie took the kids to her parents' place in Birch Falls. I don't know where Friedrich is. Gunther showed up shortly after the fracas, and the two of them took off. Haven't seen either one of them since, but I did overhear them saying something about trying to find that Renninger boy."

If anyone knew where to find a snake, it was another snake.

"I don't think you should be here when Rick gets back, Gram."

"I'm way ahead of you," Lottie said, waving toward the back door, where a large quilted bag and a small suitcase sat, waiting.

"Would you like to stay in my cottage?" Tina offered.

"Thank you, dear, but no. You've got enough to deal with. Mr. O'Farrell has kindly offered his guest room. In fact, I was just about to call a Zuber."

"You mean, an Uber?"

"No, I mean, a Zuber. Mr. O'Farrell's neighbor, Marjorie Zuber, has an enterprising grandson who provides basically the same service but without the corporate overhead."

Tina knew exactly who Lottie was talking about. "You don't have to call Tommy. I'll drive you down, Gram."

"Are you sure?"

"I'm sure. I need something constructive to do." Something that didn't involve rushing up to Sanctuary and dodging reality in Doc's arms.

Tina loaded Lottie's things into the back of her truck and helped Lottie in. Once they were on their way, she asked, "So, this thing with you and Mr. O'Farrell is serious, huh?"

"I like the way I feel when I'm around him," Lottie told her candidly. "The only other man who made me feel that way was your grandfather, and I'm old and wise enough not to pass up a second chance like that."

Tina understood exactly how she felt.

"How is our Dr. Watson handling all this drama?" Lottie asked as if reading her mind.

"Very well. He's incredibly sweet and supportive. Everyone at Sanctuary has been, honestly."

Lottie patted Tina's arm. "You deserve a good man to stand beside you, Bertina. He's a keeper."

Tina thought so, too. But there was so much going on, and her emotions were running higher than usual. "You know things are bad, don't you?"

"Yes, I've heard enough to get the gist."

"Are you okay?"

"Okay? No, I'm not okay. What they've done …" Lottie's voice faded off as she shook her head. "But I'm eighty-six years old. Time is precious, and things are just things. I'm more worried about you."

"I'll be okay."

"I don't doubt it for a minute. You've got a good head on your shoulders. Your brothers, they're not going to fare as well. You reap what you sow, and they've sown some bad seeds, to be sure."

Karma. Fate. Destiny. God's will. Whatever someone called it, it amounted to the same thing.

Tina dropped her grandmother off at Mr. O'Farrell's and then headed back toward the farm. The urge to return to Sanctuary was strong, but she forced her hands to turn the truck back to the caretaker's cottage.

She'd already leaned on Doc quite a bit, and her biggest fear was becoming too dependent on anyone. She needed to prove to him—and more importantly, to herself—that she was still a strong, capable woman.

That didn't mean she didn't spend hours on the phone with him that night, telling him about her day and asking about his. They made plans to see each other on the weekend, but as Tina curled up alone in her bed that night, the weekend felt very far away.

CHAPTER THIRTY-FIVE

~ *Tina* ~

Saturdays were typically spent at Ziegler's, where Obermachers had a permanent stand. Word had spread like wildfire through their small community, and Tina was inundated with locals stopping by for a scoop. So inundated in fact that actual paying customers had difficulty getting close enough to buy anything.

By lunchtime, Tina had had enough of the clicking tongues and nods of sympathy. She closed the stand, loaded up everything in the back of her truck, and left.

The plan was to head up to Sanctuary later that night after Ziegler's closed, but Tina didn't want to wait. She made a brief stop at her cottage, packed a bag, and drove up early, hoping Doc wouldn't mind.

Even though she'd been there several times before, she felt weird about just walking into the lobby of the main building. Those prior visits had been when she was expected or when she had someone else with her.

Did she believe Rick's assertions that Sanctuary was a stronghold of paranoid mercenaries with an evil agenda? No, not even a little. But she was a strong believer in common courtesy and respecting others' privacy, so she rang the bell on the front door and waited. Noticing a security camera pointed down at her, she offered a smile and a tentative wave.

She didn't have to wait long. Within seconds, Matt Winston opened the door and invited her inside.

"You could've come in," Matt told her with a smile.

"I didn't want to be rude. Besides, if the rumors are true, I had half a dozen sights on me, just waiting for me to make a move."

She'd meant it as a joke, only realizing after the words were out of her mouth that they sounded terribly offensive. Thankfully, Matt's grin grew.

"Good thing you have clearance then. Shouldn't you be at Ziegler's?"

"I was, but the lookie-loos and gossipmongers were out in full force today, scaring away business, so I decided to close early. Is Doc around?"

"No. He usually spends Saturday afternoons with Mr. O'Farrell."

Tina had forgotten about that. "That means he's spending the day with my grandmother, too. She's been staying with Mr. O'Farrell after Rick and

Bonnie got into a drunken fracas."

"A fracas, huh?"

"A *drunken* fracas. Bonnie ended up taking the kids to her mother's. I've been avoiding the house."

"Smart. From what I remember, Rick has quite a temper."

"That hasn't changed," Tina told him. "Anyway, when I was here the other day, Sam mentioned she uses stuff from The Mill. The back of my truck's loaded if you want it."

"That'd be great. Let me get some guys to bring it in."

Tina inwardly breathed a sigh of relief. Her muscles and joints were aching even more than usual—a direct result of poor sleep and lots of stress.

Two of the guys who came to help she recognized; two of the guys she didn't. They made short work of unloading the crates, and then Matt beckoned her toward his office.

"Come on in here, and I'll write you a check. How much do I owe you?"

She waved him off. "Nothing."

"Unacceptable."

"Seriously. Consider it a long-overdue welcome-home gift. It might be the last I can offer for a while."

Matt looked like he wanted to argue, but he wisely clamped his lips together and nodded. "In that case, thank you. You know we'll help you in any way we can, right?"

"I do, and I appreciate it. Do you mind if I hang around and wait for Doc?"

"Not at all. Make yourself at home."

"I was thinking of checking out some of the trails, if that's okay." Her hopes were that a leisurely stroll would loosen her joints and help her clear her head.

"That's fine." His eyes even twinkled a little when he winked and said, "Just give me a moment to disarm the booby traps."

She laughed and wondered if that was a running joke among everyone who lived there. At least they had a good sense of humor about it.

Tina started at the greenhouses. It was a nice day. Many of the glass panels were open, allowing in direct sunlight and fresh air to circulate. She breathed in the comforting scents of soil and plants, pleased to see that they'd added some dwarf lemon trees to their inventory. The lemons wouldn't survive outside in the northeast Pennsylvania climate, but they definitely could in a climate-controlled greenhouse. She wondered vaguely about adding natural lemon to some of her existing products.

Leaving the greenhouses, she followed the trail she'd been on before, down toward the stock pond and then farther out toward the small lake. The sun was bright and hot, reflecting off the water in beautiful, shimmering bands. When her skin began to tingle, warning her that she was approaching the limit of her exposure to direct sunlight, she opted for a fork that led into the woods.

Here, the sunlight was broken up by tall, stately evergreens and an assortment of budding deciduous trees, like oaks, maples, and massive walnuts. The trail was well-worn and clear. By the looks of it, it was used often by horses and motorized vehicles.

It was peaceful there amid the dappled sunlight, abundance of mountain laurel, and the scents of wet earth and leaves that hadn't fully decomposed over the winter.

As she walked along, Tina caught occasional glimpses of cabins through the trees and wondered if that was where some of the permanent residents lived. As the path wound back toward the lake, Tina gained a companion. A massive pit bull trotted her way, then stopped, sat down, and stared at her.

It wasn't Duke, the dog who'd approached her before, but he did look similar.

"Brutus!" called a woman's voice. "Where did you get to?"

Bree appeared on the path in front of her. Tina knew her from their coffee chats, knew that she was paired with the guy they called Cage.

"Sorry about that," Bree apologized. "He looks vicious, but he's really a big marshmallow."

"So, I can pet him?"

"He'll be your friend forever if you do."

Tina reached out slowly and scratched the top

of his head, feeling the need to explain her presence. "I'm just killing time until Doc gets back from town. Matt said it was okay to walk the trails."

"It's nice, isn't it?" Bree agreed. "Brutus and I love walking out here, but it's even more fun snowmobiling and riding horses." She laughed. "Never thought I'd say those words. I've always been more of a city girl, but this place, these people … it kind of sneaks up on you and changes the way you see things."

Bree was right. There was something about Sanctuary, something peaceful and therapeutic. Tina felt the effects after being there only a short time. She had to work on her endurance, however. The ache in her back, legs, and hips was becoming impossible to ignore.

"How long is this trail?" Tina asked.

"Pretty long," Bree told her. "It goes all around Sanctuary property, which covers a couple hundred acres at least, and that doesn't include all the offshoots and shortcuts. I've been here for months, and I feel like I've barely scratched the surface. I've even gotten lost a few times. Thankfully, Nick comes looking for me if I'm gone too long," she said with a laugh.

Tina wondered if Doc would come looking for her if she were gone too long. Warmth flooded through her when she realized that, yes, he probably would. If he was around, that was.

She looked at her wristwatch, surprised to see

how much time had passed. "Speaking of, I should start heading back. Matt said Doc is usually back by dinnertime."

"It's faster if you keep going the way you're going. Take the next fork to the right just ahead. That'll take you right past our place and toward the main building. You can't miss it."

Tina thanked her, and with one last pat on Brutus's head, she went on her way. With each step, her anticipation grew, as did her desire to see Doc again. Wanting to hear his voice. See his smile. Feel the warmth and strength of those strong arms as they closed around her. When had she become so needy?

Before long, she was walking up the final slope to the main building. She spotted the object of her current obsession talking with Matt, who was probably telling him that Tina was out and about. Her steps quickened without conscious thought.

"This is a nice surprise," he said. "Is everything okay?"

"Yes. Well, as okay as it can be, I guess. I decided to come up early."

The look in his eyes made her knees go weak. "Does this mean you're staying the night?"

"I'd like to, if that's okay with you."

"That's more than okay. Want to eat in the dining room or take things back with us?"

"It's a little early for dinner, isn't it?"

"Yes, but once we head back to my place, I

don’t plan on coming out again until tomorrow.”

A delighted thrill ran through her along with a telltale heat she only felt around Doc. She was so on board with that. “In that case, definitely takeout.”

CHAPTER THIRTY-SIX

~ *Tina* ~

"I don't know what's going to happen," Tina confided to Doc the next morning. Lying there next to him, soaking in the warmth of his body, was the only time when everything made sense. Beyond his arms, her world was pure chaos.

His hand gently stroked the length of her spine, providing the soothing comfort that enabled her to speak from her soul.

"Obermachers have lived and worked that land for over four hundred years. I can't imagine it in the hands of a developer. The thought makes me ill."

Yet there didn't seem to be any other option. Rick had them so far in debt that they'd never dig themselves out. If they didn't sell out, they'd not only end up losing the land, but they'd be destitute as well. Or as Rick had suggested, worse.

"I can't help but feel partly responsible. I knew Luther was shady. I mean, I didn't trust him with *my* personal finances. Why did I stand by and allow my brothers to trust him with the family business?"

Sure, she'd been outvoted three to one, but it wasn't the first time they'd teamed up against her. She should have fought harder. She should have demanded to see the books on a regular basis or at least insisted on an independent audit every year.

The more she thought about it, the worse she felt. The tears came, unable to be kept back any longer. Doc didn't tell her to stop. He didn't ply her with false platitudes. He just held her and stroked her back, letting her get it out of her system.

"I'm sorry. It's just ..."

"I know," he said quietly.

"And what about everyone who works for us?" she asked. "Do you know how many people are going to be out of work? It's not like Sumneyville has a lot of job opportunities. Some of them have been employed by Obermacher Farms since they were old enough to work.

"You know what the worst part is?" she asked, feeling a wave of guilt wash over her. Farming was in her blood. She loved what she did, but the physical demands were hard on her body.

"Part of me is actually relieved that I won't have that responsibility anymore. I feel like a traitor. Like a rat fleeing a sinking ship."

"You're not," he assured her.

"I feel like it though. That land has been so good to me. To my family. Not being able to work it anymore is one thing, but seeing it destroyed is going to kill a part of me inside."

Doc hummed slightly and then tapped her lightly on the backside. “Get dressed.”

“What’s the point?” she asked, punctuating the question with a sniffle.

“The point is, there’s someone I want you to meet.”

“Who?”

“Get dressed, and you’ll find out.”

Reluctantly, Tina pried herself away from Doc, immediately feeling a sense of loss. “Can’t we just stay in bed? I’ll make it worth your while.”

He leaned over and kissed her. “Tempting, but hold that thought. Go on now; get dressed. I need to make a phone call.”

Doc smiled when she pouted. She didn’t know what he had in mind, but he seemed determined to introduce her to someone. After everything he’d done for her, it was a small ask.

Minutes later, they were in Doc’s Jeep, heading away from Sanctuary.

Surprisingly, the first stop he made was at The Mill.

“What are we doing here?” she asked.

“Creating a gift basket of your finest products.”

“Why?”

“Jeez, you ask a lot of questions. Just trust me, okay?”

How could she not?

They walked around the store, picking up items as they went. Since it was off-season, most of the products were canned or preserved in some way. They gathered mead, cider, and an assortment of jams, jellies, chutney, and jars of peaches in various flavors.

Ten minutes later, they were on the road again, heading south of Sumneyville.

"Where are we going?" she asked.

"Pine Ridge."

"Who's in Pine Ridge?"

"Maggie Callaghan. She owns a farm there."

The name was vaguely familiar.

"When I was younger, my grandparents used to take me to a farm in Pine Ridge, but I knew it as the Flynn farm. Of course, that was probably twenty-five years ago. There was a girl there named Maggie. She was a few years older than me. I think she was their granddaughter."

Tina had always liked Maggie. They'd bonded almost instantly over an intense dislike of doctors. From what she remembered, Maggie had had her share of health issues, too. Those homeopathic remedies Maggie's grandmother used to make were just as effective as the medicines the doctors prescribed—plus, they had far fewer side effects.

Her father hadn't approved, however, and when he discovered where Lottie had been taking Tina on their weekend drives, he had put a stop to it.

"Might be the same one. Callaghan's her married name," Doc told her.

"And we're going to see Maggie because …"

"Because she might be able to help."

For a few moments, Tina wondered if Doc had discovered her secret. He was a medic after all, and her symptoms had been flaring as of late. She'd been explaining them away, citing her recent bout with the flu, stress, and long hours, but it was only a matter of time before he figured it out—if he hadn't already.

"Help how exactly?"

"From what I understand, Maggie was in a similar situation. She almost lost her farm to developers."

Tina inwardly breathed a sigh of relief. Things were going so well with Doc, and she didn't want to ruin it. Did she really believe he would see her differently if he knew about her autoimmune disease? No, but then again, she hadn't believed her brothers would lose the farm either.

She *would* tell Doc everything. Eventually.

"I don't see how anyone can help at this point."

He gave her a mysterious *Mona Lisa*–like smile but said nothing.

Tina didn't ask again, choosing instead to enjoy the moment. It was a beautiful morning, the drive to Pine Ridge was scenic, and she was with Doc. If he wanted her to listen to what Maggie had to say, she'd listen.

The Flynn farm wasn't as she remembered it. Some things seemed familiar. There was the traditional, old farmhouse, but it looked to be in much better shape than the last time she'd been there. The once-detached garage was now connected to the main house with a glass-paneled breezeway. Flower boxes adorned the wraparound porch, and the yard looked professionally landscaped.

Like Obermacher property, the land sloped away from the main house in a series of rolling hills and semi-flat plateaus, creating a patchwork of fields. Off in the distance, she heard the comforting purr of powerful farm tractors doing their thing. The thought that she soon might not get to hear those again was a depressing one.

Though twenty-five years had passed, Tina recognized Maggie as soon as she opened the door. Curly dark-red hair, brilliant green eyes, and a smattering of freckles. Time had been kind to Maggie. Unlike years earlier, she was the picture of health.

"Tina Obermacher! It's been a long time."

"It sure has," Tina agreed. "You look fantastic."

"Thanks! I *feel* fantastic."

Tina couldn't help but wonder if Maggie's grandmother's remedies could be credited or if there was some other reason for the change. Either way, she thought it would be rude to ask.

"And you must be Doc," Maggie said. "Please, come in. Michael is in the kitchen. I just pulled some bear claws out of the oven."

The delicious aroma of freshly baked pastries filled the foyer. “It smells wonderful.”

“I’ll send some back with you. I always make too many, and heaven knows, I don’t need the temptation,” Maggie said with a laugh.

“Oh, here. I brought you some things from The Mill.” Tina handed her the basket.

“These look amazing!” Maggie said, pulling out a jar of spiked peaches. “I can’t wait to try them. I’ve been meaning to take a trip up there. I’ve heard great things about what you’ve been doing, and I was hoping maybe you’d share some tips. Our pears and apples do well, but from what I’ve heard, our stone fruits don’t compare to yours.”

“Of course,” Tina said, wondering if this was the reason for their impromptu visit.

Perhaps if she shared some of her knowledge with Maggie, Maggie would apply it to her orchards and be willing to sell enough of her yield with Tina to keep The Mill running.

“How are your grandparents?” Maggie asked as she led them into a large, cheery kitchen. “Are they still around?”

“My grandmother is. My grandfather passed quite a few years ago now.”

“I’m sorry to hear that. They’re good people. Your grandmother was a firecracker from what I remember.”

“She still is,” Tina told her, hoping Maggie didn’t inquire about other things, too.

Thankfully, if Maggie remembered the reason for those frequent visits, she was kind enough not to bring them up.

"Tina, Doc, this is my husband, Michael," Maggie said, introducing them to the tall, handsome man in the kitchen. To Tina, she mock whispered, "He's a doctor, but try not to hold that against him."

Tina grinned. It appeared she and Maggie had something else in common. They were both attracted to men with medical training, which seemed kind of ironic since they'd once bonded over their mutual dislike for the field.

The dark-haired man smiled. Just the slightest hint of silver frosted his temples, but it only added to his good looks, especially with those brilliant blue eyes.

"Tina, it's good to meet you," he said, offering his hand and then repeating the gesture with Doc. "I believe you know my brothers."

Doc nodded. "Ian and Jake. They've been very supportive of Sanctuary."

"It's a great thing you're doing," Michael said.

"And that's George," Maggie said, waving her hand toward the ancient-looking basset hound in the corner, looking mighty comfortable in his therapeutic doggy bed. He lifted his head and offered a wag of his tail. "Don't mind him. He only moves when he has to these days."

They exchanged pleasantries while Maggie offered them coffee and bear claws, which were every bit as delicious as they smelled.

"So," Maggie said after a while, "Doc tells us Obermacher Farms is in a bit of a pickle."

That was an understatement. With Doc's gentle encouragement, Tina gave them a high-level overview of the farm's current situation. She didn't go into detail, simply saying that her brothers had made some bad investments and because of that, the farm would be placed up for auction among developers.

She had to accept that, but it hurt, and it was impossible to keep the emotion completely out of her voice.

Maggie nodded and reached over to pat her hand. "I know how you feel. I came close to losing this place, too. In my case, it was because of shady financial shenanigans and local political corruption."

Well, *that* certainly sounded familiar. Tina looked at Doc, but his hazel eyes gave nothing away.

"Thankfully, that was right about the time Michael came into my life," Maggie continued, "and he and his brothers worked miracles."

"How so?"

"Shane is a brilliant lawyer. He did a deep dive into the township's case, which was based on sketchy rezoning and tax requirements. Anyway, he found some substantial holes that got me off the hook and several township officials in hot water."

"Oh." Tina tried to hide her disappointment.

Their situations weren't so similar after all. Legal loopholes didn't exist for bad investments and illegal arms deals.

"Of course, the deal with the Celtic Goddess didn't hurt either," Maggie said and then went on to explain. The deal had allowed Maggie to retain ownership of her land and contract out huge parcels to the restaurant in exchange for exclusive rights to the fresh organic produce the farm yielded.

To Tina, it sounded like the ideal solution. Maggie was getting paid for someone else to farm her land. That was far more palatable than stripping the soil and building high-end condos.

"I'm really glad everything worked out for you." Tina summoned a smile even though her heart felt like it was breaking. "We caught a glimpse of the fields as we drove in. They look great."

"The Goddess does a good job. They're serious about sustainable farming and use only the best. Plus, they're supportive of the community. We host school field trips, promote pick-your-own events, and even run a haunted hayride in the fall."

"It sounds wonderful."

"It is, and the best part is, I can be as involved as I want. Admittedly, having kids really changed my priorities."

"You have kids?" Tina asked.

"Two boys. They're hanging out with their cousins today or I'd introduce you. Would you like to take a walk? I can show you some of the things we've done."

"I'd love to," Tina said honestly.

As they walked along, Maggie told Tina about some of the things they'd tried and what had proven most successful. Farming, especially produce farming, was something Tina could talk about for hours on end. Most people tended to get bored quickly when she did, however, so she curbed her enthusiasm and kept her answers short and relevant.

Maggie seemed keen to continue talking though and asked lots of questions about Tina's experience, especially when it came to hybrid grafts and some of her more unusual products. Apparently, Maggie was something of a mad canner, too.

As they went on, the men fell farther and farther behind.

When Tina thought it was safe to do so without being overheard, she asked, "I wanted to ask … do you happen to have any of your grandmother's old recipes?"

"All of them," Maggie said with a chuckle. "Did you have something particular in mind?"

Tina glanced behind them, finding the men engrossed in a discussion of their own. "A couple of things actually, but the one I'm most interested in is for joint pain."

Maggie's eyes softened. "I wondered if you still had issues with that. Does Doc know?"

"No. No one does, outside of immediate family."

"It must be incredibly hard to keep something like that a secret."

"Not as hard as you might think," Tina said.

She'd gotten quite good at hiding it over the years. Not having close friends or a social life made it easier. Even her brothers assumed she'd "grown out of it" or at least it had lessened in severity. But Doc … it was much harder, keeping it from him.

"He loves you, you know," Maggie said suddenly.

Tina stopped abruptly, her heart hammering in her chest. "Why would you say that?"

Maggie stopped, too. When Tina looked at her eyes, they seemed to be swirling, just like Maggie's grandmother's used to. Some people said she was a white witch; others simply said she was gifted healer. Tina's visits to the Flynn farm had ceased when those rumors reached her father's ears.

"Trust me, I can tell," Maggie said. "He's the one for you, and you, for him."

"He's a good man," Tina said carefully.

Maggie looked back at the guys, then looped her arm through Tina's, and gently urged her forward. "Do you know what a *croie* is?"

When Tina shook her head, Maggie explained, "Think of it as a soul mate. Michael is mine. I think Doc is yours."

Tina didn't know what to say to that, but

Maggie wasn't finished. "Let me ask you this. Does he seem protective of you? Do things for you for no apparent reason?"

"He showed up at my doorstep and took care of me when I had the flu. And he gives these amazing massages …" Tina paused. Was it possible? Could Doc actually feel as strongly about her as she did about him?

"And you," Maggie continued, the swirls in her eyes moving faster now, "do you think about him all the time? Feel different when you're with him?"

Those questions were easily answered. Tina nodded.

"There you go. *Croies*."

Tina wanted to believe her. She really did. But things were complicated, and Tina didn't trust her own feelings. She said as much to Maggie.

Rather than be deterred, however, Maggie nodded emphatically. "Exactly! It's no accident that Doc came into your life at this particular time. You're meant to be together."

Maggie was so earnest. But as wonderful as that sounded, she was too much of a realist to start believing in fairy-tale endings. She and Doc were still in the early phases of their relationship, and there was the potential to be so much more, but she wasn't going to jinx it by making assumptions that could end up breaking her heart.

"You'll see," Maggie said with confidence. "But to answer your earlier question, I've continued my grandmother's practice. I can make whatever you need."

"But you said your husband is a doctor."

"He is. A brilliant one."

"How does he feel about your homeopathic remedies?" Tina asked, managing to stop herself before she used some of her father's more derogatory names for the teas, balms, and poultices.

"He's come to terms with it. I've accepted that modern medicine can be beneficial in certain instances, and he's accepted that natural alternatives can be effective. I can give you some tea today that I think will help, but the poultices will take a little more time to pull together."

"There's no hurry. I can come back another day—as long as you don't mind."

Maggie's eyes were doing that swirling thing again. "No, I don't mind. I really enjoyed our visit today, and something tells me we're going to be seeing a lot more of each other in the near future."

CHAPTER THIRTY-SEVEN

~ *Doc* ~

"Too easy," Doc muttered, admiring Yaz's skill in setting up his next shot. Even Doc could sink it in with his eyes closed.

Yaz canted his head, scanned the table, and then called off a tricky double bank.

"Not a chance."

Yaz grinned. "Five bucks?"

It was worth it. "Sure."

Yaz leaned over the bumper, lined up his stick, and hit the cue ball with precision and the perfect amount of English. Doc watched in amazement as the cue hit one bumper, spun back, hit a second, then kissed the eight ball, and sent it dropping into the side pocket, just as Yaz had said it would.

"Now, you're just showing off."

Yaz shrugged as if it were no big deal. "It's just geometry."

"Right," Doc said doubtfully as he dug into his pocket and handed over a few bills. "Just geometry. Admit it. You grew up in a pool hall, didn't you?"

"Maybe. Another game?"

"Nah, I'm good."

They'd already played three, and Yaz had whipped his ass each time. A man could only take so many solid thrashings before his ego felt the sting.

"You're getting better," Yaz told him encouragingly.

"Thanks."

He *was* getting better. Not only had Doc been spending a lot of time practicing in the game room these days, but he was also learning a lot from Yaz. The guy could play professionally if he wanted to. He was that good.

Doc was heading back to his place when Church called out to him, "Got a sec?"

"Sure."

"How'd it go today? You took Tina to see Maggie Callaghan, right?"

"Right. It went well, I think. Turns out, Tina and Maggie knew each other from when they were kids."

"Did you tell her about the Goddess?"

"Maggie told her about what happened with her place but stopped short of suggesting anything that might get Tina's hopes up. We took a basket of stuff along with us, and Michael said they'd make sure it got to the right people. If the Goddess is interested, then they'll get some of the other brothers involved. One's a lawyer; another's good with finances."

Church nodded. "Sounds good. Hopefully, we can get this figured out before Tina's brothers do anything else stupid."

"Any updates?"

"Heff and Sandy had dinner at Franco's," Church told him.

Franco's was the best—and only—sit-down restaurant in Sumneyville and a favorite place to go for a night out. It was also where Sandy had worked as a waitress for years and a good place to get a rundown on townie news.

Church's mouth turned downward; he was obviously displeased with whatever intel they'd come back with. As a general rule, Church didn't condone gossip—probably because he was often at the center of speculation himself—but as a special forces man, he understood the importance of listening to chatter.

"Not surprisingly, Obermachers' financial troubles is the hot topic. No one saw it coming."

"No one, except the brothers and Renninger," Doc said, unable to keep the bitterness from his voice.

"Speaking of, Renninger's still MIA. Probably plans on staying that way, too. After word got out about Obermachers, people started taking a look at their own accounts."

"No doubt there were a few rude awakenings."

"No doubt," Church agreed.

Doc's phone vibrated. He pulled it out and looked at the screen, surprised to see Tina's number pop up. When he'd talked to her earlier, she'd said she was going to make an early night of it.

"Tina?" Church guessed.

Doc nodded and put the phone to his ear. "Hey, I thought—"

"Doc!" After his name, Tina's words came out in a jumble, barely intelligible between panicked sobs.

"Tina, breathe. Say that again—slowly, please."

On the other end of the line, Tina took a shaky breath. "The Mill. It's on fire. I'm on my way down there now."

"I'll meet you there."

Doc disconnected and moved swiftly toward the door, throwing back a quick explanation to Church over his shoulder on the way out. "The Mill's on fire. Tina's on her way there now."

Church grabbed his jacket and was right behind him. "Let's go. We'll take my vehicle. It'll save time."

Doc didn't argue. At that moment, he was of single-minded purpose—to get to Tina as quickly as possible.

The two men double-timed it out to the garage behind the main building. Over the course of the evening, the blue sky from earlier had given way to a storm front, one that was currently dousing the area in a cold spring rain. It made the curvy mountain roads slick, but Church was a skilled driver who'd grown up on these roads and knew every inch like the back of his hand.

Community volunteers had closed off the road around The Mill to all but emergency vehicles. Church made a couple of quick turns and got as close as he could. Doc was out the door before the SUV came to a complete stop and hit the ground running.

It was a hellish sight. Flames licked up into the inky night sky, defying the rain. Ghostly silhouettes moved in the reddish-orange glow, the reflective tape on the firefighters' gear catching the light. Men shouted and wielded fire hoses attached to pumper trucks, pointing them toward the blaze, but it looked like a losing battle.

Police tried to keep people back as the locals continued to crowd the scene.

Doc located Tina off to the side with several men, watching the horrific scene unfold. One of them he recognized as her brother Rick. The others bore a similar resemblance, and Doc knew he was looking at Gunther and Kiefer.

When Tina spotted him, she ran over and wrapped her arms around him. Her brothers glared at him, their expressions none too friendly. Doc enclosed Tina in his arms and glared right back over the top of her head.

"I got here as fast as I could. Are you okay?"

Doc asked quietly.

She was cold and wet and shivering. He quickly removed his flannel and draped it around her.

"Physically, I'm fine. Emotionally, not so much. Thanks for coming so quickly."

"What the fuck is he doing here?" asked Rick.

Tina turned in his arms and faced her brothers. "I called him."

"Why would you do that?"

"Figure it out."

Had the situation not been so serious, it might have been funny, watching Rick Obermacher put the pieces together. Apparently, the other two were a little quicker and glowered at him with narrowed eyes.

"Oh, *hell* no," Rick bellowed when he figured it out, taking a step forward.

"You want to get into this right here, right now?" Tina hissed.

"You're goddamn right I do."

"*My mill is going up in flames*."

"You have insurance, don't you?"

There was something in the way Gunther had said it that set off warning bells in Doc's head. Apparently, Tina picked up on it, too. One second, she was with Doc. The next, she was pushing hard against her brother's chest, shoving him backward as if he wasn't ten inches taller and at least fifty pounds heavier.

"Did you have something to do with this? Is this another one of your schemes?"

Rick grabbed Tina by the back of her shirt and yanked her away from Gunther. Doc saw red. Before he realized what he was doing, Doc had one hand on the pressure point at the base of Rick's neck, the other twisting Rick's arm behind his back. Close as he was, he got a whiff of whiskey and something else—something that smelled suspiciously like gasoline.

"Don't fucking touch her again." Doc shoved Rick away, placing himself between Tina and her brothers.

Gunther and Kiefer moved forward, but Church was suddenly there beside him.

"Think very carefully about what you do next," Church said, his voice low and deadly.

Several seconds passed in a standoff before Daryl Freed joined them. "Is there a problem here?" he asked, looking between the men and then narrowing his eyes at Tina, who'd moved back to Doc's side.

"No, there's no problem," Church said. "Just saying hello. Weren't we?"

Rick turned his head and spit off to the side, noticing that they were drawing a crowd. "What are you looking at?" he growled. "Go on now; mind your business."

A few shuffled away, but most remained, curious to see what would happen next.

"Tina," Chief Freed said, puffing up his chest, "the fire chief and I are going to need you to answer a few questions."

Doc felt Tina stiffen.

"What questions?"

"Whatever they are, they can wait until tomorrow, Daryl," Church said, handing Tina a rain slicker. "Tina's had a rough night."

Freed bristled. Whether it was Church's quiet, commanding tone or the fact that he'd called the police chief by his first name, Doc didn't know, but Freed was clearly pissed.

"Show some respect," Lenny Petraski said, appearing out of the darkness. "That's the chief of police you're talking to."

"I know exactly who I'm talking to," Church said evenly without taking his eyes off of Freed. "*Tomorrow.*"

It was the first time Doc had seen Church engage with Freed one-on-one. On those few occasions Church had felt compelled to do something—as was the case when Dwayne Freed had shown up in Heff's cabin, shooting out his mouth and a gun—Church had gone alone.

Of the two men, there was no question who commanded—and deserved—respect. Doc knew it. Freed knew it. And judging by the expressions on the people watching in undisguised interest, they knew it, too.

The former SEAL commander was calm, in

control, and focused. The hate in Freed's eyes was palpable. He looked like he wanted a reason, any reason, to yank out his night stick and start beating Church with it.

Doc could've told him not to waste his time. Nothing Freed carried would be effective against Church, including the Glock. Church could have him disarmed and facedown in the mud before Freed could get it out of his holster.

Freed was the first to look away. He glanced around, read the crowd, and then addressed Tina, "Tomorrow."

She nodded in acknowledgment. Freed walked away, and Tina moved closer against Doc.

"You all had better go on home now," Lenny said quietly, more so to the Obermacher brothers than to Church or Doc. It proved that, despite numerous examples to the contrary, Lenny did have a sense of self-preservation and a glimmer of intelligence.

Rick crooked a beefy finger at Tina. "Let's go, Bert."

"I'm not going anywhere with you."

"Bertina—"

"She said no," Doc said firmly.

"You keep your fucking—"

"Enough!" Tina said, raising her voice. "Go home, all of you. And I swear to God," she said, her voice quivering with emotion, "if I find out that you had anything to do with this, I will *never* forgive you."

Rick's nostrils flared. Gunther's eyes flicked from Church to Doc, calculating his next move. The youngest, Kiefer, said nothing and avoided everyone's eyes.

"Let's go," Gunther said, his eyes shooting daggers at Tina. "Bert's made her choice. So be it."

Gunther turned on his heel and walked away. With pure hatred in his eyes, Rick spit within inches of Doc's feet before following. The youngest brother, Kiefer, hung back.

"You okay?" he asked Tina, quiet enough not to be overheard by the others. It was the first time he'd spoken.

Tina nodded, and without another word, he turned and followed the others.

CHAPTER THIRTY-EIGHT

~ *Tina* ~

"I'm sorry, Tina."

Tina nodded and continued to stare at the hellish glow off in the distance. She was barely holding it together. If it hadn't been for Doc's strong presence, she would have lost it completely.

Doc and Matt exchanged a few quiet words, which resulted in Matt returning to Sanctuary and Doc remaining behind. Things got blurry after that.

Pumper trucks continued to come and go, filling up at the nearby creek, emptying the water onto the blaze, and then repeating the process until flames no longer licked at the sky and the fire was reduced to smoke and steam. Tina vaguely remembered some people coming up to her and saying things, but she couldn't say who or what.

Through it all, Doc remained by her side, a solid presence. He tried several times to get her to leave and go someplace warm and dry, but for a long time, she couldn't. Her pride and joy was going up in flames, and all she could do was watch it happen.

The rain got heavier as the night wore on. The crowd dispersed and went back to their beds, and she and Doc were among the remaining few. The pumper trucks had gone away, leaving a couple volunteer fire fighters behind to ensure there were no flare-ups.

“Ready?” Doc asked.

“Yeah.”

“Your place or mine?”

“Mine,” Tina said, exhaustion exerting its heavy pull. “It’s closer.”

She couldn’t remember where she’d parked her truck; at the time, her mind had been too focused on the horror of what was happening. Thankfully, Doc seemed to know where it was.

As Doc led her away from the scene, her stiff joints protested painfully, exacerbated by standing in a chilly rain for hours. It resulted in a halting, jerky gait and the inability to climb into her own truck.

“You drive, okay?”

Doc helped her into the passenger seat, then got in and drove them back to the caretaker’s cottage.

Doc carried Tina inside and right into the shower. He eased her onto the seat, turned on the hot water, and then proceeded to peel her damp clothes from her body. She hated that he had to see her like this.

“Doc …”

"Hush."

He adjusted the controls so that hot water flowed from the overhead and handheld showerheads.

"But …"

"Later, okay? Let's get you warmed up first."

"Okay."

Doc stepped away and closed the door, his expression unreadable. Tina had no idea what he was thinking, but she could guess. And it wasn't good.

When the water began to run cold, Tina reached over and turned it off. Doc was there a moment later with a large, fluffy towel and a pair of her fleece pajamas. It reminded her of when she'd had the flu, except this time, what she had wouldn't be going away in a couple of days.

Numerous prescription bottles were lined up on the sink. Painkillers. Anti-inflammatories. Steroids. The antimalarials she was supposed to take every day but rarely did. There were no cures for lupus, but there were plenty of pharmaceuticals made to control symptoms and minimize flare-ups. She'd tried them all.

"Guess you found my secret stash, huh?" she said, selecting one of the more powerful NSAIDs.

"Lupus?" he guessed.

She nodded.

"That explains a lot. Come here."

He lifted the bed covers, helped her climb in,

and then tucked the covers around her.

“Where are you going?” she asked, hating the needy tone in her voice when he walked toward the bedroom door.

“To throw my wet clothes in the dryer.”

“You’re not leaving?”

His eyes were intense. “Not a chance. Drink that,” he commanded, pointing to the mug on the nightstand. “I’ll be right back.”

Tina picked up the mug and sipped, recognizing the familiar tastes of almond milk, vanilla, turmeric, cardamom, and cinnamon. Clearly, he’d been paying attention.

When he returned, it was with a towel around his waist. The rest of him was gloriously on display. Broad, strong shoulders. Sculpted pecs. Clearly defined abs. As usual, the sight of him stole her breath.

“Scooch forward.”

She did, and he climbed into bed behind her. She resettled between his legs, the feel of him better at making her forget about her pain than anything that came in a bottle. She leaned back into him, relishing the feel of his body heat soaking through the material, wishing she were naked.

Doc’s strong hands started kneading the area between her neck and shoulders.

“Why didn’t you tell me?”

A simple question but one with many answers.

What should she tell him?

That people treated her differently once they found out?

That she didn't want to be seen as weak or sickly, just because she had more challenges than some?

That she was afraid if he knew, it would change things?

They were all true.

What she said was something that encompassed all those things at a higher level. "Because I refuse to be defined by it. Because when you look at me, I don't want that to be the first thing that comes to your mind."

He made a sound, a masculine mash-up of a snort and a chuckle. "Trust me, that is not what comes to mind when I think of you. You are one of the strongest, most capable women I've ever met. Definitely the sexiest."

She smiled a little at that, but it was short-lived. "You can't tell me it doesn't change things."

To his credit, he didn't rush to deny it. "You're right. It does change things."

Her heart sank.

"But that's not a bad thing. It just gives me more reasons to want to take care of you."

"I don't need a keeper."

"No," he agreed. "I'm not suggesting you do. What I am saying is, I want to be the one you lean on when things get to be overwhelming. The one who gives you massages and comes up with creative ways to keep your joints flexible. And just to be clear, those desires have nothing to do with the fact that you have lupus and everything to do with the fact that I'm falling in love with you."

She sat up, and with some difficulty, she twisted in his arms to face him. "You are?"

"I am."

She stared into his eyes, finding nothing but sincerity.

"Are you okay with that?" he asked softly.

"More than okay with that," she whispered. "I especially liked the part about creative ways to keep my joints flexible."

"*That* was your favorite part?"

"Well, after the part about you loving me. I'm not sure if you know what you're getting yourself into."

"I'm not sure you do either. I don't want to scare you, but what I feel for you … well, let's just say, I've never felt this way about anyone before. And I can't guarantee I'll always be able to stand quietly on the sidelines, especially if your health or happiness is involved."

His words and the intensity in his eyes set off a fluttering in her chest. There was that SEAL again. The one who would do whatever it took to achieve an objective. If his current objectives were to make her happy and keep her healthy? She was oddly comfortable with that.

"I think I can live with that," she told him. "As

long as you realize that I never have been and never will be the type of woman who responds well to heavy-handed tactics."

His hands flexed around her hips. "How about these handed tactics?"

She tucked her face into his neck and sighed. "Less talking, more massaging."

* * *

Early the next morning, Doc went with Tina to check out the damage. It didn't look quite as hellish in the light of day, but it was still a painful sight. She'd put so much time and effort into making it a success. The Mill wasn't just a business. It was her laboratory. Her baby.

Now, it was gone.

On top of everything else that had happened over the last couple of weeks, it was almost too much to bear. It might have been were it not for the incredible man by her side.

"It's no accident that Doc came into your life at this particular time. You're meant to be together."

Maggie's words seemed more insightful than the hopeful, romantic notions Tina had originally thought them to be.

After they looked around, Doc accompanied her to the Sumneyville police station to talk to Chief

Freed and Fire Chief Petraski. Doc hadn't asked if she wanted him to, but she didn't mind because the truth was, his presence didn't weaken her. It made her stronger.

Bonus: Tina didn't particularly care for either chief. In her opinion, they were nothing more than overgrown bullies with badges and—she believed—the primary malcontents behind local anti-Sanctuary sentiment.

"What's he doing here?" Joe Eisenheiser asked, narrowing his eyes at Doc when they walked into the police station together.

Joe was one of the two full-time police officers in Sumneyville. Jerry Petraski, Chief Freed's nephew and Fire Chief Petraski's son, was the other.

"Providing moral support," Doc said simply.

Joe ignored him and spoke only to Tina. "This doesn't concern him."

"It concerns *me*," Tina said, "and *I* want him here. Chief Freed said he wanted to talk to me this morning. Is he here? Or should we come back another time?"

"Follow me," Joe said, grudgingly leading them to a small conference room. "Have a seat. I'll let the chief know you're here."

Doc held out the chair for Tina to sit down before taking a seat himself.

"So, you and Joe are good buddies, huh?" Tina asked once the door closed solidly behind Joe.

Doc smiled. "We've never been formally introduced."

"But he knows who you are."

"Yes. He knows."

Tina waited for him to say something more. He didn't. Instead, Doc looked pointedly around the room.

He met her eyes and mused quietly, "Do you think they watch a lot of cop shows?"

Despite the seriousness of the situation, Tina's lips quirked. The room *did* look like something right out of a crime drama. The furniture consisted of a plain, rectangular table and a set of uncomfortable metal chairs on either side. There were no windows. The walls were painted a drab, depressing shade of off-white. The only splash of color was the black corded phone hanging on the wall next to the door.

She wondered if Doc's question was also a veiled warning that perhaps they were being watched or listened to. The room didn't have the massive two-way mirror most made-for-TV interrogation rooms did, but when Tina looked around, she did spot a security camera mounted in one corner near the ceiling.

It seemed a little over the top for their tiny, mostly rural, mountain town. As television show comparisons went, Sumneyville was more like Mayberry than Chicago or New York. It wasn't the type of place where hardened criminals made videotaped confessions to be presented in a court of law.

They preferred to handle their own business in Sumneyville. The less outsiders involved, the better. In fact, Tina could only think of one instance in recent memory that hadn't been handled in-house, and that was when the chief's son had gotten a wild hair and thought it would be a good idea to go up to Sanctuary with an attitude and a gun.

They probably would have squashed that, too, if they could have.

That could explain some of the current animosity between some townies and Sanctuary, but there had been issues even before that happened. Everyone had a different theory. Some were completely ridiculous—like Rick's ramblings about them stockpiling weapons (ironic!) and seducing women, for example.

Others seemed more plausible, like an age-old feud between Matt's and Daryl's granddaddies. Or the popular rumor that Matt had done wrong by Daryl's sister, Hayley. Matt and Hayley had been quite the power couple back in high school before Hayley suddenly left town and Matt joined the Navy.

Matt and Daryl were probably the only ones who knew for sure. Matt wasn't likely to say, and Daryl was likely to lie.

Tina and Doc waited. And waited. Tina got up and paced the small space several times—not just out of impatience, but also because when she sat too long, her joints got stiff and achy.

"What's taking so long?" she asked, though she knew the answer.

Doc's eyes followed her around the room. He knew the answer, too. Making them wait was a power play. A show of authority. Perhaps a punishment for bringing Doc along.

Well, fuck that.

"Come on. Let's go. I've got things to do."

Tina had her hand on the knob when the police chief entered with the fire chief right behind him. Neither showed surprise at seeing Doc there. In fact, they didn't acknowledge his presence at all.

"Thanks for coming in, Bertina. We just need to ask you some routine questions."

"Routine? There's nothing routine about what happened," Tina said and then asked a question of her own, "How did it start?"

"It's still an open investigation," Jerry Petraski replied vaguely, his eyes shifting momentarily to his brother-in-law. "You kept up with your inspections? Everything was up to code?"

"You know I did. You're the one who did the inspections and signed off on the permits."

"What about insurance?" asked Freed.

"What about it?"

"Do you have fire insurance?"

"Yes."

"You kept it up-to-date?"

"Of course I did."

"When's the last time you updated your policy?"

Doc shifted in his seat. Clearly, he didn't care for the chief's questions any more than she did, but he remained silent.

"What are you implying, Chief?"

"Just answer the question, please."

Tina exhaled. "About three years ago when I expanded the kitchen. Why?"

Fire Chief Petraski scribbled something into his notebook and then asked, "Have you had any trouble at The Mill lately?"

"What kind of trouble?"

"Malfunctions. Accidents. Unexpected incidents. Things like that."

"No, not at The Mill," she said carefully. "But there have been incidents at the orchards. And someone shot out my tire a few weeks ago."

Petraski stopped scribbling and looked up.

Freed's eyebrows pulled together. "What's that now?"

"Someone shot out my tire," Tina said slowly and clearly. "I was on my way up the mountain and—"

"Why were you on your way up the mountain?" Freed interrupted, shifting his eyes toward Doc accusingly.

"That's irrelevant. As I was saying, I was on my way up the mountain, and someone was following me, so I turned the tables and began following them. That's when they started throwing beer bottles back at me. They cracked my windshield, and when that didn't stop me, they shot out my tire."

It was Freed who said evenly, "You didn't report it."

"Yes, I did. I talked to Joe." Beside her, Doc shifted again. "He took the information, but said since I couldn't identify them, there was nothing he could do."

An uncomfortable silence stretched out for several long moments before Chief Petraski cleared his throat and asked, "Can you think of anyone who would have it out for you? A disgruntled employee maybe?"

"What? No, I—" Tina thought of Eddie and clamped her lips shut. Eddie, who happened to be Joe Eisenheiser's cousin *and* a volunteer firefighter. Suddenly, things became clear.

"Yes?" Chief Petraski prompted.

Beneath the table, Doc gave Tina's hand a gentle squeeze and broke his silence. "Are you suggesting the fire was deliberately set?"

Petraski's lips flattened. "I'm not suggesting anything until the investigation is complete. One more question: where were you last night, Bertina?"

She gaped at him. "Surely, you can't possibly think I had anything to do with it. Why the hell would I destroy my own business?"

"Just answer the question, please."

"I was home," Tina said through clenched teeth.

"Can anyone corroborate that?" Chief Freed's eyes flicked toward Doc.

"No. I was home *alone* until I got the call. Anything else?"

Petraski closed his notebook and sat back. "I think we've got everything we need. For now."

"Good." Tina stood up. "We're done here."

Doc's hand on the small of her back felt good as they stepped out of the police station and into the sunlight. She took a deep breath in an attempt to calm herself.

"Well, that was fun," she said sarcastically.

CHAPTER THIRTY-NINE

~ Doc ~

"Thanks for going with me," Tina said. "I appreciate it."

"You're welcome," Doc replied as he opened the driver's door for her. Thankfully, she hadn't protested his tagging along.

Not that he'd asked.

Daryl Freed and Jerry Petraski—or Frick and Frack, as Smoke called them—were morons. Morons and bullies who, unfortunately, were in positions of power. They liked to remind everyone of that, using veiled threats and intimidation tactics instead of earning respect.

Like sticking them in a ridiculous interrogation room. Making them wait an inordinate amount of time. Casting vague insinuations.

Their plan had backfired. All they'd done was highlight the corruption within their own ranks. Doc was now certain that Joe Eisenheiser was behind the attack on Tina. He knew it. They knew it. And now, Tina knew it, too.

"I'm not sure I did you any favors," Doc told her.

Maybe Eisenheiser had thought he was avenging his cousin. Maybe he had heard about Tina's visits to Sanctuary and had been attempting to warn her off. Probably both.

As she stepped up into the truck, she placed a kiss on his cheek. That one simple act of affection, so readily given in the Sumneyville PD parking lot in broad daylight, lit him up from the inside. Those idiots inside had drawn a line in the sand, and Tina had stepped over it, placing herself firmly on the other side.

"Funny," Tina said, "I was thinking the same thing about you."

"How do you figure that?"

"Well, I've just basically confirmed the rumors that a Sanctuary man has seduced yet another local female into his clutches," she said with the hint of a smirk. "I don't imagine that'll help your cause."

As if he gave a shit about any of that.

"Totally worth it," he said emphatically.

Her smirk became a genuine smile. "I agree."

As she pulled away from the curb, she said, "I should probably head to the orchards. Want me to take you back to Sanctuary first, or would you like to come with me?"

"You're offering?"

"Well, now that the cat's officially out of the bag, I suppose I can be seen with you," she said with a teasing grin. Then, the grin faded. “I can give you the grand tour before the developers come in and bulldoze everything.”

Tina tried to keep her voice light, but he felt her pain as if it were a blade in his own chest. He wanted to tell her about the Callaghans, but at the same time, he didn’t want to offer false hope. If things didn’t work out, it would be yet another cruel blow, and he wouldn’t do that to her.

“In that case, how could I possibly say no?”

After driving in silence for several minutes, Tina said, “Listen, I think we need to address the elephant in the room.”

He wasn’t sure to which elephant she was referring. There seemed to be a whole herd. “Okay.”

She gave him a sideways glance and cleared her throat. “You might have noticed that some people call me Bertina or Bert, not Tina. My real name is Bertina. Bertina Matilda Obermacher, to be specific.”

He waited for her to say more. “And?”

“And I just thought you should know.”

“Okay.”

“Okay.”

“It’s just that I really hate it,” she admitted. “That’s why I go by Tina.”

He thought about that for a moment. “You do know that Bertina means intelligent, right? And Matilda means might, strength, and battle?”

She gave him the side-eye. "How do you know that?"

He shrugged. "I find it interesting how closely people's given names reflect their personalities. I'd say yours are pretty accurate."

"Hmm," she hummed. "I've never thought of it that way. What does Cole mean?"

He laughed. "It actually means swarthy and coal black."

"No offense, but that doesn't exactly fit you, does it?"

"No," he agreed. "In my case, it's a shortened form of Nicholas, which is my father's name."

"Ah. Do you see your family often?"

"Not really, no. My parents moved to Cornwall after my father retired from the Navy. His family owns property there."

"What about your sisters?"

"They're scattered across the globe. We moved around a lot as kids, and I guess we each had our favorites."

"And you chose to settle in Sumneyville," she said with a smile. "Why?"

"Because that's where Church was building Sanctuary. And I hadn't decided on a settling-down place yet."

"And now?"

"Now, I couldn't imagine living anywhere else. Although I wouldn't mind traveling occasionally. I do miss that."

"Me, too," Tina admitted. "I got to see some amazing places in college. But farming isn't really something you can take a break from, you know?" She exhaled and offered a small smile. "I guess I won't have to worry about that for much longer, huh?"

* * *

After a tour of the orchards, a quiet dinner, and some intimate time at Tina's, she gave him a ride back to Sanctuary. Once again, she refused his offer to spend the night, promising to call immediately if anything happened.

He made his way over to the main building, surprised to find the team hanging around, waiting for word. Apparently, Church had filled them in.

"How's Tina holding up?" Church asked.

"Losing The Mill was a big blow, especially on top of everything else she's had to deal with lately."

"Arson?" asked Smoke.

"Petraski's not saying one way or the other," Doc told him, relaying the morning's Q and A at Sumneyville PD. "But I'm thinking it has to be."

Murmurs of agreement sounded from around the room.

"It's the why of it that eludes me. Someone sending a message maybe?" Doc hated the thought that it had anything to do with Tina's recent involvement with Sanctuary, but it wasn't outside the realm of possibility.

In the last six weeks, Tina had been followed, sabotaged, and shot at.

Maybe those incidents had nothing to do with Sanctuary and everything to do with the clusterfuck her brothers had created. But maybe it did.

"Insurance is my guess," Cage said.

"Tina wouldn't burn down her own mill for the insurance money," Doc said firmly.

"Relax. No one thinks she did. But one of her brothers might have. Financially, they're fucked, right? What have they got to lose?"

Doc shook his head. "That doesn't make any sense. They'd have no claim on an insurance payout. The Mill wasn't part of Obermacher Farms. It was owned and operated solely under her LLC."

"Misplaced guilt maybe?" mused Heff. "They had a moment of regret for screwing Tina out of her family legacy, thought it might be too painful for her to stick around and watch the farm go condo, so they gave her the means to start over?"

Church shook his head. "I can't see Rick doing regret. Or Gunther for that matter. They're selfish pricks. If they had anything to do with setting the fire, it was in the hopes of getting Tina to give them a handout."

"Why not burn down their own homes and collect the insurance?" Doc asked.

"I can think of two reasons," said Cage. "One, because it would be too suspicious. Obermachers are in financial straits, and the family homestead just happens to burn down? No one would believe it was an accident."

"And the second?"

"There *is* no insurance on any Obermacher Farms property. We've been doing a little investigating of our own. Friedrich let it all lapse."

"Fucking hell. Is he really that stupid?"

"Apparently," Smoke said at the same time Church said, "Yes."

"What about the other one?" asked Heff. "Kiefer? Could he have done this?"

"It's possible," Mad Dog said doubtfully, "though from what we know about him, he seems more inclined to do what the others tell him to do than have an original thought."

Doc had thought so, too, but now, he wasn't so sure. Tina's youngest brother was good at being invisible. Almost too good. While the other two had been giving Tina a hard time, Kiefer had been hovering quietly in the background, watching and listening. He hadn't said a word until they walked away.

But in that moment when he'd asked Tina if she was okay, Kiefer's eyes had turned to Doc, and his gaze had been sharp and assessing. Perhaps he wasn't the dullard he pretended to be.

"The likeliest suspects are our buddy Eisenheiser and his cousin, Eddie," said Mad Dog. "They've already demonstrated a mean streak and an appalling lack of intelligence. Based on what

Doc said about Tina talking to Eisenheiser about the truck incident, it seems pretty obvious."

"I don't know," said Cage. "Something doesn't feel right about that. Seems too easy."

"Or maybe you're just overthinking it. We're not dealing with geniuses here."

"Petraski's going to rule it an accident, guaranteed. Any hint of arson is going to bring in outside investigators, and he sure as hell doesn't want that," said Smoke.

"My thoughts exactly," Heff agreed with a nod. "Have we heard anything from the Callaghans yet?"

"Not yet."

The words were barely out of Church's mouth when the phone rang.

Cage looked at the display. "It's Ian."

"Put him on speaker."

"Ian," Church greeted. "Are you prescient or something?"

Ian laughed. "Me? No. But Maggie, on the other hand … Is Doc there? He's going to want to hear this."

"I'm here," Doc responded.

"Good. Maggie gave those items to Lex. Lex was really impressed. She'd like you and Tina to come to the Goddess and talk business."

"That's awesome. When?"

"The sooner, the better. Gunther Obermacher's at it again. He's decided the offers they have aren't good enough, and he's been reaching out in an attempt to foster competition and drive up the price of the land."

"Greedy bastard," Smoke muttered.

"He's an opportunistic prick, for sure," Ian agreed. "And too stupid for his own good. The buyer he had lined up and has now subsequently pissed off? Anthony Tollino."

Cage sat up at the mention of the name. "Tollino? As in the mobster?"

"Yeah, I thought you might recognize the name. And heads-up, Tollino is not happy with Gunther's decision to expand the buyers' club to include Tollino's competition."

"Just what we need," grumbled Smoke. "Organized crime in Sumneyville. Uh, no offense," he said, shooting a look toward Cage.

Cage, who had grown up in that world, grinned. "None taken."

"Whatever you do," Ian said through the speaker, "make sure Tina doesn't sign anything until she talks to Lex and Aidan."

Doc's conscience required him to speak up, particularly since Tina was no longer capable of producing the products their potential interest was based upon.

"Ian, you should know—"

"About The Mill? Yeah, we know about that. Can you get Tina here tomorrow night?"

"I'll do my best."

CHAPTER FORTY

~ Tina ~

"Will you have dinner with me tomorrow night?" Doc asked.

Tina was regretting her decision not to spend the night with Doc. Holding the phone to her ear wasn't the same as having his lips there. The bed felt empty without him. *She* felt empty without him.

But things were moving so fast. So much was happening. Doc was everything she'd ever wanted and nothing she'd expected to find, and yet there was still a part of her—granted, a tiny part—that was afraid to believe it could last.

She worried that, with all the bad things going on, she was painting too rosy a picture, desperate to put her hope and faith in a future with him. Simply put, Doc seemed too good to be true, coming into her life just when she needed him most. Being all caring and protective and wonderful.

Believing that Maggie was right—that she and Doc were meant to be together—was too easy. Tina had become wary of anything good that seemed easy because experience had proven time and time again that it never was.

"Sure," she answered. "Is Kate making something good?"

Doc chuckled. "Kate is always making something good, but I had something else in mind."

"Mmm, I like the something elses you come up with. We could get some takeout and get creative."

"Very tempting, but I was thinking more along the lines of going out to eat."

"You mean, like a *date*, date?" Tina asked. "I suppose we could. News of our torrid affair has surely made it out by now. Being seen at Franco's is probably the next logical step."

"Not Franco's."

She frowned into the phone. Franco's was the only sit-down restaurant in Sumneyville. Maybe Doc was talking about Andy's, the hole-in-the-wall burger place in the next town over, or maybe the diner farther out. She had been to both and would be fine with either.

"No, and no," he said when she told him as much.

"Then, where?"

"It's a surprise."

"I'm intrigued. Okay, Mr. Watson, I accept your challenge."

"Good. Wear something nice."

"How nice?"

"*Nice*."

"Now, I'm *really* intrigued."

"Tomorrow night. I'll pick you up at six. And, Tina?"

"Yes?"

"Have a bag packed and ready to go because I'm not taking you home afterward. Dinner isn't the only surprise I have planned for you."

A thrill ran through her as she snuggled into her pillow.

* * *

The next morning, Tina was questioning the wisdom of her ready acceptance for a night out as she stared into her closet. Her "nice" wardrobe was extremely limited and slightly outdated. Dressing up wasn't something she did often, mostly because she didn't have a reason to. She had one classic black dress for funerals and somber occasions, one nice flowery dress she'd worn to Rick's wedding, and another she'd worn to Gunther's.

Perhaps she could convince Doc to forego the dinner part of the surprise and move right toward the second half, which was the part she was most excited about anyway. Her best option was, when he came to pick her up, to show up at the door, naked, and distract him.

The crunch of tires on gravel was followed by a

knock on the door.

"What now?" Tina murmured.

Unexpected visitors rarely brought good news, especially early in the morning.

Tina took a deep breath and steeled herself in preparation. When she opened the door, however, she found not her brothers or the chief of police, but Kate grinning widely at her.

"Good morning! Sorry to bother you so early, but we wanted to make a full day of it."

"Full day of what?"

"Doc told us you're going out tonight, and we thought it was the perfect excuse for a girls' day. Are you in?"

Tina looked toward the sleek black SUV. Sam waved from the front passenger seat. The rear tinted window behind Sam went down, and Bree and Sandy grinned and waved from the backseat.

Spend the day worrying about not having something nice to wear or go shopping with her new friends? It was a no-brainer. "Hell yes, I'm in."

* * *

Shopping was an absolute blast. Tina couldn't remember the last time she'd had so much fun. Truthfully, she wasn't sure she'd *ever* had that much fun. Growing up with only brothers, having health issues, not having a lot of close friends meant most of her life had been more about proving herself than having a good time.

Sandy, who had her own business creating custom websites, had a client who owned a health and wellness spa in the Poconos, and that client had invited Sandy and a group of friends to experience the services firsthand. As a result, part of their girls' day was getting pampered with facials, manicures and pedicures, and even hot-stone massages. The hot stones couldn't compare to Doc's highly personalized, hands-on therapy, but it was nice.

Afterward, they hit some of the nearby outlets, and Tina managed to find a dress she was happy with. It was a classic, timeless style in a shimmery shade of dark blue that Bree said brought out the blue in her eyes.

"Doc is going to flip when he sees you," Sam said approvingly.

"I feel like Cinderella," Tina joked, looking at herself in the trifold mirror.

"You kind of look like her, too," Bree said with a grin. "Blonde hair, blue eyes, and an hourglass figure. Who knew you were hiding all that under jeans and flannel?"

Tina laughed. "I guess I've always been more of a tomboy than a girlie girl."

"Which is why you fit in with us so well," Kate said cheerfully. "But there's nothing wrong with embracing our feminine side once in a while."

"And wielding it like the strong, empowered women we are," Sandy added. "Which reminds me … where is that lingerie place Bree found last Christmas?"

* * *

Tina checked her hair and makeup one more time. It was probably the tenth time she'd done so since the ladies dropped her off. The woman in the mirror looked so different than the one she was used to seeing. Her skin was radiant and glowing. Her long hair, instead of being pulled up into a practical, functional ponytail, was loose and flowing around her shoulders in soft waves. The new dress clung in all the right places, accentuating her natural curves.

Those things could be attributed to a phenomenal girls'-day adventure. But the bright sparkle in her eyes was purely due to the anticipation of seeing Doc again and whatever surprises he had planned for the evening.

Those tingles of anticipation intensified when she heard Doc's arrival. But nothing could have prepared for the sight that awaited her when she opened the door. Bespoke, classic black suit. Silk tie. Clean-shaven. Hair combed back and away from his beautiful, sculpted face.

And those gorgeous, hypnotic hazel eyes, now gazing intensely at her.

Her normally plaid-flannel-clad SEAL medic looked more like a male model who'd just come from a photo shoot.

"Wow," they both said at the same time.

"Tina, you look stunning."

"You look pretty good yourself. Are you sure you want to do this?"

His eyes raked down her body and back up again. "No. But let's do it anyway."

"Okay then. I'm as ready as I'll ever be, I guess."

Doc took the overnight bag from her hand. "Got everything you need?"

"Yep." She hadn't packed much, just a change of clothes for the next day, some of the new silk lingerie she'd picked up, and a fresh jar of body butter.

Tina locked up the cottage with shaking hands.

"Nervous, Miss Obermacher?"

"Excited," she corrected. "Where did you say we are going again?"

He gave her a sly smile. "Nice try. You'll find out soon enough."

Her curiosity continued to grow as they drove past the Sumneyville town limits and continued southeast. When Doc pulled up in front of the Celtic Goddess and handed his keys over to a uniformed valet, she thought she was dreaming.

She'd heard of the place, of course—mostly from Giselle—but she'd never actually been there.

The restaurant-slash-resort was built into the side of the mountain just outside of Pine Ridge. Multiple levels of gleaming white stone, tinted glass, and accent lighting made her think of Greece. She'd never been there either, but she'd seen pictures.

Doc offered his arm. Once again feeling like Cinderella, she slipped her arm through his. They entered through massive Ionic columns into a fantastical, opulent lobby. Brilliant murals adorned the walls behind even more columns. Pristine white marble flooring—*are those veins of actual gold?* Elegant statues. A proliferation of lush greenery.

They stepped up to the ornately carved podium, where Doc spoke quietly to the tuxedoed man. The man lifted his hand, and a younger man appeared, also wearing a tuxedo. Tina wondered if it was the official uniform of the Goddess.

"Escort our guests to the Danann room, please."

The younger man's eyes widened slightly, then he nodded and turned to them. "Follow me, please."

They were led to an elevator, one that required a private key. A short while later, they exited on another floor and entered a balconied alcove overlooking the valley.

"The Danann room? That's an unusual name, isn't it?" Tina mused quietly.

"I'm guessing it's a nod to ancient Celtic mythology," Doc said. "The Tuatha Dé Danann were a supernatural race, often associated with the Fae."

That made sense. The place was called the *Celtic* Goddess after all.

"More name-based etymology?"

"Sort of. I grew up hearing the legends and myths."

"I thought you said your family was from Cornwall."

"My father's family is from Cornwall. My mother's family is from Killarney," Doc replied with a wink.

"Boy, when you take a girl on a date, you really go all out, don't you?" Tina murmured, stepping closer to the glass.

It was a stunning view. The sky was a dark blue, the forested mountains washed in silvery highlights, the lights of the valley twinkling like jewels.

"It's breathtaking, isn't it?" said an unfamiliar female voice from behind her. "No matter how many times I see it, I never get tired of it."

Tina turned to find a petite, beautiful woman who looked like she could have been a goddess herself.

"You must be Tina," the woman said. "Welcome to the Goddess. I'm Lexi Callaghan, and this is my husband, Ian."

"Glad you could make it," the tall man beside her said with a nod, then extended his hand to Doc.

Tina looked questioningly at Doc, who seemed determined not to meet her eyes. He hadn't mentioned anything about a double date, but she certainly wasn't going to complain.

"Please, sit down," Lexi said. Only then did Tina notice that the table was set for six. "Aidan had some business to take care of, but he and Mary will be joining us shortly."

The man named Ian smirked. "Uh-huh. *Business*."

Lexi's cheeks pinked slightly. "Tina, let me just say, I loved everything, but I think the vanilla peaches were my favorite. What was that, schnapps? Though there was something else in there, too."

Tina blinked, feeling a bit lost. "I'm sorry?"

"The basket of goodies you gave Maggie."

"Oh, uh, yes," Tina said, replaying Lexi's question in her mind now that she had proper context. "Schnapps and a touch of whipped cream vodka and some natural flavors."

"I knew it! Absolutely brilliant. The moment I tasted it, I had visions of a flambé. The peaches would pair well with vanilla bean ice cream and some toasted coconut, I think. A perfect summer dessert."

"Yes, I suppose they would," Tina said, feeling more confused by the moment.

Lexi turned to Doc accusingly. "You didn't tell her, did you?"

Doc shook his head.

"Tell me what?"

"I work here," Lexi said to Tina. "In the kitchen. I'd love to incorporate some of your specialties on the menu."

Before Tina could respond, Lexi said, "Oh good. Here are Aidan and Mary now."

Two more people joined them in the private dining area. The man had golden-brown hair and exotic eyes of an unusual shade that reminded Tina of fresh honey. Like Lexi, he seemed slightly *more* than the average guy, radiating an aura of wealth and power. Tina, who didn't typically have an issue with self-confidence, suddenly felt way out of her league. Thankfully, the woman with him seemed far more approachable, especially when Tina learned she ran a flower shop in Birch Falls.

Over the course—or seven courses, as it were—of an absolutely fantastic dinner, Tina learned that Aidan worked for the Goddess, too, though he didn't come out and say exactly what it was that he did. She assumed it was in some sort of legal capacity when Lexi explained that they were interested in contracting with Obermacher Farms.

"You mean, like you did with Maggie?" Tina asked.

"Not exactly like that, but similar," Lexi confirmed.

"As wonderful as that sounds, I'm afraid that won't be possible." Tina's heart felt like it was breaking all over again as she explained that Obermacher Farms had accrued significant debt and that her brothers were anxious to sell to an out-of-state developer.

Strangely, they didn't seem discouraged by that.

"We know about that," Aidan said. "But The Mill and everything in it is yours, is it not?"

"Yes, but as of two days ago, The Mill is out of business. There was a terrible fire, and the place was gutted."

"We know about that, too," Lexi said, surprising her. "As tragic as it was, The Mill can be rebuilt. It's you we're interested in contracting with, Tina."

Again, Tina shook her head. "Even if I did rebuild, there's the issue of sourcing. You can't just swap one bushel for another. I spent years researching and experimenting, creating my own hybrids. That's what makes my products unique. A new orchard would take years to become viable, and that's assuming you could find the right land."

"We wouldn't need to start a new orchard," said Aidan, tilting his head to the side. "As you said, you've already spent years perfecting yours."

"Yes, but as I explained, Obermacher Farms is up on the auction block." Realization dawned. "Are you saying that the Celtic Goddess might be interested in buying *all* of Obermacher Farms?"

It seemed like another thing just too good to be

true. Tina didn't dare hope.

"That's exactly what we're saying," Aidan said.

"I don't think you understand just how far in debt we are or how much land is involved. Unless, of course, you're talking about breaking it up in parcels and purchasing only the orchards."

"All of it. Your family's lands are not only designated and zoned as prime agricultural, but the slopes and drainage are ideal for farming."

Tina had come to terms with losing the family farm, but it would be preferable to have it remain a working farm in someone else's hands than paved over and built up.

"My brothers are considering several offers," Tina said carefully. "I could talk to them."

Aidan shook his head. "We're not interested in dealing with your brothers. Only you. In fact, I'd prefer if they didn't know of our interest at all."

"Then, you're *really* out of luck because I've only got a twenty-five percent say in the business. They control the other seventy-five percent of what happens next."

Aidan's lips quirked. "I don't believe in luck, Tina. The question is, are you interested?"

"Yes, I'm interested. I just don't see how it's possible."

"Leave that to me. In the meantime, please, enjoy your stay at the Goddess. It was a pleasure meeting you."

He rose to go, as did his wife and Lexi and Ian.

After saying their good nights, Tina turned to Doc. “We’re staying here tonight?”

He grinned. “That’s part of the surprise. We’ve got a private suite for the night.”

* * *

“Are you angry with me?” Doc asked as they walked through the lit gardens, away from the restaurant and toward the posh resort.

It was so beautiful, yet Tina’s thoughts were churning too furiously to properly appreciate it.

“I haven’t decided yet,” she answered honestly. Several moments passed in silence before she exhaled and said, “I love that you’re doing this, but I kind of hate you for giving me false hope.”

“If anyone can make it happen, they can.”

Tina shook her head. Maggie had a big heart and good intentions. Lexi was a chef, which meant she might have some pull in the Goddess kitchen, but they were talking about more than just shifting suppliers. And Aidan, well, she didn’t know what exactly Aidan did, though he did seem like an important man.

She said as much to Doc. He laughed softly.

“What’s so funny?”

Doc wrapped his hand around Tina’s, lifted it to his lips, and kissed it. “Lexi isn’t just a cook.

She's the master chef as well as one of the owners. Aidan is the other."

Tina felt the blood drain from her face. "We just had dinner with the *owners* of the Celtic Goddess?"

"We did. Lexi is Maggie's sister-in-law."

"Holy …" A tiny tendril of hope broke through layers of doubt. "But I still don't see how it can work." There was so much to consider, not the least of which was her brothers' combined controlling interests in Obermacher Farms and the shady corners they'd backed themselves into.

Perhaps she should have mentioned some of that to *Aidan* and *Lexi.*

CHAPTER FORTY-ONE

~ Doc ~

"How do you know them anyway?" Tina asked. "Lexi and Aidan, I mean."

"Friends of friends through Sanctuary. Ian Callaghan and his brothers served in the military themselves and have been supporting the project from day one," Doc said, hoping Tina didn't ask for details on exactly how they'd been helping. "If there's one thing I've learned about that family, it's that they have a way of making things happen."

"I'm afraid to hope." Tina was quiet for a few minutes, then asked, "Aidan—I can't believe I'm on a first-name basis with the owner of the Celtic Goddess—seemed pretty firm about not dealing with Rick, Gunther, or Kiefer or even letting them know about it for that matter. Do you know why?"

It was yet another question Doc had to answer carefully.

"Aidan Harrison didn't get to be a billionaire by chance. He's a very astute businessman. I imagine he did his research."

Tina laughed softly. "If Gunther and Giselle knew where I was right now—or more specifically, who we had dinner with—they'd be green with envy."

"You can't tell them," he said quietly.

She sighed. "I know. It is fun though, imagining the look on her face."

"No more thinking about that tonight. I've got other plans for you."

"Based on what you've managed so far, I can't wait to see what's next," she said softly.

"You really look beautiful tonight," Doc told her. "I mean, you always look beautiful, but …"

"I clean up nice?" she finished with a mischievous grin.

He laughed. "Yes."

"Funny, I was thinking the same thing about you. You cut quite a dashing figure in that suit, Mr. Watson. In fact, there's only one thing I think you look better in."

"Yeah? What's that?"

"*Nothing*."

Doc groaned and led her to the private suite. Seeing Tina in that dress and scenting that subtle hint of cocoa and coconut that clung to her skin, had been driving him crazy all night. And when she said things like that … he'd be lucky if he could control himself long enough to let her enjoy the amenities awaiting them inside.

The sexy smirk playing across her lips only

intensified his sense of urgency. He pulled the key card the bellman had slipped him earlier out of his inner pocket and held it to the keypad. The door unlocked with a snick.

"Did I mention I picked up more than just this dress for our date tonight?" she said as he ushered her inside.

"Such as?"

"When we get inside, you can take my dress off and find out for yourself."

"Fucking hell, Tina."

She laughed and then squealed as he swept her off her feet, swung her over his shoulder, and carried her caveman-style to the raised dais containing the massive bed. There was a momentary snafu in getting up the wide steps without tripping, mainly because she slipped her hands down his pants and was squeezing and fondling his ass, but he pushed through it.

It was a full hour later when he noticed how nice the suite actually was. Besides the raised king-size bed and the mirrored panels above it—which he was particularly fond of—the suite boasted three fireplaces, a living area, two Jacuzzis (one inside and one out) as well as a steam room and an in-room massage table.

Needless to say, they made use of all of it.

CHAPTER FORTY-TWO

~ Tina ~

"Miss Obermacher? This is Gretchen Meyer, Aidan Harrison's personal assistant. He'd like to schedule a meeting with you. Are you free this afternoon?"

Tina sat up abruptly. It had been less than forty-eight hours since their dinner, less than twenty-four since she and Doc had left the heaven that was the Celtic Goddess resort and returned to her tiny caretaker's cottage. She'd always liked her cozy little space, but there was something to be said for splurging once in a while.

"Yes, I am."

"Wonderful."

After Aidan's PA gave her the details, Tina hung up and turned to Doc. "Wow, that was fast. Aidan wants to meet with me this afternoon. Will you go with me?"

He pressed a kiss to her shoulder, sending more tingles into places that had already been tingling, thanks to Doc's early morning attention. "Of course."

"What do you wear to a meeting with Aidan Harrison?" Tina mused aloud, mentally reviewing her closet while Doc slipped into the bathroom.

She'd barely gotten the words out when her phone vibrated again. This time, it was Maggie.

"Word travels fast, huh?"

Maggie laughed. "You have no idea, especially in this family. But I was planning to call you today anyway. I've got those things you wanted."

"Perfect. I can pick them up since I'll be down that way."

"I'll have them ready for you. Are you nervous about meeting with Aidan?"

"A little," Tina admitted.

"Don't be. Aidan's good people."

Tina had gotten that impression, too, but it was nice to hear Maggie confirm it.

"Good to know, though I'm glad I didn't know who he was before the dinner. I would have been a nervous wreck."

"Aidan does have that effect on people," Maggie agreed. "Is Doc coming along with you?"

"Yes." Tina felt better when Doc was with her. Like she could face anything. And dinners and business meetings with billionaires and master chefs were definitely something.

She hadn't meant to say that aloud, but she must have because Maggie said, "Of course you feel that way. He's your *croie*. I guarantee he feels the same way about you."

Tina had a hard time believing that. Doc seemed so capable. So in control. But it was a nice thought.

She changed topics and posed the wardrobe question to Maggie. "You've been there before, right? I have no idea what to wear."

"Jeans are fine. Business casual if you're worried about it."

"Seriously?" Tina asked doubtfully.

"Seriously. Lexi wears jeans every day. She wouldn't work there if she couldn't," Maggie said on a laugh.

"Lexi is the head chef. She can wear whatever she wants."

"She's also incredibly down-to-earth. Don't stress over it, okay?"

That was easy for Maggie to say.

"I'll do my best."

Tina hung up with Maggie just as Doc was coming out of the bathroom. Sadly, he'd put on jeans, but his chest and feet were bare, and that was something, especially with that sexy bit of dark scruff along his jawline.

"I need to head back to Sanctuary for a few hours. Want to come with me?"

"I would, but I should go to the orchards and check on things. I haven't been around much the last two days."

"All right. Be careful. I'll be back around

noon."

"Sounds good. I'd like to stop at Maggie's either before or after the meeting. She's got some things for me."

"You got it."

Less than thirty minutes later, Doc was gone, and Tina was on her way. Each day, there were fewer people working the fields than the day before. Boxes of Japanese beetle traps sat untouched along with a delivery of organic soap waiting to be hung on the trees—a natural deterrent for the deer and other animals who liked to munch on tender young shoots. The grass hadn't been cut lately either, giving the place an unkempt appearance.

She didn't like it. These were still her orchards—at least for a little while longer.

With plenty of time before she had to go back to her place and prepare for her meeting, Tina opted to do some mowing. She started up the commercial zero-turn, stepped onto the back, and zipped between the stately rows.

It was impossible to imagine paved roads and half-million-dollar homes there. Hopefully, with the help of the Celtic Goddess, that would never happen. Letting go would be hard but easier if she knew the farm was going to be in the hands of someone who would take care of it.

For a few hours, Tina lost herself in the fresh air and scents of freshly mowed grass and peach blossoms. Her temporary sense of peace was shattered when she returned the mower to the shed and found Rick waiting for her.

His greeting: “What the hell are you doing?”

“What does it look like I’m doing?” she asked, stepping off the mower and removing her gloves.

“Wasting your time. Did you sign those Tollino papers?”

“No.”

“Why not?”

“Because I haven’t had time to read through them.”

His expression was one of annoyance. “What’s the point?”

“The point is, I don’t trust you or Gunther to do what’s best. You’ve already proven all you care about is saving your own selfish asses.”

Rick’s face turned beet red. “We’re losing the land, Bert. There’s no getting around that.”

“Thanks to you. But selling out to a big-city developer with mob ties? Is that really our only option?”

“It’s the smartest one.”

“Yeah, well, you and I clearly have different opinions on what smart is.” She looked at her watch. “Anything else?”

“Sign the papers. Tonight.”

* * *

The Celtic Goddess offices were located in the same complex as the resort, which, according to the internet research Tina had done, spanned several hundred acres. In addition to the restaurant and the exclusive, private suites, there was also a five-star hotel, a spa, several high-end shops, a world-class business center, and plenty of distractions to keep guests occupied and entertained.

The business offices had the same general theme as the restaurant—lots of gold-veined, gleaming white marble; tinted glass; and an abundance of lush greenery.

After she gave her name at the front desk, Tina and Doc were taken up to a conference room on the top floor. One entire wall was made of glass, providing an exceptional view of the valley and surrounding mountainside. The rest was exactly as she'd pictured a billionaire's private meeting room to be, with dark wood and plush seating that probably cost more than her truck.

"Tina, Doc, please come in," Aidan said. He and the other two men in the room—neither of whom Tina had met before—rose with Tina's arrival in an old-fashioned, gentlemanly gesture.

They sat down again only once she did. Lexi, the only other woman present at the table, smiled knowingly.

"I'm sorry. Am I late?" Tina asked.

"No, not at all. We wanted to have everything

hammered out for you."

Aidan made the introductions. "Lexi, you know. This is Shane and Kane Callaghan."

"Just how many Callaghans are there?" Tina blurted out.

Lexi laughed. "Seven, though sometimes, it seems like a lot more."

Like the Callaghans she'd met thus far—Ian and Michael—Shane and Kane were large, well-built men with dark hair and striking blue eyes. Shane had a warm, friendly smile. Kane didn't. His gaze was watchful and assessing.

"Shane is a lawyer. He's been looking into the legalities of your particular situation, and he's drafted the proposal we'll be reviewing today." Aidan tapped on the closed leather portfolio in front of him. There was one in front of every occupied seat, including hers.

"Kane is a financial advisor. He's reviewed the financial holdings of Obermacher Farms and your LLC as well as those trying to buy your land. Both men are quite familiar with the process, as they've been actively involved in a similar situation."

"Maggie's farm?" Tina guessed, receiving nods in response.

"Would you like something to drink before we begin?" Aidan asked.

"Water would be great, thanks." Tina's throat already felt dry.

Aidan's PA got her bottled water and a glass

and then moved back into the shadows.

"Kane," Aidan said, nodding at the large, stoic-looking man, "why don't you begin?"

"As you know, Obermacher Farms, Incorporated is in a deep financial hole. The personal accounts of the co-owners, present company excluded, are equally insolvent. While filing for bankruptcy might alleviate some debt, it will do nothing for the substantial *illegal* debts accrued."

Kane turned those icy-blue eyes her way. "Your brothers have been doing business with some bad people, Miss Obermacher. The ones who've put in the offer your brothers are currently considering aren't much better."

Tina nodded and squeezed Doc's hand under the table. Kane wasn't saying anything she hadn't known or hadn't already figured out herself.

"They know your family is desperate for cash, and they're using that to their advantage. What they're offering is pennies on the dollar for what the land is actually worth, and then they'll make a killing, stripping the land and turning Obermacher Farms into a high-occupancy residential and commercial area. Believe me when I tell you that no one in this room wants to see that happen."

The truth was painful, and hearing it put out there so succinctly was hard. Tina sipped her water and cleared her throat. "So, what do you propose?"

His response was equally brief and to the point.

"Contract with the Goddess. Allow them to farm sections of it and preserve the rest."

He made it sound so easy.

Tina turned to Aidan and asked the question at the forefront of her mind, "Why not just buy the land yourself? What do you need me for?"

"Because we want you more than we want the farm," Lexi answered.

"You mean, my hybrids."

"No," Lexi corrected. "We mean, you."

"You offer something no one else does," Aidan said. "Superior produce and unique end products not available anywhere else as well as multiple patents based on your work. That is exactly what the Goddess is about—providing the best experience possible. Simply put, we want you to align exclusively with us."

"Everything is spelled out clearly in the proposal," said Shane, opening the portfolio in front of him. "Let's review it together, shall we?"

* * *

Less than an hour later, Tina was shaking hands with everyone and then stepping onto the private express elevator on wobbly legs.

"Pinch me, will you?" she said to Doc.

He didn't. Instead, as soon as the elevator doors closed, he pulled her into his arms and gave her a breath-stealing kiss. The close contact centered her and sent her into the stratosphere at the same time. Kind of like the meeting she'd just stepped out of.

If everything went according to plan—and there was no reason to believe it wouldn't—she couldn't have asked for anything more. It would be a best-case scenario for everyone involved. Her. Her family. The town.

Much the way they'd done with Maggie's land, the Celtic Goddess would use Obermacher Farms as a primary source of fresh, organic produce. They would supply the equipment and staff needed to do so. Aidan and Lexi had made it quite clear that they preferred to stay local, which meant that anyone currently working for Obermacher would keep their job if they wanted it. As employees of the Goddess, they would also be eligible for benefits far beyond what Obermacher had been able to offer.

Unlike the Flynn-Callaghan farm, however, the Goddess would own the land outright. Had Tina been the sole owner, they would have contracted with her for use of the land, as they had with Maggie. However, they'd made it quite clear that they had no interest in partnering with Rick, Gunther, or Kiefer.

Tina couldn't blame them for that.

As for Tina, she'd keep her LLC and her patents and serve as the overseer of the Goddess's orchard division—not just for *her* orchards, but for Maggie's as well. In exchange, she'd agree to give the Goddess non-exclusive rights to her products, which meant she could also rebuild her mill.

All she had to do was get her brothers to accept the Goddess's offer … without them knowing it was the Goddess.

The offer would come in not under the name of the Celtic Goddess franchise, but from one of the many subsidiaries owned by Aidan Harrison's family. He believed that if Tina's brothers knew the Goddess was interested, they'd get greedy and demand more.

Sadly, they were right about that, too. Gunther would see the Goddess name, get visions of grandeur, and then pull Rick and Kiefer into one of his schemes.

Tina's only regret was, she wished she could have discussed the offer with Lottie and gotten her perspective before signing. Things had moved so quickly. However, Tina thought Lottie would approve. Her grandmother would be the first person she called once everything was official.

* * *

Tina and Doc made a quick stop at Maggie's farm on the way back to Sumneyville. Maggie was thrilled; apparently, Lexi had already called her with the good news.

"I just hope I can pull it off," Tina confessed.

"You can," Maggie told her, her green eyes swirling hypnotically. "Everything is going to work out. I know it will."

Tina wished she shared Maggie's confidence, but she knew her brothers. Gunther, especially, had a nose for scheming.

"I took your advice and told Doc about my autoimmune issues," Tina told Maggie as she accepted the bag of teas and herbs and pastes.

"And?"

"And he was every bit as supportive and accepting as you'd said he would be."

"I knew it," Maggie said with a wide smile. "Invite me to the wedding, okay?"

Tina laughed, but inside, her heart filled with joy at the thought. "If there is a wedding, you will definitely be invited."

"Good. Listen, I can't believe I'm saying this, but … would you consider talking to Michael about your health issues?"

"Oh, I don't know …"

"I get it. I really do. But he's not like other doctors, and I'm not just saying that because I'm sleeping with him. He's a brilliant biochemist. He might be able to help."

Maggie was so earnest that Tina was tempted to believe her. After all, Maggie had been right about everything else so far.

"I'll think about it, okay?"

* * *

“You should go,” Tina told Doc after they arrived back at her cottage. “Aidan said he’d fax the offer over right after we left. Gunther must have received it by now.”

Doc’s mouth turned downward. “Maybe I should stick around, just in case.”

“That’s exactly what you *shouldn’t* do. Just seeing you will get their backs up. If my brothers think you’re influencing me in any way, it’ll just make them that much harder to deal with. Trust me, okay? I’ve got this.”

“I do trust you. It’s them I don’t trust.”

Tina stepped close and wrapped her arms around Doc’s neck. “*I’ve got this*. I’ll call you later, okay?”

“You’d better,” he grumbled.

“I will. And later tonight, after everything is said and done, I’ll thank you properly for being there for me today.”

“Thank me how?” he asked, the familiar heat lighting up his eyes, his big hands flexing just above her backside.

“How else? Sexual favors.”

Doc groaned and left reluctantly.

Tina had barely started unpacking Maggie’s bag of goodies before Kiefer showed up at her door.

“Rick wants you down at the office.”

Tina exhaled. She had to play her part. If she

acquiesced too easily, her brothers would get suspicious. "Do we really have to do this right now?"

"Yes. Right now. He said to tell you the papers are getting signed tonight whether you're there or not."

"What's he going to do? Forge my signature?"

Kiefer's mouth twisted, suggesting that was exactly what he would do. Or more likely, Gunther would.

"Over my dead body. Let's go."

* * *

"Threatening me now, Rick? Really?" Tina asked, striding into the office with Kiefer in her wake.

Gunther was already there.

Rick shrugged unrepentantly. "It got you here, didn't it? Did you finish reading the offer?"

Tina tossed the papers on his desk. "I did, and even I can see it's a bad deal. They're offering a fraction of what this land is worth, and you *know* they're going to make a killing."

Gunther raised his eyebrows. "Since when did you start caring about land value and profit margins?"

"Since I started my own business," Tina shot back, rolling her eyes. "One that wasn't on the brink of financial collapse until you geniuses decided to play fast and loose with the family assets."

All of her brothers scowled at that one.

"What are you bitching about?" Rick muttered. "The Mill was insured, wasn't it?"

"Yes, but rebuilding won't do me any good if there aren't any orchards to supply the product now, will it?" She dropped into a chair, disgusted. "The only reason I was able to make a profit was because my overhead was so low. If I have to contract with someone else for produce, I'll barely be able to keep my head above water."

Tina waved toward the desk. "It's bad enough we're losing the farm our family's had for generations, but giving it away to a bunch of mobsters? That's adding insult to injury."

"Baby sister has some teeth after all," Gunther murmured.

Tina ignored him. "Is that seriously the best offer we have?"

"It was," Rick said slowly, sitting back in his chair. "But another offer came through this afternoon."

"*And*?"

"And … they're offering slightly more than Tollino."

"Let me see."

Rick exchanged a glance with Gunther, who nodded. Rick picked up the paper in front of him and handed it to her.

It was Aidan's offer. Tina scanned over it, verified everything was exactly as Aidan had said it would be, then tossed it back on the desk, and snorted. "EHI Properties? Never heard of them."

"They're based in Georgia," Gunther said.

"So? What do they want to buy land up here for?"

"How the fuck do I know?" Gunther snapped. "They're from Georgia. Maybe they have a thing for peach orchards or something."

Tina shook her head, playing her part. "It still seems low to me."

"Because you're thinking with your heart and not your head. We're never going to get what you think the land is worth," Gunther told her plainly.

"Well, forgive me for giving a shit." Tina crossed her arms and took several deep breaths to calm herself.

Rick exhaled heavily. "We have to sell. There's no way around that. It sucks, but there it is."

Long moments passed in tense, heavy silence.

When she figured enough time had gone by to be believable, Tina uncrossed her arms and exhaled heavily. "Fine. I guess I have no choice."

Tina stood, grabbed the EHI offer, and scribbled her name and the date at the bottom. Then, she tossed the pen on the desk. She didn't have to fake the shaking of her hands or the tears welling up in her eyes. Four hundred years of family history gone with a few strokes of a pen. Up in the family cemetery, generations of Obermachers were probably turning in their graves.

"Are you happy now?"

Rick looked at the paper, verifying her signature. "You made the right decision."

She nodded somberly and turned to go. Before she got to the door, she turned around, grabbed the Tollino offer, and put it into the paper shredder.

"What the hell, Bert?" exclaimed Gunther.

"Just so you don't get any clever ideas about using the EHI offer to get Tollino to up theirs."

The guilty look on Gunther's face confirmed that he'd been thinking of doing exactly that.

She pointed at the EHI contract. "I want this over. Now. Sign it."

Tina watched as each of her three brothers signed their names above hers. Then, she pulled out her phone and took pictures of it.

"Jesus. Is that really necessary?" asked Gunther.

"With you, yes. This ends right here, right now. I'll expect notarized copies of the final sale papers by the end of business tomorrow. If I *don't* have them, I'm going straight to a lawyer to file fraud charges. And *then* I'm going to call the ATF and leave an anonymous tip about what you have hidden in the root cellars."

The veins in Rick's neck pulsed. "You wouldn't."

"Try me. I'll never forgive you for this. Any of

you."

Tina walked out of the office, her heart pounding like a jackhammer in her chest. She made it into her truck and climbed in, then leaned her head and arms over the steering wheel, willing the sick feeling in her stomach to go away.

The eerie feeling of being watched made her lift her head. Kiefer was standing by her driver's door.

"Jesus, Kief! Are you trying to give me a heart attack or something?"

"Did you mean what you said in there?"

"Every word."

Kiefer nodded, something like respect flashing in his eyes. "Good for you. You take care of yourself, okay?"

Then, without another word, he walked away.

EPILOGUE – 6 Months Later

~ Tina ~

Tina surveyed the orchard with approval. It was small but perfect, a blend of old history and new beginnings. The young trees had taken root, and in another year, they'd be producing gorgeous peaches, maybe her best ever.

In the meantime, some of the older trees—mostly apples but some pears, too—had been keeping her busy. Over the last few months, she'd been doting on them with lots of TLC. They were responding even better than she'd hoped.

Happy orchardist, happy orchard, she thought with a smile.

And she *was* happy. Why wouldn't she be? She was doing what she loved and living with the love of her life.

As if on cue, Doc stepped up behind her and wrapped his arms around her waist. "How are they looking?"

"Beautiful. Is it time to go already?"

"It is. Are you ready?"

"Ready as I'll ever be, I suppose."

"Good. Your grandmother and Mr. O are meeting us there."

The new and improved Peach Mill would be having its grand opening in just a few hours. It would be Tina's first public appearance in months. She'd been psyching herself up for it ever since the last of the Amish craftsmen left the week before.

They'd really outdone themselves, too. It was even better than before. In addition to the state-of-the-art kitchen and professionally designed shop, the new place also had a small indoor/outdoor café, where visitors could sit and enjoy some of the unique offerings, including not only Tina's patented recipes, but also some new specialty items created by Lexi Callaghan herself.

The real centerpiece was the old-fashioned cider mill press in the back. Visitors could watch as various ciders were made right before their eyes, using centuries-old methods and just a touch of modern technology. The type of cider featured on any given day would vary, based on what crops were available. In addition to the usual—apple and peach—Tina was also working on crafting the perfect blends of the unusual, like black currants, cherry, and pear ciders.

As they drove down the mountain, Tina wasn't sure what to expect. She knew many locals would be coming around, more out of curiosity than anything else. So much had happened, but for anyone on the outside, looking in, not much had changed.

Obermacher Farms was still a working farm, supplying the area with fresh produce. Obermachers might not be running it anymore, but many of the same people who'd been working there their whole lives still did, now with bigger paychecks and better benefit packages.

Tina couldn't help but wonder how her brothers felt about that or if they knew or even cared. She'd moved in with Doc shortly after the sale went through and not seen or spoken to any of them in months. Part of her was sad about that, but it wasn't a big part. Mostly, she just felt relieved. Being able to wake up in the morning happy and looking forward to the day instead of dreading it was a huge improvement.

Beyond her little ten-acre orchard at Sanctuary, Tina didn't spend much time in the fields these days. When she did, it was as the lead consultant of the Celtic Goddess Orchard Division. Aidan and Lexi had offered her more—what essentially amounted to a VP position—but she'd turned them down. Her greatest joy came from getting her hands dirty, whether that be creating new hybrids in the Sanctuary greenhouses or experimenting with new recipes in the kitchen with Kate. Lexi'd had her back on that, saying she understood completely.

Tina believed she did, too. The master chef had become not only a business partner, but a good friend as well. In fact, Tina had a lot of good friends now. Doc often said that the men and women of Sanctuary were like family, only better.

He wasn't wrong. They were there for each other, always and without question, and now, she was fortunate enough to be included among them.

"Holy cow," Tina said as Doc was forced to slow down to a crawl half a mile before the Peach Mill. "What's with the traffic jam?"

Doc grinned at her.

"Oh, hell no. This can't all be for the Peach Mill. Can it?"

"I hear they're giving away free stuff," he said with a wink.

They were. As part of the grand opening, they were offering free samples of several signature items, including Tina's new vanilla-peach ice cream, peach tea, and of course, bite-sized baked peaches topped with zabaglione. They'd been working extra hard to make sure everything was perfect. In fact, she probably would have pulled an all-nighter had Doc not literally tossed her over his shoulder and carried her out to the cheers of the staff.

Her man was a patient man, but he had his limits, especially when she tended to push herself too hard. That was when her gentle medic stepped back, and her commanding SEAL took over. She didn't mind so much—as long as he didn't do it *too* often. Her SEAL was hot AF.

People smiled and waved and slapped the Jeep when they saw Tina.

"This is insane."

Eventually, they made it to the mill and were waved through by the volunteers handling traffic control.

"I hope you don't mind, but we started without you," Aggie said, ushering Tina and Doc in through the back service entrance where Lottie and Mr. O'Farrell were waiting with smiles and hugs. "The natives were getting restless."

"It's not even supposed to open for another hour."

"Honey, some people have been sitting out there since early this morning."

"Why?"

Aggie grinned and looked at Doc. "She still doesn't get it, does she?"

"Get what?"

Doc laughed. "Come on, Peaches. Your public awaits."

~ Doc ~

She was so fucking beautiful, inside and out.

And she had no idea.

All day, she was in a constant state of

amazement, shocked that so many people would come out for her grand opening.

"I told you, didn't I?" Lottie said to him, beaming at her granddaughter.

She had, but he hadn't believed it.

"I'm counting on you to watch over our girl, Dr. Watson," Lottie had said.

"She doesn't need anyone to watch over her," he'd said in response. "Tina's one of the strongest, most capable women I know."

"That's what Tina wants everyone to believe, but inside"—Lottie had shaken her head—"there will always be a part of her that feels like she's not good enough. That's why she works so hard at everything. Because she doesn't believe she is."

He'd thought that was ridiculous and told her so.

"It is," Lottie had agreed, "but it's true. Her whole life, she's been told she's not good enough, not strong enough, not healthy enough. First from her father and then her brothers. You hear that often enough, and you start to believe it. Her grandfather and I tried to tell her different, but it's far easier to believe the bad things people tell you than the good, eh?"

* * *

The grand opening was a huge success. At one point, it seemed as if the entire town had converged on Tina's new business—with a few notable exceptions.

Doc never strayed far from Tina, his eyes watchful and his ears alert. He wasn't expecting trouble, but he wouldn't be surprised if there was someone out there who wanted to ruin Tina's special day.

Sadly, Tina's oldest brother was at the top of that list. Rick Obermacher was still skulking around Sumneyville, licking his wounds and blaming everyone else for his bad choices. He was living in the other half of Lenny Petraski's double-block these days and picking up the occasional odd job. According to Sandy's Franco's connection, he'd become even more of a dick after his wife filed for divorce and forced him to pay child support.

Cage had tracked Gunther and his wife to Vegas. Gunther had taken a management position in one of the casinos out there—ironically enough, for one of Anthony Tollino's biggest competitors. He was on Ian Callaghan's watchlist, so if he ever decided to return to the East Coast, they'd know about it.

Kiefer had simply disappeared. No one had seen hide nor hair of him since the night they signed the contract with EHI. For all intents and purposes, he'd gone completely off the grid. Even Ian hadn't been able to pin him down. Given the digital resources at Ian's disposal, that was saying something.

Throughout the day, Church, Mad Dog, Smoke, Heff, and Cage had been watching, too. They'd shown up, not only to support Tina, but to make a statement as well. One that said Tina was one of them, and they took care of their own.

"I can't believe we sold out of just about everything," Tina said later as the last customer left.

"I can," he said, lightly resting his arms around her waist. Not touching her all afternoon had been hard, spoiled as he was. "You have a way with peaches, Miss Obermacher. Speaking of, did you save some of that zabaglione for me?"

She gave him a wicked smile. "You know I did."

"Good. Ready to head home?"

"So ready. You are going to give me one of your special massages, right? I worked very, very hard today."

"Count on it. Hey, what's that?" He pointed to a small wrapped package on the counter.

"I don't know. Someone must have left it."

"Check it out. Maybe it's got a name on it or something."

Tina picked up the box and frowned. "It's addressed to me."

"Huh. I guess someone got you a present to celebrate your grand opening."

"But who?" She turned it around in her hands.

"It doesn't say who it's from."

"Maybe you should open it and find out."

Her brows drew together. "I don't know. Aren't you the one who told me never to open any unmarked packages?"

Shit, he'd forgotten about that. It was a cautionary warning he'd issued months earlier after Obermacher Farms was sold. Unsurprisingly, Anthony Tollino had not been pleased to discover he'd been outbid by EHI. Plus, there were a few window lickers—a term of Tina's Doc had become quite fond of—like Eddie Schweikert, running around.

Not Eddie himself though. Not too long ago, he had been picked up in the next county on a DUI, but only after he'd sideswiped several vehicles, including one driven by the daughter of the state attorney general. After he failed a sobriety test and resisted arrest, the police discovered he had been driving with a suspended license and no insurance. They hadn't been too happy about the unregistered guns they found in the back of his truck either.

Eddie's cousin, Joe Eisenheiser, was keeping a low profile these days, too. That might have had something to do with the fact that Joe's truck had somehow taken a *second* tumble down the mountainside.

"Right," Doc said to Tina. "Better give it to me then."

She didn't, narrowing her eyes at him instead.

"Why? Are you less likely to be harmed than me?"

He made a halfhearted attempt to reach for it, but she spun away and pulled on the ribbon. Had he not bought and wrapped the present himself, that would have bothered him. As it was, he loved *and* hated that she was as protective of him as he was of her.

"Well? What is it?" he asked.

She pulled out something and regarded it with interest. "It's another box in the shape of a peach. Clever."

He thought so. It had taken him forever to find that, but it had to be as unique and fitting as the custom engagement ring it held. Anna Mueller—the Sumneyville jeweler who'd designed rings for Sam, Sandy, Kate, and Bree—had outdone herself.

Tina lifted the lid and looked inside. Blinked twice. Then looked at him questioningly.

He went down on one knee. "Bertina Matilda Obermacher, will you marry me?"

Her fingers came up to her lips, and she nodded.

"Is that a yes?"

She nodded more emphatically. "Yes!" she yelled suddenly, launching herself at him and knocking him to the ground in the process. It was a good thing he had been prepared for it.

"Yes! A thousand times yes!" she said, straddling his waist and peppering his face with kisses.

"We should go," he whispered against her lips, "or I'm going to end up taking you right here."

She gazed down at him with heat in her eyes and a smirk on her lips. "So? It wouldn't be the first time."

"Don't tempt me," he growled.

"Oh, I'm going to tempt you all right," she said with a wicked grin. "Where's your sense of adventure?"

"You do realize, everyone's watching, right?" he said softly.

Apparently, a guy couldn't have an engagement ring made and plan a surprise proposal without the whole town knowing about it.

Tina looked around, her cheeks turning a lovely shade of rose when she saw the grinning faces peering in through the windows. Then, she laughed.

"Put it on."

From there on the floor, Doc obediently slipped the ring onto her finger. It fit perfectly. She held up her hand for everyone to see. Happy cheers and applause ensued.

She looked down at him, her eyes filled with love and happiness. "Doc?"

"Yeah?"

She said the three words he'd wanted to hear most—after saying yes, that was—"Let's go home."

Thanks for reading Doc and Tina's Story

You didn't have to pick this book, but you did. Thank you!
If you liked this story, then please consider posting a review online! It's really easy, only takes a few minutes, and makes a huge difference to independent authors who don't have the mega-budgets of the big-time publishers behind them.

Do you like free books? How about gift cards?

Sign up for my newsletter today! You'll not only get advance notice of new releases, sales, giveaways, contests, fun facts, and other great things each month, you'll also get a free book just for signing up ***and*** be automatically entered for a chance to win a gift card every month, simply for reading it!

Get started today! Go to **abbiezandersromance.com** and click on the **Subscribe** tab to sign up!

Also by Abbie Zanders

Contemporary Romance – Callaghan Brothers

Plan your visit to Pine Ridge, Pennsylvania and fall in love with the Callaghans

- 🕮 Dangerous Secrets
- 🕮 First and Only
- 🕮 House Calls
- 🕮 Seeking Vengeance
- 🕮 Guardian Angel
- 🕮 Beyond Affection
- 🕮 Having Faith
- 🕮 Bottom Line
- 🕮 Forever Mine
- 🕮 Two of a Kind
- 🕮 Not Quite Broken

Contemporary Romance – Connelly Cousins

Drive across the river to Birch Falls and spend some time with the Connelly Cousins

- 🕮 Celina
- 🕮 Jamie
- 🕮 Johnny

🕮 Michael

Contemporary Romance – Covendale Series

If you like humor and snark in your romance, add a stop in Covendale

🕮 Five Minute Man
🕮 All Night Woman
🕮 Seizing Mack

Contemporary Romance – Sanctuary

More small town romance with former military heroes you can't help but love

🕮 Protecting Sam
🕮 Best Laid Plans
🕮 Shadow of Doubt
🕮 Nick UnCaged
🕮 Organically Yours
🕮 Prodigal Son (Jan 2022)

More Contemporary Romance

🕮 The Realist

- Celestial Desire
- Letting Go
- SEAL Out of Water (Silver SEALs)
- Rockstar Romeo (Cocky Hero Club)
- Finding Home (The Long Road Home)
- Cast in Shadow (Shadow SEALs 2022)

Cerasino Family Novellas

Short, sweet romance to put a smile on your face

- Just For Me
- Just For Him
- Just For Her

Time Travel Romance

Travel between present day NYC and 15th century Scotland in these stand-alone but related titles

- Maiden in Manhattan
- Raising Hell in the Highlands

Paranormal Romance – Mythic Series

Welcome to Mythic, an idyllic communities all kinds of Extraordinaries call home.

- Faerie Godmother
- Fallen Angel
- The Oracle at Mythic
- Wolf Out of Water

More Paranormal Romance

- Vampire, Unaware
- Black Wolfe's Mate (written as Avelyn McCrae)
- Going Nowhere
- The Jewel
- Close Encounters of the Sexy Kind
- Rock Hard
- Immortal Dreams
- Rehabbing the Beast (written as Avelyn McCrae)
- More Than Mortal

Howls Romance

Classic romance with a furry twist

- Falling for the Werewolf
- A Very Beary Christmas
- Going Polar

Historical/Medieval Romance

📖 A Warrior's Heart (written as Avelyn McCrae)

About the Author

Abbie Zanders is the author of more than 55 published romance novels ranging from contemporary to paranormal and everything in between. She promises her readers two things: happily ever afters, always, and no cliffhangers, ever.

Born and raised in the mountains of Northeastern Pennsylvania, she has degrees in Computer Science and Mathematics. She worked for more than twenty-five years as a software engineer, designing and writing financial applications, though she has also held second jobs as a deli clerk, pub waitress, restaurant baker, and secretary that she draws upon to give real-life dimension to her characters.

Abbie has been crafting stories since elementary school, though she has only recently decided to start sharing them with others. When she's not escaping into another world of her own creation, she's a busy wife and mother of three, including a set of identical twins. Besides being an avid reader and writer, she loves animals (especially big dogs), American muscle cars, and 80's hair bands.